CHEAT MOUNTAIN

by

K. P. Hayden

Edited by: Rebecca Stroud

Editorial Assistant: Kimberly Hayden

ISBN 978-0-9857915-6-8

Cover Design: Ott & Associates

Richmond, VA

DEDICATION

Dedicated to Florence Cheatham and Wirt Chambers; memories are ghosts trapped within the souls of the living. Because of them you and many wonderful moments will never be forgotten. And to US History Professor Richard Couture for exposing a youthful mind to the beauty and tragedy of the American experience as though it were the most incredible story ever written. Your works upon this earth are finished, good people; now delight in the fellowship of your God and fathers.

Bring up the Twelve Pounders!
All the horses are dead her, sir.
Bring 'em up by mule then.
All the mules are dead here, sir.
Well bring 'em up by hand boys.
All the battery men are dead here, sir.
I need them Twelve Pounders.
There ain't no artillery left here, sir.

Bring Up the Twelve Pounders by Paul Kennedy
White Mansion
Copyright 1978, Rondor Music (London) Ltd.
US & Canada by Irving Music, Inc. (BMI)

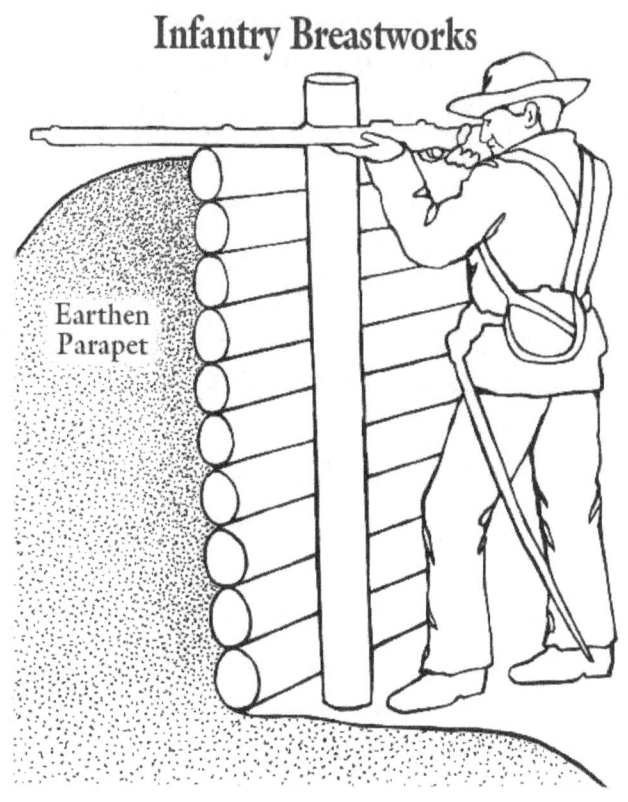

Infantry Breastworks

Earthen Parapet

Chapter 1

Not one of my better ideas...

Lexi Willow blotted the sweat from her palms against the thighs of her faded jeans, one hand at a time, quickly returning each to the leather grip of the steering wheel. Although she possessed the cool, measured reflexes of a champion equestrian, this road had her completely unraveled: today of all days.

She focused her attention on the expanse of twisted, ascending pavement that stretched before her: Highway 250 trailing west out of Staunton, Virginia and into the rolling mountains of the Shenandoah.

Lexi flicked her eyes at the travel atlas lying on the front passenger-side floorboard, opened to the legend describing the quality of the state roadways.

Since when did 'principal through-highway' mean looped

5

about the countryside like a spaghetti noodle tossed from an
airplane?

The heavy Ford Expedition she was driving broached another narrow patch of straight and level road. Lexi tossed a glance at her husband, Chet, reclined in the seat beside her sound asleep and suppressed an urge to wake him.

"No, moving up here was your idea, Lexi Willow," she told herself. "Now deal with it. Shoulders square, eyes straight, both hands on the wheel and keep the hood ornament centered between the white lines. It's just a road. Your new mountain neighbors do this every day."

She slid her foot off the accelerator, covered the brake and carefully banked left into anther climbing hairpin turn. One moment she was staring at a rugged, gray, drilled-granite rock face; the next she was peering over the saw-toothed tops of a mutiny of pines with nothing between the Expedition and a hundred-foot vertical drop but an old guardrail that looked like it once served as the line of scrimmage in a shootout between the Hatfield's and McCoy's.

She sucked in a deep breath and exhaled in a series of short, even spurts. "Rationalize your anxieties," her analyst had often told her. "Mold each into a definite shape, and then build a ladder to climb up and over it...one by one."

"The move to Monterey," Lexi reassured herself. "That's all it is. Just the stress from the move."

Lexi eased into another hairpin curve where yet another misty, mountain vista flashed before her, the precipice just inches from the Ford's passenger side door panels. Every muscle in her body curdled and she slowed the vehicle to a crawl. When she finally managed to exit the curve, she reached with her right hand to give Chet's knee a brisk shake. She wouldn't ask him to drive but at least he could provide some conversation to help calm her nerves.

Tires suddenly shrieked on the pavement behind; Lexi's heart leapt up into the back of her throat. Renewing the death grip on the steering wheel, she cut her eyes to the rearview mirror: the whole width of it was filled with the grill, hood and windshield of an old red pickup.

"Where did that come from!?" Lexi exclaimed. She gave the Expedition a punch of gas; the pickup remained jammed to her bumper. "Come on, pal! Give it a break."

She slowed to let the pickup pass but it slowed right along with her. She came to a dead stop; the pickup stopped. She stuck her hand out the window and motioned for it to pass; the pickup remained, its driver raced the engine.

"What kind of asshole are YOU?"

Lexi padded the accelerator and the Expedition lurched forward, a geyser of Diet Pepsi shot from the mouth of a twenty-ounce plastic bottle resting in the beverage holder on the center console. Foam and a groping nebula of viscid, brown fluid landed on the leg and crotch of her jeans.

"Oh, shit!" she squawked, and fished a box of tissues from under the seat. "Now it looks like I've peed my pants."

The tissues were of little help; the Pepsi stains were set. "Lovely. Just lovely." Lexi threw the wadded tissue onto the passenger floorboard; it landed with a wet thud on the travel atlas.

The red truck lagged behind for a moment, then came roaring up before slamming on its brakes again.

Lexi bolted upright in her seat. "We're in the mountains, for God's sake, not the Bonneville Salt Flats."

Chet began to snore.

"Chet, wake up," Lexi called. She flicked his thigh with the back of her hand. "Come on, Chet! Wake up!"

No response.

The red pickup raced up behind her again and slammed on brakes a third time. Lexi unwillingly increased speed and continued up the mountain into another set of hairpins, taking each new curve a little faster than the one before.

She kept calling to Chet but he simply would not wake. Her breathing elevated to a pant. Tires squealing once again, the truck behind her suddenly swerved into the oncoming lane as if attempting to pass, and then darted back behind her just before the onset of the next curve. Lexi deflected another wave of panic.

"Keep moving," she told herself. "You can do this. There's bound to be a town or a gas station up ahead with someone who will help."

Exasperated, she tried to backhand Chet's knee again but misjudged the distance and jammed her wrist against the center console; pulses of pain shot through her hand, wrist, and forearm in perfect rhythm with the beating of her heart.

Ahead, the road leveled off again before it took a sharp right turn and started up another incline. A grove of budding treetops partially obscured her view but Lexi thought she spotted a stretch of shoulder just beyond the first curve wide enough for her to pull over. She placed her throbbing hand back on the steering wheel and decided to give it a try.

When the road flattened, the truck swerved out into the left lane again and the driver gunned the engine. Instead of darting back in behind at the next curve as he had done the other time, he pulled alongside and plowed into the curve with her, two abreast. Lexi squeezed the steering wheel so hard that she forced all the blood from her fingertips.

It was a blind, climbing left curve; Lexi couldn't see more than fifteen feet of the road ahead. The pickup had the inside lane and, if the driver couldn't hold the turn, he could quite possibly force her off the road and over the side of the mountain.

To her right, the shoulder of the road disappeared. Lexi fixed her eyes straight ahead, hugged the guardrail, and fought to maintain control of the Expedition and her nerve. The front of the red pickup was dead even with her driver-side door.

For some obscene reason, a lyric from the song *Hot Rod Lincoln* popped into her head: "Fenders were clicking the guardrail posts; the guy beside me was white as a ghost." She ran her eyes to Chet again, his snoring resumed. *Deaf as a post was more like it.*

Lexi detected a flash of movement in front of her. She cut her eyes forward and a gasp escaped her throat. A towering, black tractor-trailer was headed right for her. Straddling the yellow line, it was setting up to cut the radius of the curve as it descended the mountain.

As the first few molecules of chrome on the Expedition's front bumper reached the wide spot in the road, Lexi whipped the steering wheel hard to the right and crushed the accelerator.

If God protected babies, drunks, and bleached-blondes, the Expedition might just manage to squeeze through. But, unless the driver of that pickup was the pope out on a redneck sabbatical, he didn't have a prayer.

Lexi's brain suddenly registered two shapes along the side of the road; her eyes jetted from the truck to the road, and then to the two new figures. At first, she thought her eyes were tricking her. But, no, there they were...exactly where she needed to pilot the Expedition to avoid crashing into the tractor-trailer. It was a man leading a horse.

"Watch out!" she shouted. She made the split-second steerage correction necessary to avoid hitting the man and horse though now she was certain to ram into the rear of the trailer.

Tires screamed to the left beside her. Lexi glanced in the rearview mirror and saw the pickup knife back in behind the Expedition and continue around onto the right shoulder, placing the man and the horse directly in its path.

For a nanosecond, she and the horseman locked eyes. That's all it took to sear his image into her brain forever: disheartened blue eyes, chest-length black beard flecked with gray, and a gray coat with three large red splotches on it. He was certain to have seen the pickup hurtling toward him but didn't show the slightest trace of urgency.

Lexi braced for impact. She heard the tire screams of the impending collision, not sure if they were her own, the pickup or the tractor-trailer. As if in slow motion she watched the nose of the Expedition pass within millimeters of the trailer but there was no crash. To her amazement, the huge truck passed by and continued down the mountain completely unfettered. *Impossible*.

To her right, a dense cloud of dust boiled into the air. The red pickup rocketed from the cloud like an errant missile and flew back onto the road in front of her.

The driver of the pickup had just slaughtered two living creatures and was not making any attempt to stop or even slow down.

Halfway through the next hairpin, Lexi managed to bring the Expedition to a complete stop, her mind still reeling. The first thought she wrestled back to solid ground was MURDERED. She made a sweeping left turn and headed back down the mountain; the red truck had sped through the next set of hairpins and accelerated up the mountain and out of sight.

Lexi returned to the wide spot in the road, expecting to find the worst. But there was no sign of the man or the horse. She crossed the westbound lane and pulled over. She really didn't want see what was awaiting her but had to render whatever assistance she could.

She leapt out of the Expedition and peered over the edge of the mountain, anticipating a landscape of mangled gore. To her surprise, there were no broken bodies, no battered flesh, and no clumps of horse hair or tattered clothing...not even a single drop of blood.

Lexi searched the ground where the impact was certain to have occurred. There was no blood anywhere; not on the ground, not on the guardrail. "That's impossible."

Chet rushed to her. "What's impossible?"

"Where's all the blood?!" she cried.

"What blood?" Chet asked.

"That guy in the red pickup just smashed into the man leading the horse. There should be blood everywhere."

"Honey, you've repeated the phrase 'man and a horse' three times now. I didn't see a man leading a horse."

"Of course, you didn't," Lexi snapped. "You were in some kind of trance. I swerved, but that pickup was headed right for them."

"Sweetheart, I swear, there was no man leading a horse."

Further down the mountain, the tractor-trailer laid into its air horn and disappeared around an outcropping of drilled rock.

"I suppose you're going to tell me that semi doesn't exist either," Lexi said.

Chet examined the four sets of thick, black skid marks in the road. "No. That truck was definitely here, alright. The driver will probably need to stop somewhere at the bottom to change his underwear."

"And so was the horse and the man with the beard," Lexi insisted. She turned to her left and took two large steps. "They were right here. When that red truck skidded around us, it was barreling right for them. There's no way it could have missed."

"Sweetheart, if that old rust bucket hit a horse it would have burst into a hundred pieces. At the very least, there would be some broken glass or spilled radiator fluid."

Old rust bucket! Lexi thought. She searched over the guardrail again. How did Chet know that pickup was an old rust

11

bucket? He never even saw it, couldn't have seen it; he was sound asleep. But that part of his argument did make sense. There would be some sort of debris from the impact.

"Wait a minute, Lexi," Chet said. "Let's turn around and retrace your steps. Which side of the truck did you get out of?"

"What do you mean which side?" Lexi pointed up the mountain to the next hairpin curve. "I stopped up there, turned around, drove back down, pulled off the side of the road, got out on the *driver's side* and looked over the guardrail for the man and horse."

"No, sweetheart, you didn't," Chet replied softly, his expression loving but serious. "I was driving. You've been asleep ever since we passed through Lexington. You must have awakened just as we encountered the tractor-trailer."

Lexi knew what she had seen. "You were driving? Don't be ridiculous. I was driving. I jammed my wrist on your knee and spilled Pepsi all over my pants." She looked down at the front of her jeans; there were no wet spots and no caramel-colored stains. She tested her right wrist; there was no pain.

She stared at Chet and then gazed back at the Expedition. "No...That's not how it...I was driving..." She took another deep breath. "You don't suppose...do you expect me to believe I dreamed the whole damn thing? Is that what I'm supposed to think?"

"You got the part about the red pickup truck right. It's been on our bumper ever since we started up the mountain."

Lexi threw her hands into the air. "I don't sleep in cars. I can hardly even sleep in my own bed."

She didn't realize she was trembling until Chet wrapped his arms around her. "So there was no horse and no man with a black beard?"

Chet shook his head.

12

CHEAT MOUNATAIN

"I'm telling you, Chet, I saw them as plain as day. He had red stains on the front of his coat that looked like gunshot wounds."

"No blood, no antifreeze and no smashed truck," Chet repeated. "Just a couple Herculean skid marks."

Lexi felt drained. She didn't know whether to be embarrassed or disappointed. The move to Monterey was supposed to ease her anxieties, not magnify them. She held Chet's embrace for several moments and then walked to the Expedition. Back inside, she spied her bottle of Diet Pepsi—full—sitting in the beverage holder with the cap still on...the seal wasn't even broken. Now she *was* embarrassed. She sat and snapped on her seatbelt.

Two-thirds down the other side of the mountain they came across a set of flashing blue lights. A Highland County patrol car had the shabby red pickup pulled off onto the shoulder of the road. Chet slowed the Expedition as they approached.

A rotund deputy and a twentyish kid were standing nose-to-nose behind the truck. Judging from the way the officer's head was jerking up and down, he was giving the kid a royal face-chewing.

As they eased past, Lexi placed the back of her hand against the window. The kid looked at her and grinned sheepishly. Lexi snapped her fingers into a tight, clenched fist; all of her fingers, that is, except the middle one.

Chapter 2

By the time Lexi arrived in Monterey, she had mounted a full recovery from her brush with dreamland mortality. And why not? The beauty of this slice of planet Earth exceeded every possible description.

She stepped away from the Expedition and gazed southward through a lush valley where boot-top meadow grass swayed in synchronized rivulets under a pristine, azure sky. Insulated from the outside world by flanking peaks of ancient mountains Mother Nature had deceivingly softened in a tapestry of pines, fledgling-leafed maples and oaks.

"The panorama from that ridge is absolutely breathtaking," Lexi said to Chet. "What a fantastic place to build a new life."

Chet pulled a light jacket over his wide shoulders and stepped from the driver's side of the Ford. "No traffic jams, no psychotic cabbies, no high-rise office buildings or police sirens screaming through the night. The guys back at Parker, Burns & Puckett say we won't last sixty days."

"And what do you say?" Lexi asked, truly not knowing what

14

reply to expect.

"Twenty years, maybe. Thirty with good behavior."

Lexi's cheeks flexed into tight round balls as she smiled and blew him a kiss. "That's what I hoped you'd say."

She returned to the white, two-story, clapboard building with a red, tin roof which Chet had parked in front of. A sign attached to the railing of the second-floor balcony read:

JB General Merchandise
Monterey, Virginia
Down Home Hospitality
Frank Opinions at No Extra Charge

"I don't see Audrey's car anywhere," Lexi said.

"She'll be along," replied Chet. "Let's go inside and see what opinions Frank is serving up today. My treat."

Monterey was a charming little village at the crossroads of two highways and the last flat spot on Route 250 in Virginia before crossing into West Virginia. Main Street was a collection of antique stores, gift shops, JB's, a Texaco, two restaurants, a double-wide that served as a bank and three country inns. Lexi and Chet had visited only once before to view the Blaylock estate before making an offer on it.

Culture, as Lexi's mother once put it, was a function of divine preference and selective exposure. D.C., Baltimore and New York had plenty of the high culture and all were only a short flight away. But one of the most important things Monterey offered couldn't be found in those other places: low population density.

The tragedies of September 11 had caused Lexi to become increasingly weary of New York City, the ruthless side of the human experience having never directly impacted her before. Not that a

15

repeat of that day was likely; instead, she realized how vulnerable she was to forces beyond her control. There were few, if any, of those influences in Monterey and she felt safe here.

A gust of wind tasseled her thick, blond hair. She pulled it back into a ponytail and turned toward the Expedition. A speckled nose and a pair of hairy feet belonging to a liver-and-white Springer Spaniel were pressed against the inside of the passenger-side window.

"Beecher, be a good boy until we get back," Lexi said. "In a few minutes, you can run until your ears flop off."

Lexi offered Chet her arm and he escorted her up the short incline to JB's front steps. A bell tinkled overhead as she pushed the door open.

Half a dozen parallel rows of bare fluorescent tubes suspended from exposed joists illuminated the interior of the store. The perimeter walls were layered from floor to ceiling with shelves displaying shirts and pants, straw hats, fishing tackle, hunting supplies, and boxes of nuts and bolts. Across the center were aisles of bread, pastries, canned goods, potato chips, paper products, hand tools and automotive accessories. Lexi zeroed in on a rack of post cards.

"Where's Ike Godsey and the jar of sourballs?" Chet joked.

A woman dressed in slightly faded bib-overalls with braided, gray hair twisted back into a bun and gold-rimmed glasses set half-way down her nose stepped out from behind the frozen food case and walked with purpose over to the cash register.

"I'm a month of Sundays better looking than any Ike Godsey. And if it's sourballs ya'll come for, the jar's back here."

Lexi looked at Chet and grinned.

Chet blushed and sank his hands into his coat pockets. "That was rather inappropriate," he said. "I apologize."

"I'll be called worse before the day's over, I reckon," the

woman replied. "I'm JB. Audrey Pepper called to say she'd be about a half hour late. Said something about a funds transfer."

"You know who we are?" Lexi asked.

"Either you're a month late for ski season up to Snowshoe or you're the folks who just bought the old Blaylock place. Audrey said there'd be a handsome young couple driving a big, green suburban assault vehicle equipped with New York tags. Since that thing out front and the two of you match the description, figure you gotta be them."

Lexi was impressed, if not a smidgeon flattered. She angled toward the cash register holding a fan of post cards she had taken from the display, noting that JB had a very smooth complexion for a woman her age. She had probably been a very beautiful woman in her day.

Chet plucked two packs of cheese crackers from a shelf on his way over from the beverage cooler.

"You have a fascinating shop here," Lexi remarked. "Such an eclectic selection of merchandise."

JB's eyes bounced back and forth between Lexi and Chet. "Well, it's no Wally World. But I've got everything from frozen turkey gizzards to weed whackers; they'll just cost ya half-again as much. After a dozen or so trips across them mountains to Staunton, you'll thank your stars I'm here."

"We're accustomed to high prices," Chet replied. He placed two twenty-ounce bottles of soda and the crackers on the counter.

"Well then, let's see here," JB said. She swiftly tapped her fingers across the cash register keys. "That'll be three hundred and ninety-two dollars for what you got, and them post cards are ten bucks apiece. That comes to a grand total of four hundred sixty-one dollars and eighty-nine cents, with tax."

Lexi bit her lip and tilted her head at Chet. "He's buying."

"That's a bit steep for pop and crackers," Chet said as he reached for his money clip. But the Chet Willow she knew wasn't going to roll over on an invitation like that. "Can you break a seven-hundred-dollar bill?" Chet asked.

"Be glad to, young fella," answered JB, not skipping a beat. "How'd ya like your change? In twenty-fives or forties?"

Lexi burst into laughter. It appears Chet may have met his match. She took an immediate liking to JB.

Chet grinned wryly. "I see you've spent a little time in New York yourself."

JB patted the bun on the back of her head and crowed. "Lord have mercy no; never been farther north than Winchester." She waved her hand at him. "Put your money away. I'll have plenty of it before the leaves fall. And let me give you your first lesson on country-speak." She swooped up a Pepsi and a package of crackers. "Around here, we call this a drink and a pack of nabs. Pop is what an old woman's hip does when she hoists herself out of the bathtub."

Chet's smile bloomed into a hardy laugh. "JB, it's going to be a pleasure knowing you. My name is Chet Willow. This is my wife, Alexis."

JB's eyes narrowed. Lexi detected a slight glimmer to them; the kind a person has when they're party to an inside joke.

"You best hold onto this one tight, young lady," JB said. "If one of these mountain vixens gets one talon in a handsome, brown-eyed chunk of man like this, you'll have to burn her off with a blow torch. Why, if I was ten years younger, I might flip you for him myself."

Lexi hooked Chet's arm and pulled him to her, the point of his chin grazed the top of her head. "For the next several years, this one's all mine. Once I finish filling this valley with children, you can have what's left." She looked to Chet for reassurance. He gave her that same distant smile he always did when the discussion turned to kids.

"Don't think there won't be a line of 'em waitin'."

Lexi held up one of the cards she had found. "This post card has a picture of our farm on it. Why does the subtitle read Cheat Mountain?"

An unshaved man wearing a soiled butcher's apron and a tattered, black baseball cap with a 'Remember Number 3' logo above the bill stepped from a room behind the meat case and leaned against the doorway. All Lexi could see was the left side of his face, but guessed him to be forty-five to forty-seven years old.

"On account of the filthy lucre that built the damn place, that's why," he said.

"Porter, return your parts to that back room there and finish traying up them chickens like I told ya," JB snapped. "Nobody out here needs any of your foolishness today."

Porter pulled a cigarette from his shirt pocket and dipped his head to light it. He exhaled a thin, laminar jet of smoke and looked Lexi square on. The right side of his face was sunken in and discolored with a large, purplish-red birthmark. His right eye didn't have a pupil; it was just a white glaze with a murky yellow center.

Lexi felt her stomach twist but resisted the urge to look away. Porter ambled back into the back room.

"Don't pay that old skunk any mind," JB said, still visibly agitated. "What he lacks in social grace, he more than makes up for in aggravation."

"Who was he talking about?" Lexi asked.

"Oh, dear." JB glanced at Chet and then back at Lexi. "I reckon you'll hear of things soon enough, though." She pulled up a stool, plopped down and leaned an elbow on the counter.

"The Blaylocks owned this entire valley. It was once a forest filled with virgin timber. Most of the town and surrounding pastures were cleared by Titus Blaylock—that was the old man—or his son, Deacon. Titus made a fortune in various business endeavors but you couldn't tell it by the way he paid his help. The old-timers say he cheated every man who turned a hand for him out of half his wages. Money was hard to come by back in those days, so most took what he gave them and were thankful for it, but the nickname "cheat" stuck. Soon everyone was calling the place Cheat Mountain. Tourists get a real kick out of it."

"A thievin' slave-driver is more like it," added Porter from the back room. "Had to keep his Jezebel in caviar and silk stockings."

"Porter, if you keep flappin' your trap, I'll show you a Jezebel. I'm not gonna warn you again."

"He's still up there, too," Porter replied. "Seen his ghost myself. It ran them others off and it'll do the same to you."

This day was providing a bounty of unexpected surprises, Lexi thought.

"I swear," JB hissed. She marched over and slammed the back room door. "That boy's got more vinegar than a batch of Maude Atkins' pickles. If I had any sense, I woulda fired him ten years ago." JB returned to her stool. "Now where were we? The Blaylock place. You folks plan on working it?"

Lexi's editorial instincts told her the exchange between JB and Porter had been dialogued before, probably to give the tourists a juicy piece of local flavor to talk about during the ride home. Lexi certainly wasn't about to forget it either.

"We have some renovations to make first, but we intend to raise horses," Lexi said. She was still contemplating what Porter had said. A thought occurred to her. "Titus Blaylock didn't have a beard, did he? How about horses?"

JB's eyes narrowed again. "No, I believe Titus was always

clean-shaven, as I recall," she answered. "But I suspect his stables were full of animals; both work and pleasure. Most folks kept horses back in those days. What makes you ask?"

Lexi realized she was blushing. The house was built in the early 1900s so, of course, he had horses—the notion didn't seem stupid until she actually verbalized it.

"My wife has a delightful imagination, JB," Chet interjected. "One of these days, she's going to be a widely-celebrated author."

Audrey Pepper came bursting through the front door, almost ringing the bell off its hook.

"Sorry I'm late, Mr. and Mrs. Willow. I got halfway here and realized I'd left my gate key at the office. Imagine that." She marched up to the counter. "Mr. Willow, your money came through right on schedule and everything's absolutely hunky-dory down at the bank. The closing is set for ten o'clock tomorrow morning. Now, if you'll give me a minute to catch my breath, we can all head on up the mountain."

Audrey was another intriguing slice of humanity—half Granny Clampett and half Edith Bunker. She couldn't weigh more than a hundred pounds if dipped in lead, and was always in a rush as though her hair was on fire.

"I see you've met JB," Audrey said. "She's such a captivating local historian. I don't know how she manages to do all the things she does. Why, she's a grocer, a hardware store operator, a gas station attendant, and auctioneer and, during the summer, she'll cut and bale your hay. Was the Postmaster once, too, before they built the new post office."

"A woman's got to survive," JB said. Her tone sounded like she was defending herself.

Audrey put a hand to her chest and took a deep breath. "There, that's better. We can shove off any time you're ready. We

21

mustn't dawdle though. It looks like we're in for another little 'ole shower."

JB glanced out the windows. "Clouds are still gathering. You've got a good hour or so before any hard stuff rolls in."

Lexi collected a small paper bag from the counter. "Thanks for the cards, JB. Soon as we get settled, I'd love to have you over for coffee. Maybe you can share some more local history with us."

"It's gossip mostly," answered JB. "People in these parts like to tend everybody's business but their own. Y'all have a wonderful day. And welcome to Monterey."

The entrance to the Blaylock estate was to the left a mile west of JB's store: two hairpin curves up the western rise and just past a small sheep farm.

The first three hundred feet or so of driveway leading up to the house were rather steep. After that, it leveled onto a wide terrace of solid rock chiseled out of the mountainside. Ten feet to the right of the drive, there was a towering face of weeping granite with a drainage culvert cut at the base to channel the runoff down to the ditch along the main road. On the left, there was a line of thick cedars, shallow-rooted to help anchor the soil. Two paces beyond the cedars, there was a waist-high cut-stone wall that ran the entire length of the upper and lower terraces. On the other side of the wall, on this level anyway, the property dropped sharply to the floor of the valley.

The view of the valley was riveting but nothing compared to what waited just ahead.

Audrey stopped at a security gate, inserted a card into the control panel and punched in her code. Two ten-foot-high wrought-iron gates retracted from the center and disappeared behind two stone walls to the right and left, equal in height to the gates.

On each side of the opening, stood a six-foot lion, front feet perched on a pile of rocks, elevated somewhat higher than the rear feet, challenging all who entered. Both sculpted from blocks of solid black West Virginia coal. The craftsmanship was fabulous, equal to any gallery sculpture Lexi had ever seen. One of the lions had a 'B' etched into its outside cheek; the other had a 'J'. Lexi remembered Audrey earlier referring to them as "Shepherd's lions," calling them the guardians of the estate.

Beecher bounced from side to side in the back of the Expedition, smudging all the windows with his nose. Chet was excited, too.

The driveway continued up another incline—gradual this time—for another hundred yards to the second terrace. This level was expansive enough to accommodate the two-story mansion with generous front and back yards, and a garage area. Several smaller outbuildings which at one time had served as quarters for the mill and timber bosses and a large barn were situated in linear fashion a comfortable distance from the south end of the house.

From this elevation, the view of the valley, Monterey, and the opposing line of mountains were nothing short of spectacular, worth every penny of the 2.6 million-dollar price tag.

Chet wheeled the Expedition parallel to the garage and parked. Lexi pushed her door open and she and Beecher hit the ground. Beecher dashed for the nearest tree, cocked his leg, and then bounded off behind the house in hot pursuit of a gray squirrel. It took every ounce of self-control Lexi could muster to contain herself from jumping up and down with excitement.

Audrey padded over, the heels of her shoes clicking the pavement like a drum roll. She pointed at Beecher. "Looks like someone's already made himself a new friend. As you know, the upper terrace was formed mostly by Mother Nature, but the lower one had to be dynamited from the mountainside. The rubble was used to build the house and wall. Nothing but the best for Mrs. Andrea...that was Titus Blaylock's second wife. It was barely finished before she and Titus departed for the big house in the sky."

"Was there some kind of accident?" Lexi asked.

"I'll say. A big boat named *Titanic*. My, oh my. Mr. and Mrs. Blaylock, Sr. traveled extensively. I guess it was just their time to go. Tragic, positively tragic."

Chet winked at Lexi. He obviously found Audrey amusing as well.

"Did I ever mention that the house has been renovated twice?" Audrey asked. "The second time was before the bank sold it after Deacon killed himself."

"Killed himself? How did that happen?" Lexi wasn't thrilled with the fact that the words 'killed' and 'departed' kept turning up in conversations, especially after the morning she'd had. Funny none of this was ever mentioned before.

"Some say he did, some say he didn't," Audrey answered. "Personally, I think it was all that alcohol. I understand he got pasted every evening before sundown."

"The Blaylocks certainly had their share of adversity," Lexi said. She thought of JB; being a local historian must be a grisly pastime.

"You folks are so lucky to have so much money at such a young age," Audrey replied, adroitly changing the subject. "Why, one of these days I expect to see this place on that Rich and Famous television show. Now, I don't mean to rush you the tiniest little bit but I am just dying to have another look inside."

Great, another death reference, Lexi thought. Chet took her hand and followed Audrey—though at a considerably more leisurely pace—up the walkway past the northern entrance and around to the front portico. Audrey already had the door open and was clip-clopping around inside the foyer.

Lexi paused at the doorway and gazed into the foyer. It was semi-rotunda shaped, modeled after Thomas Jefferson's Monticello and the rotunda on the campus of The University of Virginia, with a slightly elevated landing decked in a glossy black, natural-cleft slate. Overhead, the dome was painted atrium white and was accented with hand-painted pink dogwood flowers. Eastern facing transom-styled windows flooded the foyer and adjacent rooms with a refreshing, bright light.

Two steps down, the foyer widened into a sea of red-oak hardwood flooring. A formal dining room was located on the right, with a layered Tiffany chandelier suspended from the center of the twelve-foot ceiling. A sitting room and study were on the left, a wide staircase with a cherry banister and white pickets elegantly flowing up the rear of the rotunda to the second floor and back down the other side. Centered beneath the balcony railing was an arched hallway leading to the kitchen; the sound of running water echoed off the walls.

"There's a little blood in the water," Audrey said from the kitchen. "Nothing a dash of Clorox can't remedy." She came clipping back out into the foyer.

"Blood?" Lexi asked. This was starting to get morbid.

Audrey immediately recanted her description. "It's just rust. The house has been vacant for two years. Water left in old pipes sometimes gets stagnant and turns red. Porter was to have drained them last week and made certain everything was shipshape. We hired him to take care of odds and ends around here for us and maintain the grounds."

Lexi turned to Chet. "First thing we do is change the locks." Chet nodded in agreement.

Audrey clamored up the stairs. "Every time I go up these, I

feel like I'm Scarlet O'Hara. Mrs. Willow, if I was a writer like you, this place would have me just brimming with romance novels."

Cheesy romance novels, Lexi thought.

Audrey's continued sales routine was wearing thin. These were precious moments, a dream that was finally coming true. Lexi wanted to share them with Chet and Chet alone. But Audrey seemed to be enjoying herself and, for the moment, she decided not to spoil it for her.

"You're certain to find a whole bunch of little extra amenities I have failed to mention." Audrey completed the circuit around the stairs and then clipped back into the kitchen and turned off the water.

Chet eased up behind Lexi and wrapped his arms around her. 'Let's invite her back for a drink after closing to celebrate."

"Make it Bloody Mary's," replied Lexi. "We could invite Porter, too. Maybe hold a séance and contact the bearded guy with the horse."

Chet took her by the hand again and trudged after Audrey once more.

The tour lasted another ten minutes. Audrey led them out a rear kitchen door, across the backyard and was explaining, for the third time, how drainage channels cut in the terraces above kept mountain runoff from washing everything away.

Lexi hooked Chet by the arm and hurried him around the south end of the house, stopping at the cut-stone wall overlooking the valley. Instead of a steep drop like on the lower terrace, here a lush-green meadow gently rolled downward into the valley.

"I figure that's where we'll put the landing strip," Chet said, pointing. "Between the base of the mountain and that knoll over to the right. That way I can easily clear the power lines along the road and we won't see it from the house. The mountain will provide a natural break from crosswinds." He pointed again to a spot down the valley to the south. "The main arena will go there with the pasture just behind it. The horses can use the natural fall from the back of the terrace as a ramp to the stables. We'll just need to build things down there sturdy enough to withstand an occasional gully-washer."

Lexi put her arms around Chet's neck and kissed him fully on the mouth. "I know you're doing all this for me," she said warmly. "But we are really going to connect with this place. I just know it."

For the first time in years, Lexi felt like the past was truly behind her and it was time to embrace the future once again. At thirty-five years old, there was little time to waste.

"A man needs to call some place home." Chet stuffed his hand in his pockets and gazed out over the valley again. "Mine might as well be here. It's certainly remote. You'd have been the envy of Nathaniel Hawthorne. The teleconferencing hookup will help make civilization feel a little closer. Besides, where in New York City can a guy park an airplane in his own front yard?"

"Mr. Willow! Oh, Mr. Willow!" shouted Audrey, hurrying across the yard, the heels of her shoes sinking into the soft ground like a tree climber's spikes. "Your truck is gone. I mean, it's not where it was. I went looking for you and Mrs. Willow and found it rolled down the hill."

"What?" Chet yelped. He took off in a dead run toward the garage, Beecher lapping at his heels.

When Lexi caught up, she discovered that the Expedition had rolled down the side of the terrace and hit a tree. Chet was standing at the rear, examining the bumper with a perplexed look on his face. Lexi hurried down to join him.

"There's not even a dimple," he said. "The whole back end should be smashed in."

Lexi examined the impact zone. Neither the tree nor the truck was the slightest bit damaged.

27

Chet walked around to the driver's side and opened the door. "The emergency brake's still set."

Lexi noticed Chet had left the keys in the ignition. "You don't suppose Titus Blaylock knows how to drive an automatic, do you?"

"I didn't hear it start. Did you?" Chet asked. He closed the door and walked to the rear again. "Surely Beecher would have barked or something." He squatted and ran his hand across the moist ground. "There're no tire marks in the soft ground either. It's as though the entire vehicle was picked up and carefully placed here."

"With Mrs. Speedy Gonzales chattering the whole time we were inside, an armored tank division could have rolled by unnoticed."

Audrey called down from the edge of the parking area. "Is everything okay down there?"

Chet started the engine, switched into four-wheel drive and powered back up the hill, spinning the tires a couple times.

"Everything seems fine," Lexi said. "Not even a scratch."

"Oh, thank goodness," cheered Audrey. "I just hate filling out all those pesky insurance forms."

Lexi followed the truck up the hill. It was obvious someone had intentionally done this. A two and one-half-ton vehicle doesn't roll thirty feet down a hill and come to rest against a tree and not damage something. It was a pretty slick trick.

"I have no idea how such a terrible thing could have happened," chattered Audrey. "Well, if you folks are finished here, I need to rush back to Staunton for a four-thirty showing. I'll just go lock up the house." She turned and started clipping toward her car, walking even faster than before, if that was humanly possible. "Meet you down by the gate. Y'all just take your sweet little ole time."

"What's her hurry?" Lexi asked.

Chet glanced back at Audrey. "Probably saw her commission taking a header down the mountainside."

"Well, she can just wait," Lexi said. A fine mist began to fall. "I want to check out the barn again before we leave."

Chapter 3

For the next four weeks, a steady flow of heavy trucks loaded with building materials, furniture, appliances and construction equipment lumbered through the twisting sections of Route 250, headed for the flat spot on the eastern face of Cheat Mountain.

The architect had recommended a local contractor, Drexel Yeatts, with Landmark Restorations in Harrisonburg to oversee the renovations. Drexel's portfolio included projects at Monticello, Mount Vernon, the Virginia state capitol and homes in Philadelphia, Baltimore and Charleston, South Carolina. He was a master carpenter.

The first project Lexi wanted to complete was the corral so Paragon, her eight-year-old black Thoroughbred stallion, could acclimate to his new home.

Since the house was basically situated on solid rock, there was no basement—only a shallow crawlspace with a serrated bottom littered with the crispy carcasses of a million dead bugs—and the kitchen flooring had to be completely removed in order to replace the old plumbing, much of which was original material.

The plaster on the walls was four inches thick in places,

making it a nightmare for the electricians to install additional outlets. Drexel, God bless him—with his impish smile and unfailing diligence—always found a way to resolve each dilemma, achieving results that made it impossible to detect that the original construction had been the slightest altered. In retrospect, Lexi could not fathom undertaking this project without him.

In addition to the kitchen, the laundry room, guest bathrooms and master bath had all been gutted and were awaiting retrofit: a stainless-steel oversized dishwasher and a cooking sink; three re-enameled, vintage four-paw cast-iron bathtubs; granite counter tops and mahogany cabinets; a restaurant-style double oven, gas range and a Jen-Aire grill...most of which Lexi had selected from showrooms in New York.

The demolition went fast but the reconstruction, at first, was painfully slow. Most of the time Lexi was left with one operable toilet, one shower and one usable sink—though not always in the same bathroom or even on the same part of the house.

When the master bath—with a family-sized Jacuzzi, separate shower, sun lights, and white marble floor—was nearly completed, Lexi could begin to see the light at the end of the tunnel.

The fifth week deposited six days of continuous rain, bringing construction on the airstrip to a sloppy halt. Lexi knew that single delay bothered Chet more than all the others combined. If the rain held off through the night, the bulldozers were set to resume again tomorrow. In the meantime, Chet rented hangar space for his single-engine Moony Bravo at the municipal airport near Staunton.

Lexi was expecting JB for coffee today at two. She was eager to delve into the Blaylock family history and was already circling her computer in contemplation of a new novel.

JB arrived at two o'clock sharp, brandishing a fresh, homemade maple pie—a local delicacy—and a bottle of Bordeaux from the Shenandoah Vineyards.

"The gate was open," JB said. "I hope you don't take exception to me letting myself up."

"Not at all," Lexi said. "We keep it open during the day so the construction crews can come and go as needed."

JB stopped at the bottom of the landing and gazed around the foyer. "Heavens, I haven't set foot up here in nearly thirty years," she said. "It's exactly as I remember; the most handsome structure for a hundred miles in any direction."

"We've tried to keep everything original but the kitchen and bathrooms," Lexi replied. "There are a few pieces of the city we couldn't bear to leave behind."

"Those areas are different. Modernization is a wonderful thing, long as it saves a body a step or two. When the first part of the house was built, there wasn't even running water. It had to be carried up from the spring. I bought me a dishwasher fifteen years ago and haven't scrubbed nary a fork since."

Lexi led JB into the study and sat her down on the sofa.

"Hope you don't mind visiting in here," she said. "The kitchen won't be fully functional for a couple more weeks."

"The view's better from here anyway," JB replied.

Lexi glanced around to make certain everything was relatively presentable. "Let me run to the kitchen to get coffee and some plates. I'll be just a minute or so."

She returned several minutes later and found JB examining a framed promotional poster on the wall next to the computer desk.

"Audrey Pepper tells me you're a writer," JB said. "Is this one of yours?"

"I wish," Lexi replied. "I worked for a New York publishing house before I began freelancing. DARKSAIL was my first literary project to crack the bestsellers list. Editors seldom get credits so the

32

author gave me this. He signed it there at the bottom."

JB flipped up her glasses and scrutinized the signature. "What kind of books do you write?"

"Novels mostly, but I never seem to finish them. I wrote a weekly personal finance column for the *Times* called *Virtual Cents*, and computer articles for a variety of women's magazines."

"Women need to stay abreast of changing technology," JB said. "Ya never know when ya might need to fend for yourself in this world. I read Popular Mechanics cover-to-cover every month. I've gotten pretty handy with toolin' around on the Internet, too."

JB returned to the sofa and Lexi poured them each a cup of coffee.

"Mr. Willow didn't come in for his paper and cup of Joe this morning. Figured he was sleeping in."

"He had to drive to Harrisonburg early to meet with the architect," Lexi said. "We've decided to make a few more changes to the barn and corral areas."

JB sipped her coffee. "I didn't know city folks had such a knack for horses."

"I'm from Long Island originally," Lexi said. "My parents boarded horses on a small farm we owned on the eastern end. My father gave me my first horse when I was seven."

"If you could keep your animals there, why move to Monterey?"

Lexi considered telling JB about the robbery at her parent's home but decided against it. "The rural part of the island is quickly disappearing," Lexi replied. "We simply couldn't acquire enough land in one place for the size of operation we wanted. So I started researching listings on the Internet. Chet's father graduated from Virginia Military Institute in Lexington and at one time dated a girl from Monterey. He often reminisced about how beautiful it was here.

So I located a handful of realtors in Harrisonburg and Staunton, found this place, and here we are."

JB tipped her cup to her lips again; Lexi noticed JB's hand tremble ever so slightly as she returned the cup to the saucer.

"Did Mr. Willow ever mention the girl's name?" JB asked. "I've known just about every stalk of flesh that's lived in these parts the past sixty years. At least those that stuck around long enough to pin a name on."

Lexi thought for a moment. "Jandy. I believe he said her name was Jandy."

JB took another quick sip of coffee. Her hand didn't shake this time, but her eyes narrowed the same way they did back in the store when they first met.

"Nope, can't say that I remember that one," JB said. "When the mills were running, workers arrived in the spring and left when winter set in. Some brought their families, some didn't. By the time the last mill closed, just about everybody had moved on for good. If Mr. Willow, Sr. ever makes it out this way, you'll have to bring him by the store."

"Gentry Willow died from leukemia shortly after Chet and I were married," Lexi said. "Chet took it real hard. I believe that's why he didn't object when I suggested looking at this place."

JB relaxed a bit. She reached over and patted Lexi's hand. "May he rest in dearest, heavenly peace knowin' your home is now made so dear to his heart."

Lexi felt a tear well up. JB's simple sentiment was expressed with such honesty that it struck a nerve. "Thank you, JB. That was a very kind thing to say."

JB cracked open a scrapbook she had brought with her. "You said you wanted to hear a little more about the Blaylock family history. So I brought along some old pictures and newspaper clippings I've collected over the years."

She turned to an old but well-preserved picture of a man in a gray military uniform. He had magnetic, light-colored eyes and a chest-length black beard flecked in gray.

Lexi swallowed a wad of air. "I've seen this guy," she exclaimed. "His beard was grayer. He was on the side of the road the day Chet and I first met you, leading a horse. I thought I had dreamed him up."

JB's eyebrows arched but she remained cool. "And a doozy of a dream it was, too. Seeing how he's been dead for nearly a hundred and fifty years. Your question about Titus and a beard the other day got me thinking. "

Lexi was certain this was her man, fifteen pounds lighter and not so well-kept. But the shape of the head, the eyes, the beard, the uniform—minus the blood stains—was identical.

"His name is Major Shepherd J. Blaylock," JB continued, "of the 12th Georgia Regiment of the Confederate States Army. He was the first Blaylock to set foot in the Shenandoah Valley. He and his men were sent here by General Stonewall Jackson to cut off Union Army advancement eastward through the Shenandoah Mountain Pass. He was assigned to General Edward "Allegheny" Johnson and oversaw the construction of Fort Johnson, atop Shenandoah Mountain."

Lexi listened intently.

JB straightened a dog-eared corner. "He and his boys dug and built more than a mile of trenches and earthen parapets up there and fortified them in such a way the Union Army was never able to penetrate. They called them breastworks because they come up about chest high and allow the soldier to fire his musket standing and reload in relative safety."

"During those days, the Staunton Rail Yard was a major

Confederate Army staging area. Route 250, or the Staunton-Parkersburg Turnpike as it was known then, was the only road through this part of the mountains. Whoever controlled it, controlled access to Richmond from the west. General Jackson intended for it to stay in Confederate hands."

"In May of 1862, General Johnson marched his troops into the town of McDowell, about ten miles west of the Breastworks, and nine miles east of Monterey. They linked up with another regiment of Stonewall Jackson's men to intercept two regiments of Union troops, commanded by General Robert Milroy, pushing in from West Virginia.

"On May 7, skirmishes broke out across the banks of the Bull Pasture River. The next morning, May 8, the main body of Milroy's force forged the river and attacked the center of Johnson's line, charging right down the throat of Major Blaylock and the men of Georgia 12th. It was a God-awful battle, but the Major and his men managed to hold the northern troops off until reinforcements arrived. By the end of the day, twenty-five hundred brave Confederate regulars had defeated a force of four thousand Union soldiers. It went down in the history books as the Battle of McDowell.

"In all, more than seven-hundred and fifty men were killed; nearly five hundred of them were Confederates, many no more than thirteen years of age. Among the dead were Major Blaylock and every last man of the Georgia 12th. It was told that the major and his lions were the last ones to fall into the arms of death."

JB paused for a moment. "I suspect they took a frightful share of Union soldiers with them, too. Young men sacrificed by a bunch of fat, money-grubbing politicians in Washington and Richmond. Why, if those bastards were the ones toting the hardware, the whole friggin' Civil War wouldn't have amounted to a turkey shoot. Slavery is the stick people use today to beat down the Confederate culture but, if they bothered to read the history for themselves, they'd find slavery wasn't exactly the iron, coke and crucible of the whole southern upheaval."

JB's eyes became glassy and Lexi was again struck by the conviction of her words. She found herself absorbed by everything JB said; however, her random access memory was filling fast.

"You said Major Blaylock and his lions were the last of the Georgia Twelfth to die during the Battle at McDowell," Lexi said. "When we first visited here, Audrey Pepper called the statues down at the gate "Shepherd's Lions." She said they were the guardians of the Blaylock estate."

"Benaja and Junta, twin brothers," JB said without hesitation. "Mandingos and two of the biggest, most powerful men the Good Lord ever covered in flesh. They were slaves on the Blaylock plantation in Georgia. As kids, the two of them and Shepherd were inseparable. You might say they were his bodyguards, tough and fearless fighters, but more like family than slaves. Given the times back then, that was quite a remarkable relationship."

"The trader Shepherd's father bought them from branded a 'B' on Benaja's right cheek, and a 'J' on Junta's left so he could tell them apart. I suspect that act of cruelty is what so endeared the boys to Shepherd. Sealed their fate at a young age, too, I reckon.

"Before Shepherd headed off to war, he freed Benaja and Junta. They turned right around and enlisted and went along with him, leaving wives and children behind. Years later Titus Blaylock commissioned a sculptor in West Virginia to carve the statues as a tribute. Since there were no pictures of Ben and Juni, as I like to call them, he had them cast as lions. Branded just like the real brothers. It was a right smart piece of workmanship, too, if you ask me."

JB finished her coffee. Lexi poured her another half-cup.

"The trenches at the Breastworks are still there," JB said.

"The National Forestry Service has preserved right much of it. When you and Mr. Willow get a chance, you might drive up there and walk the lines for yourself. Parts of the McDowell battlefields are still accessible as well. People can think what they want about the Civil War, right or wrong, but to an old bird like me, it's quite an honor to stand where so many gave so much for a cause so few fully understood. For Shepherd Blaylock's sacrifices, a local landowner deeded a twenty-five acre tract of land to the major's widow. She had no use for it, being so far from home, and later sold it to Shepherd's older brother, Thomas Horatio Blaylock. Thomas homesteaded it a few years after the surrender in Appomattox.

"Mr. Thomas had a hound's nose for commerce. He cut the timber and used the proceeds to start buying up additional tracks of land. He cut, sold and bought one end of this valley to the next; up into West Virginia as well. A few years later, coal was discovered and his wealth snowballed."

JB turned the page to a picture of a large, stern-faced gentleman wearing a checkered vest and black coat standing next to the open driver's side door of a boxy black car. A striking woman with dark hair, a delicate nose and wide cheekbones was perched on the driver's seat.

"Thomas Blaylock died in June of 1885 and left everything to his son, Titus. Titus shared his daddy's knack for commerce and continued to expand the family interests. Some say, at one point, he was richer than the Rockefeller's. This is Titus Blaylock and his second wife, Andrea, taken in the fall of 1911. Titus's first wife, Margaret Anne, died several years earlier giving birth to their son, Deacon. The car is a Pierce Arrow touring sedan, one of Titus's most prized possessions; the first of its kind in the area. Woodrow Wilson, who incidentally was born just down the road there in Staunton, didn't get his Arrow until 1919.

"The roads weren't much to speak of then but Titus drove it everywhere he could; he wouldn't let anyone besides Andrea so much as touch it. Not even Deacon. I understand it took a whole set of tires just to make one trip to Richmond and back."

"They don't look very happy," said Lexi.

"People didn't smile in photographs much those days. Then again, these two certainly had more than their share to frown about. Every three months or so, Titus would make a business trip to Richmond. One time, he came back with Andrea. By all accounts, she was the most beautiful thing that ever graced the valley, not to mention the most trifling. Nobody ever spoke badly of her out in the open, though. Titus would fix them good if'n he ever found out about it. He pitched one of his stone cutters over the upper terrace wall just for cussing near her."

Lexi examined the picture closer. "So this is Porter's Jezebel?"

"That's what some folks called her, in private of course. Didn't matter how much old Titus did for her, she always scowled like she had a load of rock salt in her drawers. Titus fell in love with her looks, you see, and Andrea fell in love with Titus's money.

"Andrea absolutely hated it here, the isolation and all, and was always threatening to pack up and move back to Richmond. The only way Titus could keep her around was by taking her on lavish trips to Europe or out west to San Francisco. She treated poor Deacon like a bastard son, too. But ole' Deacon loved her to pieces; likely in a way a son shouldn't love his step-momma. None of those Blaylock men ever had any sense when it came to women. I suspect that played a big part in the whole works coming unglued up there."

"Audrey said they died on the *Titanic*," Lexi said.

"I'll give ten-to-one odds Andrea Blaylock was telling the captain how to drive the very moment he hit that iceberg." JB cut into

39

one of her shrill laughs. "When that woman dipped her toes in hell, I guarantee it spiked Satan's thermometers."

JB crowed again and turned the page to a newspaper clipping. "This is the article that ran in the Staunton paper after their death. It goes on about all the good things Titus did but mentions none of the bad. Nobody but Deacon knew they were even gone, least not until they had been away for a week or so."

"Titus had started selling off parts of his empire. I suspect he thought it best to liquidate as much as possible before leaving things for Deacon to squander away. The mineral holdings were sold to J.D. Rockefeller and a gentleman named Henry Flagler with Standard Oil."

"Henry Flagler?" replied Lexi. "I spent a semester at Flagler College, named after Mr. Flagler in St. Augustine, Florida. We were working on a Timucua Indian archeological project. Henry Flagler was an amazing man."

"I don't know much about Mr. Flagler. But I know he and Mr. Rockefeller laid-out some serious cash for Titus's mines and the adjoining real-estate. Probably was worth ten times what they paid for it."

"The winter Titus and Ms. Andrea disappeared was warmer than most, but Titus closed the mill December through February just the same. So there weren't many other people around that would have seen them leave. I guess the Arrow ended up somewhere in Richmond. That's supposedly where they caught the train to the coast."

Lexi was beginning to lose track of all the details. She jumped up and rummaged through her desk for a pad of paper. "Do you mind if I take notes? If I don't, I'll never keep it all straight."

"No, go ahead. I'll be glad to fill in any holes you might find later."

"Porter said he's seen Titus's ghost."

"Some claim its Titus, some claim its Deacon. Porter wouldn't know either of them from a porcupine in a prom dress. You can call it Titus if you'd like."

Lexi stopped writing. "Audrey said Deacon killed himself. Did that happen on the farm?"

JB's brow furrowed. "Now that's a sad tale if there ever was one." She flipped several pages to a picture of another large-framed man dressed in a bathing suit and white pullover shirt sitting under a beach umbrella with a glass in his hand.

"He died about a month after the fire which destroyed the mill. Threw his self into a spinning blade at the old saw house, or so most believed at the time. Titus left Deacon pretty well fixed, with the various businesses and all. But he didn't leave behind a map or papers saying where he had hidden most of his money. Titus didn't put much faith in banks with his personal finances, you see. The old timers claimed he exchanged all his script for gold and stashed it around the mill somewhere. Andrea collected silver, I do know that. But Deacon was never able to find much of it.

"Deacon wasn't anywhere the businessman his daddy and Thomas were. He gambled, drank too much and chased anything that could titter and bat an eyelid. He went through money like a drunken sailor with six arms. Had himself four wives, too. I suspect each of them took a good chunk of what money he had at the time when they departed.

"Deacon possessed an explosive temper, too. He got that naturally from Titus and, I suspect, having Andrea around helped him hone it. When his money started running thin, he'd sell off a parcel of land to keep things running on even keel.

"Mill production was down to a fraction of what it was during the glory years. In the end, the only plant running was the small steam mill down behind the barn...that's where the saw was Deacon supposedly jumped into. Personally, I think he burned the mill to collect the insurance money. But I suspect something else happened that night of the fire. Something much more tragic; sinister even. Deacon's only son, Raymond, disappeared. I'm sure there was a young floozy involved in it somewhere, as well as a liberal amount of elbow bending; at least on Deacon's part...Deacon didn't do anything without first consulting the bottle.

"Raymond, on the other hand, was the strong, quiet type. Aside from Shepherd, I've always considered him the most noble of the Blaylock men. Some believe he found Titus's gold and hightailed it out of here, causing Deacon to finally strike a match to it all. There was never a formal investigation which wasn't too surprising. From the day Titus Blaylock skimmed his first dollar, he began greasing the palms of every lawman within five counties. It helped cover a world of indiscretions; Deacon's probably more so than Titus's.

"A banker down in Staunton eventually acquired the property. From there, it changed hands a number of times. A senator from Iowa once owned it, but his wife preferred rubbing elbows with the Washington, D.C. folk. Nobody stayed more than a couple years. The last owners, the Madison's, hardly lasted a winter. I so hope you and Mr. Willow can make a go of it."

Lexi was writing notes at a furious pace; JB had stopped talking for several moments before she even realized it.

"Oh, I'm sorry," Lexi said. "This is all so fascinating. Half of me wants to take notes and the other half is outlining a story."

"We'll have plenty of time to backtrack," JB said. She placed the scrapbook aside and raised her cup. "This is going down pretty good. Mind if I help myself to another cup? Haven't talked this much since I sold the livestock market."

"That's right. Audrey said you were an auctioneer."

JB rolled off a spiel of perfect auctioneer tongue. "Sold to the man in the green hat with the whiskey nose and chewing tobacco-stained teeth."

Lexi laughed and poured JB another cup of coffee. "You're the one that should be writing stories. Is there anything you haven't done?"

"A woman's got to take care of herself in this life."

"Did you ever marry?"

"I had my share of men when I wanted them," JB answered. "You can't tell it now but I was a pretty hot babe back in the day. Marriage and me just never boarded a train heading in the same direction. The only men I can get now either have more natural gas than the continent of Texas or are just too blasted ornery to live with. Tell the truth, I'd rather share quarters with a hog. That way when I get tired of him, I can boil his hair off, salt 'em and hang 'em in the cellar to eat off all winter." JB crowed again.

"Maybe you're better off single." Lexi wrote on her pad in capital letters GHOSTS, and underlined it. "Has anyone seen the ghost besides Porter?"

"Several claim to, including one or two of the previous owners. It's all a crock of horse hockey, if you ask me. Just an effective way for the women folk to get their men to haul their parts out of here, regardless of whose idea it was to come in the first place. Find me a mansion on a cliff where completely explainable things have happened, surround it with country bumpkins who can't keep their mouths shut, and I'll show you a house that becomes Spook Central Station."

"You sound pretty certain of that." It would have been impossible for Lexi to conjure up the real Shepherd Blaylock in such perfect detail without even knowing he once actually existed. She wasn't an active believer in ghosts, but didn't completely dismiss the notion either. Something had implanted his image into her dream.

"Titus Blaylock built my store. I bought it from Deacon before he killed himself. He ain't never come around haunting me. If I was you, I wouldn't go believing' Porter any farther than you can spit fishing hooks."

Lexi could tell JB was uncomfortable with this line of conversation. She spied the maple pie sitting on the coffee table. "This pie looks absolutely delicious. Let's take a quick break and have a slice."

"My recipe maple pie has captured first prize at the Spring Maple Festival three year's running."

Lexi cut JB a big piece. "You truly are a wonder," she said. The thought of pie made from pure maple syrup made her stomach shrivel. But she didn't want to seem ungrateful so she cut herself a small sliver.

"Go on and fix yourself a piece worth messin' up a plate," JB said. "If you're planning to birth a pile of children, you'll need plenty of meat on your bones. There's hardly enough of you now to trap between the sheets."

Lexi put a second sliver on her plate. She tasted it. It truly was divine and probably no less than two thousand calories a mouthful.

"How many children are ya planning to have?"

"Two, maybe three. We lost a baby a year ago this May. I had ruptured membranes and delivered at twenty-three weeks, a little girl. She died in Chet's hands. It had taken us several years to conceive. Since then, we haven't had any luck getting pregnant again. Chet doesn't even like to talk about having children anymore."

"I'd reckon your luck's about to change then. If there's one piece of magic this valley still holds, it's that a fertile woman can get pregnant by simply following a man across a parking lot."

"I don't know, JB. We've tried everything, even in vitro. I don't want to get my hopes up."

"Ever tried walking the dandelions?"

"Dandelions?" Lexi wasn't certain she'd heard right.

"Yes, ma'am. Dandelions reproduce at a clip that can shame rabbits. When and where you least expect them, too."

JB set her pie aside. "Now you do exactly as I say. Seven days before you start your cycle, walk the dandelions, barefoot, first thing every morning when the dew's the thickest. Get the soles of your feet good 'n yellow. Then let your skin completely absorb the juices before you wash it off."

"What will that do?" Lexi asked.

"It softens the egg so that a man's base runners can tag home plate with a little more authority. Wear a thin nightgown in case that handsome man of yourn' is watching; let him get a good look at all your parts. Men love seeing women nearly naked outdoors. Makes them feel less domesticated...gets the right juices flowing where you need them. But don't let him have at ya until you're ovulating. Oh, and one last thing, feed him lots of local honey. Not that processed stuff from the grocery stores; it's got to have the nectar of the valley in it. That's the secret...the dandelions, the bees and the honey...all from the same place. Gives a man's little sperm wigglers an extra whip in their get-along. Got some down at the store, case you can't find any that's fresh."

Drexel Yeatts knocked on the foyer doorjamb. "Mrs. Willow, we're ready to connect the emergency generator and new distribution panel. I'll need to shut the power off for forty-five minutes or so."

Lexi received Drexel's transmission, but her tuner was still stuck between honey and dandelions. "Oh, the power." She glanced back at her computer. "Should I unplug anything?"

"No, ma'am. We've wired in a voltage conditioner and surge

45

protection. When the power comes back on, it will flow like silk."

"Wonderful," Lexi replied. "Now if you could just do something about the telephones."

He smiled. "I'm working on it."

"Drexel, have you met JB?" Lexi asked.

His eyes shifted to JB and his smile widened. "Only across the lottery ticket display."

"JB, this is our contractor, Drexel Yeatts. It's absolutely amazing what this man can accomplish with a saw and some nails."

"Coffee, black, one sugar and a frosted honey bun," JB said. "Becoming a regular customer. Never caught the name though, it's a pleasure."

"I've got men standing in line to work up here just to get at JB's lunch specials." Drexel smiled again and started to leave. "I'll let you know when we're finished with the test. Be seeing you, JB."

After Drexel was gone, JB gave Lexi a wink. "Might just need to boost my prices a tad."

"Your fried chicken is a bargain at any price," Lexi replied. "How about a tour of the house?"

JB stood. "Thanks kindly, but I'd best take a rain check. Porter's likely downed a whole six-pack of Budweiser by now. If I don't get back, he'll run off all my cash-paying customers." She started collecting the dishes.

"Leave those," Lexi said. "I'll take care of them later."

"Much obliged for the hospitality, Mrs. Willow. Hope I didn't wear out my welcome with all my foolishness."

"Not at all, JB. And, please, call me Lexi."

JB nodded and held out the scrapbook. "Why don't you hold onto this for a while? It might help put a face to everybody."

Lexi was hoping JB would offer and graciously accepted. "Thanks again for the pie, JB. Chet will absolutely love it."

She showed JB to the door and then settled back on the sofa with the scrapbook and her notepad. The first picture she turned to was Major Shepherd Blaylock. This was definitely her man.

Chet returned an hour later and Lexi couldn't wait to fill him on the high points of her visit with JB.

"Sounds like the Blaylocks were a pretty spirited bunch," Chet said. "I just hope all their spirits stay put."

"Maybe Titus's ghost will grant me an interview."

Chet grimaced. "He'll probably demand royalties. Say, I caught Drexel down by the road. He said the generator test went off without a hitch."

Lexi nodded her head. "We didn't even need to reset the clock on the microwave."

Chapter 4

The rainy days finally came to an end and, by eight-thirty the next morning, the metallic clatter of bulldozers filled the valley. By ten o'clock, Lexi had wallpaper samples draped across every piece of furniture in the study; Chet was helping her develop color schemes for the guest bathrooms.

Drexel rushed in with red Virginia clay caked up to his knees. "The bulldozers have uncovered something down at the airstrip. You might want to come take a look."

"What is it?" Chet asked.

"A car. A really old car."

Lexi trailed Chet out the door and jumped into the six-wheel John Deere Gator—a toy Chet bought to drive back and forth to the valley—and took off toward the stables.

The sun was out in full splendor but the air still had a brisk edge to it. Lexi found it refreshing. "I wonder why there's a car buried in our meadow," she asked.

"I don't know," Chet replied. "Maybe Deacon got hammered one night and forgot where he parked it."

48

CHEAT MOUNATAIN

The pavement stopped at the gate next to the barnyard. Lexi opened it so Chet could drive through, then immediately closed it; her black stallion, Paragon, was still new to his surroundings and she didn't want to provide him any enticement to break out and go exploring.

The Gator bumped along the dirt path past the barn and a tin-roofed shed that housed the old sawmill. Beyond that, the stone wall ended and the terrace sloped back down to the valley floor.

Drexel and a group of men were standing around a large, dark rectangle on the ground; two of them were carefully digging with shovels along one edge of it.

"It's definitely a car," Drexel said. "Some type of old sedan, I'd guess. A half-inch lower and the bulldozer would have peeled back the roof like a can of sardines."

The men uncovered the top portion of a side window; Chet grabbed a shovel and dug down another foot.

"Does anyone have a flashlight and some paper towels?" he asked.

Drexel returned from his truck with a black Mag-Lite and a torn blue rag. Chet wiped the dirt off the window and fiddled with the switch on the flashlight. Once he got it working, he lay on his stomach in the hole he'd dug and peered inside.

"There's an emblem on the dashboard," he said. He wiped the window some more. "It says Pierce Arrow."

"JB said Titus Blaylock owned a 1911 Pierce Arrow," she exclaimed. "I've got a picture of it at the house."

A barrel-chested man in a white hard hat—Norman Evans, the paving crew foreman—squatted next to Chet. "Well, it's right in the middle of your airport, Mr. Willow. Either we move the runway, or we dig it out."

Lexi got an uneasy feeling in her gut. "There isn't anybody in

49

it, is there?"

Chet shone the flashlight into the rear of the cabin. "Can't tell from here." He crawled out of the hole and brushed himself off. "This baby's coming out." He looked at Norman. "What will it take?"

"I suppose we can excavate around it with the small Cat," Norman said. "Have to do the close work by hand. If it will still roll, we can hook a chain to the undercarriage and drag it out. Two, maybe three hours."

Chet was grinning like he'd just gained controlling interest in Microsoft. "Add it to my bill. I'll give each of you an extra hundred bucks if you don't put any scratches on it. Haul it up to the garage for me and I'll throw in a case of Scotch."

"Make it Dewar's and I'll give it wax job, too." Norman replied.

Chet reached out and clasped Norman's hand. "Dewar's it is. And if you find a chest filled with gold down there, we'll split it sixty-forty." He put his arm around Lexi. "If there's enough of it left to salvage, we just got a new addition to the family."

On the trip back to the house, Lexi revisited her conversation with JB. *Titanic* sank in April of 1912 on its way from London to New York. Obviously, Titus and Andrea first had to get to England. They must have left Monterey about the same time the mills were getting set to reopen. No competent business manager would leave at a time like that, especially one as controlling as Titus Blaylock seemed to have been.

But if they went to Richmond, like JB said, either someone brought the car back—which was unlikely because Titus wouldn't let anyone else touch it—or they didn't take it in the first place. Deacon could have found it later and brought it back. But why hide it? He could have sold it to help finance one of his divorce settlements.

"Don't look so glum," Chet told her. "It's only a car."

"I want to know why Titus Blaylock's most prized possession ended up buried in the valley."

"Maybe Deacon ditched it to aggravate the old man. I've got a friend in Trenton that may know a competent restoration shop."

When they got back to the house, Lexi showed Chet the picture. "Maybe JB can shed some light on it."

"If anyone knew that car was there, it would have been exhumed years ago," Chet said. "Add another chapter to your Blaylock mystery file."

Lexi flipped through her JB notes. "Deacon was the only one who knew Titus and Andrea had left for Europe. Other people didn't find out for several days. He would have had plenty of time to stash the car. Maybe Deacon learned that Titus was going to cut him out of the business. So he killed him and Andrea, then dumped the car. The mill wasn't in operation so there would be nobody around to see him do it. JB also said that winter was warmer than usual; the ground may not even have been frozen. He dug a hole, pushed the Arrow in, and filled it back. A month or so later, the *Titanic* sinks and three-quarters of her passengers drown. It's the perfect cover."

Chet mulled that over for a couple moments before speaking. "Titus and Andrea would have been listed on a passenger manifest."

"Hundreds of last-minute passengers didn't get recorded."

"Why didn't Deacon ditch the bodies with the car?"

"Because he disposed of them before realizing he needed to hide the car."

"Andrea was bound to have had servants. They would have known she was missing."

Lexi could tell Chet was weakening. "Titus gave them the week off."

"That would have raised suspicions. Besides, Andrea would need to cook and do the housework. She would have ripped Titus a new one for letting them go."

"More reason to kill her."

"Deacon or Titus?"

"Deacon."

"Great answer. Hopefully you'll be able to keep your characters straight. I'm running down to JB's to grab some lunch." Chet rose and kissed Lexi on the forehead. "Sweetheart, you've got a wonderful imagination. One of these days, Oprah Winfrey will be begging for an interview." He headed toward the foyer. "JB's got roast beef and gravy on special today."

Lexi couldn't believe Chet was simply willing to accept all this. "I thought you were a big Marine Corps officer. Aren't you even the least bit curious if a crime's been committed?"

"Curious, not suspicious," Chet said. "There's a perfectly logical explanation, somewhere. There always is. You coming?"

"All you can think about is your new toy." Lexi started writing in her notepad again. "I need to get this down while it's still fresh in my mind. Tell JB I'll give her a call later."

Chet returned with an extra plate of roast beef and gravy. JB had gone to Staunton for the day and Chet decided not to tell Porter what they had found.

After lunch, Chet made several phone calls; Lexi returned to her notes. An hour later, Chet drove her back down to the dig.

The workers had completely uncovered two sides of the Arrow and were cleaning dirt from around the third. The sheet metal was somewhat pitted and in generally rough shape, and the tires had rotted. But the windows and everything else appeared to be intact.

Lexi was relieved to learn there were no bodies inside, although the men did find an old steamer trunk full of ladies clothes. It wasn't Titus's gold but it gave credence to her theory that, if Andrea was going away for several months, she would have taken plenty of clothing and personal articles. For that, she would have needed her trunk...something Deacon apparently realized, as well.

When the last of the dirt was cleared away, one of the bulldozer operators crawled under the car with a grease gun and lubricated the wheel and axle bearings. Another carefully opened the driver's door and tied the steering wheel with a rope to keep it from turning. They attached a chain to the front and then rocked it back and forth several times to free up as many moving parts as possible. Finally, Norman inched the Arrow from its resting place with the bulldozer.

The axles squealed a bit until the grease found all the right places but, soon, it was out. Chet carefully opened the driver's side door. The air inside was stagnant yet, remarkably, the interior was in mint condition; the leather on the seats was even still supple. Mother Earth had provided a perfect hermetic seal.

Drexel eased open the hood. "Ten bucks says if you give it a crank, she'll turn over."

"I found a shop in Silver Springs, Maryland that specializes in these," Chet said. "After it's restored, I'll take you guys for a spin."

"Let's load it up on the low boy and take it up the hill," said Norman. "We need to backfill this hole and get these bulldozers back on the job."

Norman eased the Arrow onto a trailer, hauled it out to the main road, around to the driveway and up to the garage.

Chet was like a sixteen-year-old kid with his first car. He carefully washed it, twice, with warm soapy water. Lexi helped him towel it dry. He already had a truck lined up to transport it to Maryland.

Lexi still had an uneasy feeling. The Arrow was definitely an important piece of the puzzle. Someone had buried it and the steamer trunk because they were linked to a crime.

"I think we should notify the police," she said.

"Why do that?" Chet asked. "We'll end up with half the county poking around up here. Word will spread fast enough."

Lexi chased Chet around the car with the water hose. "You're beginning to sound like Titus Blaylock. Next you'll be pitching construction workers over the wall."

"Let's go for a jump in the back seat. It'll make you feel like a high school girl again."

"Excuse me?" Lexi exclaimed. "I was not deflowered until my sophomore year in college, I'll have you know."

Chet opened the door and grinned. "Honey, if you had known me back in the day, I'd have owned that prize before the end of ninth grade."

Lexi shot Chet with the hose. But he was right about the people of Monterey. Many were already quizzing JB about the goings on up here. Still, she had a feeling a serious crime had been committed and the location of the Arrow was a critical piece of evidence. Maybe even the key to series of crimes.

Chapter 5

After dinner, Chet tuned the television to a Yankees pre-season game. The teleconferencing equipment also provided high-speed satellite Internet access so Lexi decided to surf the net and see if she could access any area newspaper archives. She searched for over an hour without any success.

That night, a powerful storm rumbled over the mountain. Thunder echoed northward through the valley like the sounds of an approaching battle. A vanguard stroke of lightning deposited an eerie regiment of crooked shadows across the bedroom walls like a horde of demons marching off to battle. In a matter of moments, the house was under siege; lightning flashed and thunder exploded all around.

After the initial fury passed, a steady rain impacted the mountain face behind the house, making the sounds like a tropical waterfall. Usually the memories of September 11 fought for control of her sleep. This night, she actually managed to relax and soon felt herself drifting off.

She was awakened by Beecher barking downstairs in the

kitchen. The sun was just peeking through the windows and Lexi rolled to her side to look at the clock—the dial was blank. From the corner of her eye, she saw the red battery indicator on the security panel blinking. She reached for the phone; it was dead, too.

Beecher came barreling down the hall. He leapt into the middle of the bed, dug his nose under the covers, jumped back to the floor and started barking again. Chet clutched a pillow over his head.

Lexi lifted a corner of it. "The power's out again."

"That's impossible. We just installed an eighteen-thousand dollar emergency generator," he groaned.

"Improbable, not impossible." Lexi slid out of bed and hurried down to the kitchen to let Beecher out. Beecher made a beeline for the barn and began barking like the sky was falling.

Chet came down a minute later dressed in jeans and a black sweatshirt. He grabbed a stale pot of coffee off the counter and stared at it longingly. "Maybe someday someone will invent a battery-powered coffee maker," he said with a frown. "What's up with Beech?"

Lexi looked out the door. "Maybe something's wrong at the barn."

Chet stepped into the laundry room and got his jacket. "Let's take a look."

Lexi walked over to him. "This first. Open your mouth."

Chet did as directed and Lexi stuck a saltine cracker loaded with honey on his tongue.

"What's that for?" he asked.

"Breakfast, every morning. And another one before bed. Taste good?"

Chet shrugged his shoulders as he walked toward the door; Lexi pulled a raincoat over her robe, put on a pair of rubber boots and followed.

Beecher's barking got louder as she and Chet neared the north end of the mill's boss house. Lexi heard the sounds of a large animal struggling and ran ahead. When she rounded the other side of the house, she saw where a large branch had fallen from an oak tree and smashed the fence which bordered a soggy expanse of ground near the base of the mountain. Paragon, her prized black stallion, was trapped in the mud two-thirds of the way up his withers and was fighting to free himself; eyes electric with fear. His flailing only entrapped him deeper.

"Oh my God!!" Lexi shrieked.

Chet ran to the edge of the mud. The ground under his feet gave away and he started sinking. He jabbed at Paragon's halter with his right hand but couldn't reach it.

"Stay here and try to settle him down," he said quietly. "I'll go get the truck. Don't venture past the fence. The ground is too unstable."

Chet collected Beecher and took off in a dead run. Lexi stepped up to the fence and started talking to Paragon in a low, gentle voice. It was difficult to contain her anxiety but she had to remain calm for the horse's sake.

Paragon's tremendous strength was fading...no telling how long he had been trapped. His muzzle was covered with muck and his nostrils were flaring franticly, blowing forth a fine spray of muddy froth. When he heard Lexi's voice he relaxed a little, but then began to struggle again.

Lexi tested the ground inside the fence with her foot to determine where it was firm enough to support her weight, then knelt down face-level with Paragon and continued talking to him.

Audrey Pepper had said the mud was just an area of spongy sod, probably caused by an underground spring. The fence had been built to keep the mill worker's children from playing near it. But it wasn't just spongy sod; it was obviously a quicksand pit.

As Chet drove up in the Expedition, Paragon began to flail again and Lexi feared the ground was going to swallow him right before her eyes. She started to cry.

Chet backed the Ford up to the fence, shut off the engine and jumped out. "I'm going to the tack house and get some lead lines," he said. "Just hold on, I'll be right back."

"Hurry! Please, hurry," Lexi pleaded, trying to keep from becoming hysterical. "Everything's going to be fine," she repeated to herself, although the mud was now just inches from the top of Paragon's back.

The few moments Chet was gone felt like hours. Paragon's breathing was getting faster and faster, the force of the mud against his chest was preventing his lungs from fully expanding. He was slowly suffocating.

Chet directed Lexi to take one end of the line and run it through a split in the top of a fence post, and then loop it around the ball on the Expedition's trailer hitch. He took the other end and waded out into the mud and clipped it to Paragon's halter.

"Everything is going to be fine, baby. Just start the engine and ease the truck forward to take the slack out of the line. Stop when I tell you."

Lexi couldn't keep her hands from trembling and fumbled with the keys trying to start the engine. Once she got it running, she tossed Beecher into the back seat and put it into gear. Keeping one foot on the brake, she slowly inched forward. She had moved about two feet when Chet yelled for her to stop. Lexi stomped on the emergency brake and threw the door open, tears flowing freely down her cheeks.

"Okay, Lexi, here's what we do," Chet said, still calm and collected. "We might injure his neck if we try pulling him by the halter. So we'll just keep the line tight and let him work to the edge himself."

Several minutes passed. Paragon was exhausted and simply didn't have the strength left to pull himself out. At least—for the moment—he wasn't sinking any deeper.

"Okay, we're going to need some help," Chet said. "I'll stay here and keep him calm. You go to the house and call JB's."

Lexi wiped the tears from her eyes. "I can't. The phones are dead."

"Okay, not a problem. Get my keys form the truck, run to the garage and take the BMW. Get Porter or anyone else that's there. Everything's going to be fine here. Paragon and I are just going to talk about all the frisky young fillies he soon gets to play stable tag with."

Lexi didn't want to leave but realized there was no option. She took the keys from the truck, ran to the garage and opened the door. The BMW started on the first try. She backed out, swung around, and gunned the accelerator down the mountain.

Suddenly, she remembered the gates...they would not open without electrical power. "Ram them," she told herself.

But when she reached the lower terrace, the gates were open. It might have just been the angle of her eye or adrenalin pumping through her brain but, for a moment, she swore she saw them retracting. "Thank God."

The lights were on in JB's store, her pickup and one other car in the parking lot. Lexi leaped out of the BMW and rushed through the front door—a gas generator was humming somewhere behind the building.

JB and Porter were standing behind the counter talking to a woman about JB's age.

"Chet and Paragon are stuck in quicksand by the barn!" Lexi

59

exclaimed. "Please! You've got to help us."

"Porter, haul your parts into the back and get me two coils of Number-5 double-braided," JB ordered. "Irene, call Tallmadge and have him meet us up at the house. Mind the store while I'm gone."

JB grabbed her coat and headed for the door. Porter met her on the front porch with a coil of rope over each shoulder.

As Lexi climbed back into the BMW, she saw Drexel's truck pull into the parking lot. She got out and raced over to the driver's side window.

"Chet and Paragon are trapped in a quicksand pit by the barn! Hurry!" She didn't wait for a reply.

Drexel's engine roared and his tires slung a shower of gravel until they gripped solid pavement, then peeled rubber up the highway. JB and Porter pulled out right behind him.

By the time Lexi returned to Chet, the line had slipped off the fence post and the mud was up over Paragon's back. JB replaced the line and Lexi pulled the Expedition forward again.

Another pickup arrived and Tallmadge Price, Irene's husband, jumped out with another coil of rope.

"Looks like you brought the cavalry," Chet joked, though there was little humor in his tone.

Chet and Paragon had obviously had a struggle. Chet was covered with mud up to the tops of his ears and there were thin ribbons of dried muck around his eyes where he had to scoop it away to see. Lexi kneeled by the edge of the pit and started talking to Paragon again; Porter stood by the fence, not three feet away from her, gawking with his one good eye like a spectator at a house fire.

Drexel found an old, wooden wagon wheel leaning against the back of the boss house and cut the metal tread off with a cordless circular saw.

JB reeled thirty feet of cable off the winch, attached it to the front bumper of Drexel's truck, and removed the pin from the U-bolt holding the hook—she commanded Porter to remove the fallen branch and haul away the broken fencing.

Tallmadge threw Chet another rope and he wrapped it around Paragon's hindquarters, and then tossed it back. Tallmadge tied one end to the right side of his truck's bumper, pulled in the slack and, tied the other end to the left side.

Drexel quickly cut the wagon-wheel tread in half and drilled a hole in the end of each piece. He pinned one end of the cut tread to the winch cable and passed it through the fence to Lexi. She tossed it to Chet and he carefully slid the rim under Paragon's belly. JB looped another rope around the base of a fence post and tossed one end to Chet who threaded it through the hole on the other end of the tread and knotted it. The sling was almost complete.

The rest of Drexel's men drove up and rushed over to see what they could do to help.

"You guys grab that line on the back of the Expedition and keep a steady tension on it," Drexel said. "Pull back when I tell you to."

After everything was set, Drexel goosed the winch and drew the cable taut.

"Ready when you are," Chet shouted.

Drexel engaged the winch and began drawing-in the cable. The wheel tread splayed out flat under Paragon's belly and lifted him a couple inches. Chet hooked his arm around Paragon's neck and speared his foot into the slop alongside Paragon's belly to release the suction that built up as they rose. There was a loud slurp and Paragon popped up another six inches.

"JB, have Mr. Price pull forward. Slowly," Drexel shouted. He pointed to his men. "Heave back on that lead line."

As Mr. Price eased ahead, Paragon kicked himself toward the

edge of the quicksand pit; Drexel bumped the winch, keeping the sling tight. Lifting and pulling, inch by inch, Paragon finally made it to the edge. With one last incredibly powerful burst of strength, he climbed out of the pit with Chet still holding onto his neck. Drexel released the clutch on the winch and the sling fell to the ground.

Paragon stopped abruptly and Chet lost his grip, landing on his back with a loud groan.

Lexi rushed to him. "Are you okay?"

He scooped a handful of muck off his face. "I can't believe women actually pay to have this done."

Lexi kissed the top of his head, the only part of him not caked with goop. "Not quite the way John Wayne would have made his entrance but you're my hero just the same."

Chet said something else but Lexi was only vaguely listening. Paragon was kicking his left rear leg; the hoof was covered with blood.

"Paragon's bleeding," she exclaimed. She crawled on her hands and knees for a closer examination. The wound was deep; there was something wrapped around his fetlock. Lexi ran her finger across it. Hard and segmented like a chain; Paragon must have stirred it up from the bottom of the pit.

Chet braced his back against the horse's flank and lifted the injured hoof. Lexi sent Jimmy Grubbs, one of Drexel's men, to the barn to get a bucket of water to rinse the wound.

Lexi carefully removed the chain and traced it back into the pit where she discovered a pointed stick jutting out of the mud.

"There's something else in there," she said.

Chet gave the chain a hard tug. The stick moved a couple inches, then settled back.

Drexel unshackled the sling and hooked the chain to the U-bolt.

"Bring it in," Chet ordered.

Drexel started the winch and the stick cut through the mud like a shark's fin. Suddenly, another shape broke the surface and Drexel halted the winch. As the mud oozed downward, the object began to look like fingers and a hand. JB didn't so much as bat an eye.

"Oh my God," Lexi gasped. "It's an arm."

Drexel goosed the winch again and a head and shoulders broke the surface; he slowly delivered the body onto solid ground. The chain was wrapped around it from chest to feet. The stick proved to be a broken pitchfork handle and all three tines were buried to the hilt in the corpse's chest.

"Who do you suppose it is?" Lexi asked.

Jimmy came back with two buckets of water. Chet took one and rinsed the mud off the head and upper body.

The eyes were wide open though the orbs had shriveled to the size of grapes; the lower jaw slung open in a wide yawn. The skin was the texture of moist tanned leather.

JB crouched beside it. "It's Raymond Blaylock. I'm almost certain of it."

Lexi attempted to interpret JB's reaction. Her pursed mouth could have been either shock or dismay but her narrowed eyes seemed to convey something else. Anger, maybe...or disgust.

Chet poured the second bucket of water on the body and sent Jimmy for two more.

Raymond was still fully clothed. JB reached into his pants pocket and extracted a gold watch and chain like she knew it was there.

"It's Raymond alright," she said. "Deacon gave him this watch the day he graduated from high school. When I was a young girl, he'd hook the chain around my neck and let me wear it like a necklace."

Lexi was taken aback. It never really occurred to her that JB may have actually known the Blaylocks socially.

JB stood. "Porter, get my cell phone and call Sheriff Godsey."

Porter didn't move. His good eye was darting between Raymond and the ice pit. Lexi zeroed in on what he was looking at. Barely discernible from all the mud, there was a rope caught in Raymond's chains near his feet.

Porter looked at Lexi and smiled. His murky eye had turned a peculiar shade of dark pink, almost a blush. "Wonder what's at the other end."

He gave the rope a yank; there was no resistance. He spat a wad of tobacco juice and said, "Nothin'." He dropped the rope and walked back to the truck.

Lexi pulled in the line anyway and found the other end tied to two heavy straps of soggy leather. After she wiped the mud off, they looked like the handles of an old duffel bag.

"I reckon Raymond's been down there since about 1950," JB said. "Figured this old ice pit had long dried up by now." She turned around and looked at Lexi. "Titus had two of them dug in the summer of 1911. Power lines hadn't been run this far yet so there was no such beast as electric refrigerators. Folks used to freeze blocks of ice in the winter and placed them in pits covered with wood shavings for use during the summer months. There was a larger pit down in the valley but, of course, Andrea wanted one closer to the house.

"When they dug this one, they hit a spring at about thirty feet. The sides caved in and the whole thing filled with water. Heavy rains fell later that summer and washed a mudslide down from the mountaintop. Titus attempted to drain it but the pit's like a huge stone basin and he hit solid rock every way he dug. So they just left it."

64

"Exactly where was the other pit?" Lexi asked.

JB looked into the valley. "Right about where your airstrip is going."

"Right where we found the Pierce Arrow?" Chet asked.

This time, JB was visibly stunned. "You found the Arrow?"

"I called you yesterday afternoon but you weren't back from Staunton," Lexi said. "The bulldozers uncovered it. Chet had it pulled out and moved to the garage."

"That find was a lot better than this one," Drexel remarked.

"May I see it?" JB asked with her hand curled around the point of her chin.

"Absolutely," Lexi replied as the sound of sirens wafted up from the highway.

JB's eyes roamed back to Raymond. Her expression turned to sadness. "We'd best tend to your animal first," she said. "I've got sulfur salve and bandaging down at the store. We should call Doc Buchanan in case he needs stitches and a tetanus shot."

JB shot a look at Porter. "Grab those water buckets and clean Raymond up a little before Sheriff Godsey gets here."

As Porter trudged past the Expedition, Beecher bounced from the back seat to the front, barking frantically. Similar to the same way he had been barking earlier that morning.

Porter just ignored the barking but Lexi didn't.

Chapter 6

The rescue squad loaded Raymond's body into the ambulance and Sheriff Godsey slammed the rear doors. "What's wrong, Tommy?" he smirked. "Ain't ya gonna ride in the back with this one?"

Tommy kept walking. "Ain't so sure it's dead," he called over his shoulder, climbing into the cab as his partner drove off.

Godsey chuckled to himself and waddled over to Lexi and Chet. "The state police will conduct a follow-up investigation to take statements. Standard procedure really, nothing to get in a lather about."

He adjusted his gun belt so that everyone could see the stainless-steel Springfield Arms 1911 automatic gleaming in the black-webbed holster; the threads on the bottom button of his shirt gave away at the same time, exposing a flap of dimpled, pink skin. "I'd suggest drainin' that pit, though. Hate to be dragging one of you out of it one day."

Sheriff Godsey was about a double-frosted doughnut shy of three hundred pounds. If his predecessors were anything like him,

66

Lexi doubted that it took much of a bribe from Titus to get them to look the other way.

"Drexel and I were just discussing that," Chet said.

"Be right interested to see what else's down there. There's been a heap of stories over the years. Let me know what you decide." Godsey trundled back to his car. "Y'all certainly have a beautiful place here. Yes sir, ya do. Some folks in this valley would confer their souls to swap places with ya." His eyes meandered across JB, and then trickled down behind the barn toward the old sawmill. "I understand you folks found Titus Blaylock's Pierce Arrow. What ya planning to do with it, if ya don't mind me asking?"

Chet glanced at Lexi. "We're sending it to Maryland to be restored."

Godsey nodded his head. "My grand pappy had a '22. That's the last year they made them. Like to see it after your get it back, if'n you have the time." He dipped his bulbous torso into the squad car and yelled out, "Y'all have a peaceful day," and backed onto the road but slowed as he drove by the house.

"I think I saw that guy on *Dukes of Hazard,*" Drexel said.

"And why's he so interested in our ice pit?" asked Lexi.

"This is probably the highlight of his career," Chet replied. "It must get pretty boring around here for such a skilled crime investigator."

Lexi suspected the appearance of Raymond Blaylock's body raised more questions than it answered. It was time for her to become acquainted with the editor of *The Staunton News Leader.* With a little luck, he might give her access to the paper's microfiche archives.

"How long will it take to drain that quicksand?"

"We'll need to dig to the bottom and cap the spring," Drexel replied. He measured with his eyes from the pit to the wall. "And cut a drainage ditch. That's thirty to thirty-five feet down, and about a hundred feet to the ledge. If its solid rock like JB says, it could take a track hammer and a medium-sized excavator eight to ten days. More if it keeps raining. A slurry pump would be faster but it could take that long just to get one here."

"The sooner the better," Chet said.

"I'll have the office call Norman. He could probably have a digger here tomorrow."

Lexi and Chet returned to the house. Chet stripped down to his boxers by the back door; Lexi went inside, pulled off her nightgown, tossed it in the utility sink and used the last drizzle of water from the faucet to sponge the mud off her legs. Death had entered her life once more; it was becoming a common theme. She quickly dismissed those thoughts, put her coat back on and grabbed a laundry basket.

Chet's appearance provided a much-needed comical reprieve. The mud on his muscular body had dried to a powdery white and, in his drooping boxer shorts he looked like one of those famous Greek statues.

Lexi shifted the basket on her hip. "I thought they carted you off in the ambulance."

"Ha, ha. Very funny. And just how do you suggest I get cleaned up?"

She handed him the basket. "Wait right there." Lexi dashed into the kitchen and returned with a towel, a stiff brush and a bar of soap. She pointed to the mountain. "There should be plenty of water in the drainage ditch. You can rinse out your clothes while you're at it."

Chet grimaced. "So this is how you Long Island women treat your heroes. And just where do you plan to bathe?"

Lexi flashed open her raincoat exposing her naked body. "I'm waiting until the electricity's back on."

Drexel popped around the corner of the house at that exact moment. "That should be in about five minutes." When his eyes encountered Lexi's nudity, he ducked his head and did a hundred-eighty-degree turn. "Whoa, sweet Mother of Mary. Sorry if I'm interrupting anything, folks."

Lexi slapped the raincoat closed and jumped back inside the house.

Chet burst out laughing. "Serves her right. Now, what was that about five minutes?"

"Power will be back on," Drexel said. "But I can leave if off if you want me to."

Lexi cracked the door open an inch. "That won't be necessary. You can turn around now, Drexel. Lady Godiva's back in the house."

Drexel was grinning from ear to ear. He ran his eyes from Lexi to Chet. "Why do I suddenly feel overdressed?" Chet started laughing again.

"The generator is fine, Mr. Willow." Drexel said. "I must have switched it off-line the other day by mistake. But just to be on the safe side, I think we ought to run a test before applying the load. Lady Godiva should have hot water in about twenty minutes."

"Thanks, Drex," said Chet.

Drexel was still grinning. "Guess I win."

"Win what?" Chet asked.

Drexel blushed. "Oh, the boys were taking bets on whether or not Mrs. Willow was a natural blonde. I wagered ten bucks that she was." He walked away cackling, "I just love my job."

Chet covered his mouth to conceal his laughter. Lexi glared at him. "I get the house; you get the ditch...Mr. Droopy Drawers." She yanked the door shut and flipped the deadbolt.

As soon as the water was ready, Lexi drew herself a hot bath,

69

hoping to soothe away the morning's troubles.

At least the disappearance of Raymond Blaylock was now solved. So much for the sawmill theory or his running off with all of Titus's money. Now the pressing question was 'why'?

Lexi couldn't chase the image of Raymond's decomposed body out of her mind...the pitchfork in his chest, the shriveled eyes, mouth wrenched open like he was screaming the name of his murderer from the bottom of his cold, muddy grave: DEACON BLAYLOCK!

She closed her eyes and tried one of Dr. Fontenberry's mental relaxation techniques. After a few minutes, it began to work.

The police told her that her parents had died instantly; there was no sign of a struggle. It was September 11.

She had called her mother from her cell phone at the office several times after the plane had struck the second World Trade Tower to let her know she was safe. But there was never an answer and that was unusual. Since college, she and her mother's morning telephone conversations had become a cherished ritual. The only other time her mother had missed one was the day of her father's first heart attack.

Lexi knew something was wrong; she had to get home. She was on the bridge when a plume of dust and debris mushroomed into the sky behind her. The voices on the radio aptly conveyed the face of mayhem; the world behind her was collapsing, the world in front of her was silent. What was she to do? How many of her friends had gone to work early that day? How many managed to get out? Where were her parents? She drove on through the tears, attempting to contact her mom every two or three minutes. Her anguish only heightened.

When she arrived at the farm, she found the front door

unlocked as it would normally be that time of day. Her mother's Volvo and father's pickup were both parked in the driveway.

There was a clinging dampness to the air inside the house. No television or radio was playing in the background and that was unusual. Her father's pipe was on the table next to his recliner; he hadn't smoked in years but still carried a pipe in his left shirt pocket, often clenching it in his teeth. Her mother called it an oral fixation caused by having been breastfed too long.

Lexi found them both face-down on the kitchen floor; the pools of blood surrounding their bodies had merged into one. They were holding hands: each shot in the back of the head execution style. The robbers had made off with a few thousand dollars in cash and jewelry and some household trinkets. That was all the lives of two loving, caring human beings were worth to the robbers...pocket cash and trinkets. The nightmares Lexi had afterward were often unbearable.

She snapped back to the present. It had to be the money. Booze and women can come and go but money was the one thing Deacon Blaylock needed most. He had sorely mismanaged the mills and the Blaylock empire was in shambles. Titus's gold would solve all his problems. But if Deacon never found it, either it didn't exist or was still hidden somewhere.

Lexi rubbed her temples, diligently trying to keep the past from impinging upon the present. Her parents' death had nothing to do with Raymond Blaylock.

Porter didn't get five feet from the pit until he had discovered what was at the end of that chain. He'd probably canvassed the entire mountain with tweezers and a magnifying glass looking for Titus's fortune. Sheriff Godsey wasn't any better. He practically volunteered to drain the ice pit himself.

Her thoughts began to collapse. She dipped her head under

the bath water; it was relaxing at first. Then she developed a perfect
mental video of the pitchfork being rammed into Raymond
Blaylock's chest, so vivid she practically leapt out of the tub. This
was lunacy.

Lexi's thoughts switched to Paragon. How had he gotten out
of his stall? When she and JB returned him to the barn, the stall door
was wide open but nothing was damaged. She was absolutely certain
she had bolted it after feeding him last night—being around horses for
nearly twenty-five years, bolting a stall door was as natural as closing
the refrigerator. He must have gotten spooked by the thunder and
jarred the bolt loose.

Chet rapped on the door and came in. "Enjoying yourself?"

"I wish," Lexi replied. "I keep seeing Raymond Blaylock
everywhere."

"Maybe you should try washing in the drainage ditch. It's
difficult for your thoughts to wander very far with your testicles
drawn up into your stomach. I shouldn't require sex for two or three
months."

Lexi caressed his leg and left a wet handprint on his pants.
"Come join me and we'll test your theory."

"Sorry, but you're already spoken for. The veterinarian is
here. I sent them him on down to the barn. Finish up and I'll walk
with you."

"Would you hand me that robe, please?"

Chet ran his eyes across her body and grinned. "Since when
did you become a natural blonde?"

Lexi snatched the robe from his hand. "It was supposed to be
a surprise."

"It was a surprise alright. Drexel's going to be crushed when
I break the news to him."

She held up a fist and said, "One more word about that and

you won't need sex for another *six* months."

Chet sucked in his lips, winked and sauntered out of the bathroom. He stopped at the door and looked at her. "Are you sure you're alright?"

Lexi nodded.

Lexi introduced herself to Dr. Buchanan and held Paragon by a lead-line while the vet and his assistant assembled a tray of instruments and donned rubber gloves. Buchanan was about fifty with a close-clipped brown beard sprinkled with gray and he spoke with a distinct Midwestern accent. His assistant, or wife as it turned out, was considerably younger—late twenties at most.

"This is one fine-looking animal, Mrs. Willow," Dr. Buchanan said. "If you're planning to stud him, I have a thoroughbred mare who might appreciate his company."

"You can be our first customer," Chet interjected.

The vet cleaned the wound and began the examination while his wife went outside. Paragon typically didn't take to strangers but this man had a slow and gentle touch, continuously stroking and talking. Mrs. Buchanan returned from their truck with a medical bag and three syringes.

"You obviously know your way around horses, Dr. Buchanan," Lexi said. "I believe Paragon actually likes you."

"I was a faculty member at the School of Veterinary Medicine at Virginia Tech before we bought this practice. My specialty was large animals. Kimberly here was one of my star pupils."

She looked up and smiled, her face radiating genuine warmth. "I couldn't resist a man who smelled like horse manure. Practically had to drag him away from Tech, though."

Dr. Buchanan stood up. "The cut's really not all that bad. Ten stitches should close it. The problem's the location and trying to keep it free of infection. You'll need to limit his activity until the wound fully scabs over, and keep his stall as clean as possible."

Kimberly gave Paragon an injection of steroids to reduce the swelling, some antibiotics, and a tetanus shot.

Dr. Buchanan used a local anesthesia to numb Paragon's lower leg; his wife shaved the hair and then assisted her husband with the stitches. Paragon didn't flinch.

When they were finished, Kimberly applied a purple topical spray and wrapped the leg and hoof with gauze and a rubberized Ace bandage.

"You need to apply this antibacterial spray every day when you change the bandage," Dr. Buchanan said. "Call me if it starts bleeding again. Either Kim or I will check back with you in three or four days."

"Thank you both," Lexi said. "I don't know how he got out in the first place. I'm positive I latched his stall."

Kimberly and her husband exchanged a brief glance. "Sounds like Deacon's up to tricks again," she said.

"Not you guys, too," Lexi replied.

"We've heard the stories," Kimberly said. "The previous owner, Mrs. Madison, had five white Persian cats. During office visits, she frequently complained about things missing or being moved around. Eventually, she had the electric gates and the security system installed. But nothing seemed to help."

"Things like generators being switched off and trucks rolling down hills?" Chet asked.

"Yeah, mostly small stuff. Then one of her cats disappeared and that was the last straw. She was convinced Deacon Blaylock wanted her off the mountain so she insisted on moving back north to Alexandria."

"The Madison's didn't find little muddy footprints around the litter box did they?" asked Chet. Lexi shot him a disapproving look.

"Her fear seemed genuine enough," Kimberly said. "Not that I believe in ghosts or anything."

Dr. Buchanan waded in and changed the subject. "Paragon is going to be just fine, Mrs. Willow. Let me know when you're ready to start breeding him. If his documentation looks as good as he does, I'd be happy to place him on the registry at Tech."

"Oh thank you, Dr. Buchanan. That would be wonderful."

"Call me Terry. I get enough of that Dr. Buchanan business at the clinic. Most of the time, I don't know which one of us is being spoken to."

"We hope to have fifteen horses here by fall," Lexi said. "I was planning to contract an equine specialist in Charlottesville. If you're interested in being our house veterinarian, maybe we can work out a deal."

"So Deacon is partial to cats, too," Chet joked. "Let's dress Beecher like a sexy Tabby and see if we can lure him into the open."

Lexi paused in the driveway next to the ice pit. "This is serious, Chet. If people can get by the gates and a security system, what can we do to stop them?"

He wrapped his arms around her. "Look, sweetheart, I assure you there's a logical explanation for everything."

Lexi pushed away. Chet was always the realist, one of the things she loved most about him. But right now she wasn't looking for reassurance.

"Mrs. Madison was probably absent-minded," Chet said. "If she spent her days dreaming about ghosts, any number of things could have happened."

Lexi began walking again.

"Cats get lost every day. Paragon kicked his stall door and popped the latch. It's that simple."

"Explain the truck then," Lexi replied. "There wasn't even a dent on the bumper. I'm not an expert in physics but that doesn't seem possible. And what about Raymond?"

"He got drunk, speared himself in the chest with a pitchfork, and then went for a dip in the quicksand pond. Happens all the time in the country." Chet stopped and cupped Lexi's hands in his. "Look, some strange things have happened. I don't want to sound calloused but I think you're reading too much into it. But if it will make you more comfortable, I'll hire security."

Lexi looked him in the face. "I've always dreamed of owning a place like this. A life with fresh air and wide open spaces, a place where I can raise a family and horses and feel safe. That was taken from me once before." Lexi felt the frustration welling up at the corners of her eyes. "Whoever is behind this wants us off this mountain. Just like they did the Madison's and the others before them. But I'm not going to run this time, Chet. I won't."

Chapter 7

Lexi barely slept. The slightest sound, either inside or out, funneled straight into her brain like she was wearing a cosmic stethoscope. Beecher had gone to his food dish three times during the night and, each time, his nails clacked across the kitchen floor like a box of spilled marbles.

Noises here were different than they were at her parents' place on Long Island. The mountains captured each sound and wrung every decibel from it until it drifted to the valley floor spent and deflated. She never realized how many vehicles traveled Route 250 during the night.

Chet climbed out of bed at seven to meet the truck coming to collect the Pierce Arrow. He tried not to disturb her but, like most men, he was usually loudest when trying to be quiet.

At eight-fifteen, two bulldozers cranked up down in the valley, squeaking and rattling and scraping across rocks. The truck came for the Arrow and there was a resounding metallic crash as a ramp was dropped, the high-pitched whirl of a winch, and someone shouting, "WHOA! OKAY! TEN FEET! KEEP COMING! WHOA,

THAT'LL DO!"

Lexi sandwiched her head between two pillows.

After the first truck left, two more lumbered past the front of the house and stopped somewhere down by the barn: air brakes squawking, more ramps slamming, and another pair of revving diesel engines joined the ones in the valley. Lexi was determined to get another thirty minutes of sleep.

At nine, Drexel's men started hammering in the kitchen; Lexi pulled another pillow over her head. Beecher slapped a wet tongue across the palm of her hand; that was the last straw.

"All right, I'm up!" she shouted. "I hope everyone is satisfied."

The dog sat next to the bed, poised like a coiled spring, a sloppy tennis ball clamped tightly between his teeth.

"Sorry, baby. Not until I've had two Excedrin, a shower and a pot of coffee."

Lexi kicked off the sheets and marched into the bathroom. She turned on the shower and steam billowed over the top of the frosted enclosure. Then, suddenly, the showerhead sputtered and gurgled. When the flow resumed, the water made a frothy, splattering sound when it hit the floor of the stall.

She opened the shower door and found the back wall streaked in thin rivulets of red mud. The drain looked like a slotted ladle filled with regurgitated minestrone, what little water still emanating from the fixture fell in a coagulated drizzle.

*There's blood in the pipes...*Audrey had said.

Lexi put her hands to her face—maybe if she didn't look it would go away. She spread her fingers and peered down again. The drain had eaten its fill and now the floor pan was filling with red muck, too.

The pressure began to build somewhere south of her stomach,

the place where the most primeval of human emotions are held captive. It was an anger she hadn't experienced since age fourteen when her younger brother intentionally seared her arm with a hot pizza pan.

As the mass worked its way upward, Lexi managed to partially deflect it with her vocal cords, slightly clipping the volume and depressing the tone such that—when it slithered from the back of her throat—the words sounded surprisingly like the venomous ejaculate Linda Blair directed at a Catholic priest in the movie *The Exorcist*. Expletives included. It lasted only a few seconds.

Lexi turned off the water and backed toward the sink. It took several deep breaths but she managed to gain complete control of herself.

She closed the shower door and stomped back into the bedroom, pulled on pair of jeans under her nightgown, and grabbed her tennis shoes. Beecher was still coiled with the ball in his mouth. At that moment, throwing something as hard as humanly possible seemed the perfect remedy.

"Come on, Beech. Let's see how far you can run."

Chet had returned and was talking to Drexel in the kitchen. She fumed passed them without saying a word.

"Where ya headed?" Chet asked.

"For your information, Beecher and I are going outside to stomp some dandelions into oblivion. And when we return, that slaughterhouse upstairs in my shower had better be gone."

"Not wearing shoes," asked Chet?

"No. I need to feel the dandelion brains squish between my toes."

Chet uttered something but all Lexi wanted to do was get out of that house. She pushed the back door open, held it until Beecher was clear of the steps, and then let it slam closed behind her.

Chet turned to Drexel. "She's usually not that pleasant in the mornings." He stuffed the last slice of JB's honey-bread into his mouth. "Let's go have a look."

Chet led Drexel through the bedroom and into the bath, not the least bit certain what was awaiting him. He opened the shower door and saw red residue on the walls and a pool of glop in the bottom.

"I don't suppose we can blame this on the water company, can we?"

"Nope," Drexel replied, half-heartedly attempting to stifle a grin. "You're the President, Vice-President, Board of Directors and Chief of Groundwater Operations of the Cheat Mountain Potable Services Corporation."

Chet cracked the cold water valve. The shower head gurgled and spat another mouthful of mud. "Okay, so how do we fix this one?"

"The problem's either at the well or in the line. We'd best go throw the breaker so this crap doesn't get circulated through the whole house. Then we walk down the hill and check out the pump house."

"How much will this cost me?"

Drexel let his grin get the best of him. "Can't say for sure. It's been a long time since I added numbers that big with my shoes on."

Lexi watched Chet and Drexel leave the house and head down toward the stables. She pulled on her shoes and ran to catch up.

"You look more relaxed," Chet said. "Those dandelions must have done the trick."

"I'm sorry for getting so emotional. But if I wanted a mud bath, I'd have joined Raymond."

Chet planted a kiss on her forehead. "Better enjoy the mud pond while you can. Norman's men are getting set to start trenching."

Lexi walked with him around the side of the tenant house and encountered the new pieces of heavy equipment—a pair of crook-necked yellow dinosaurs with tracks like bulldozers. One had a long-hinged arm with a wide bucket on the end; the other was almost identical to the first, except it had a stubby chisel instead of a bucket. Two men were chalking off the twelve-foot-wide furrow to be excavated to a depth of 30 feet.

"So, what's the problem with the water?" Lexi asked.

"Drexel thinks it's the well or a broken pipe."

With the exception of a few trips to inspect progress down at the airstrip, Lexi hadn't really explored the land beyond the barn. The pump house was behind the corral, a hundred feet or so above the old sawmill; the well itself was slightly further down the terrace.

Drexel studied the piping arrangement in the pump house and then opened a valve on the bottom of the pressure tank. Muddy water spewed out. "Mud out means mud in. The problem's between here and the well."

Lexi's eyes were drawn to the sawmill—*women need to know machines.*

The saw blade was about four feet in diameter and had a swirl of rusted but vicious-looking teeth. When Deacon's body came in contact with those, they probably sliced through him like a steak knife.

Chet obviously knew what she was thinking. "What a way to go," he said.

Lexi nodded. About ten feet beyond the blade, there was a horizontal boiler mounted on iron wheels

Boilers were a common source of heat in New York but she had never seen one quite like this: cylindrical and black with long, double-riveted seams on the sides and ends. There was a series of gauges and valves on one end; on the other was a flue that ran up through the tin roof. Halfway down one side was a large wheel with a ragged belt attached to it that ran back to a smaller wheel connected to a series of gears. Above the gears, there was a platform with levers poking up through rotted floorboards.

"The racks along the sides are where the logs travel back and forth as they are cut," Drexel said.

"Does it still work?" Lexi asked.

"If you can find someone who knows how to run it," Drexel replied. He turned the handle on a water spigot but nothing came out. "Water for the boiler is gravity-fed from the holding tank at the pump house. Fill the boiler, oil the log carriage, light a fire in the furnace and you're in the sawmill business."

Lexi followed Drexel another fifty feet down the terrace to where a large cement cylinder was jutting out of the ground. Another circular piece of cement was resting on top of it.

"Well, here's your problem," Drexel said. "The well tile is broken."

Lexi walked around for a closer examination. A rock the size of a portable television was resting against the side of the well tile. There was a U-shaped crack in the tile that widened to about half an inch before disappearing under the ground.

Drexel hiked up the incline to the drainage channel. "There must have been a rockslide during that last storm that filled the ditch causing the runoff to overflow." He looked up the rock face. "That one must have bounced over the ledge and struck the well tile, filling the well with good old Appalachian Mountain mud."

"The gook in the shower was red, like the soil at the airstrip," Lexi said. "All the mud here is gray. Shouldn't the muck in the shower have been gray, too?"

82

Drexel had to ponder that for a moment. "Maybe when the rocks came down they brought some red clay with them."

Chet muscled the cement cap off and peered down into the well. "It looks clear from here."

"It's all settled to the bottom by now," Drexel replied. "That's where the pump feeds from."

"So we pump it all out and replace the well tile," Chet said.

"Then drain the pressure tank, a couple thousand feet of water line, the water heaters and all the plumbing in the house," Drexel said. "It'll take a day, maybe a day and a half. Be a good idea to build a barrier around this tile to keep it from happening again."

Lexi was still trying to rationalize the different colors of mud. Drexel's theory was plausible but, if there was red mud up the mountain, there would be red mud on the terrace. That certainly wasn't the case. The mud in the ice pit was gray as well, and she recalled JB saying most of that had washed down from the mountain, too.

"Alright," Chet said. His voice was resigned, as though asking himself if this was ever going to end. "Get a new well tile here as soon as possible and get started."

"I've got a tile at the shop that should work. Just need to charge for the backhoe and labor."

"Whatever it takes."

On the way back to the house, Drexel paused on the road near the ice pit. "I have an idea. If that spring has enough volume, we can cap it, build a second pump house and use that water to service the house. Then we can dedicate the old well to the barn. Tie the two systems together for back up, connect the pumps to the generator circuit, and you'll never be without water again."

"I'm not going to drink dead-man water!" Lexi exclaimed.

"Dirt is dirt," answered Chet. "It's all worm poop and

ground-up dinosaurs."

"Install a water filter and a softener and you won't taste a thing," Drexel added. "It will keep your skin from drying out, too. With all new piping inside the house, you'll have a brand new system. Hey, we might dig up a little of Titus's gold in the process."

Lexi turned and looked at Drexel. "You know about Titus's treasure, too?"

"Mrs. Willow, everyone in the western half of Virginia knows about Titus Blaylock's gold."

Chapter 8

After lunch, Lexi returned to her computer. She desperately wanted to take a nap but the little writer's voice in her head had begun shouting PUT YOUR FINGERS TO THE COMPUTER KEYS... NOW! The urge was stronger than ever before. It wouldn't be denied much longer.

Beginning a novel, any kind of novel, was exasperating at best. What was her premise? A young couple moves to the country so they can...dig up old cars, find bodies in their backyard, and throw selected local villagers into the jaws of a ripsaw. On second thought, maybe a nap was a better idea.

Perhaps she should work on the back story. Everything else would build from that. She opened JB's scrapbook to the article on Titus's and Andrea's death. It was dated May 15, 1912, more than a month after the sinking of the *Titanic*.

She skimmed to the more pertinent information. Titus Alexander Blaylock, born 1871...Andrea Day Blaylock, born 1881...timbered the valley...coal mines...provided funding and materials for the construction of the Monterey United Methodist

Church in 1908...responsible for road improvements and electricity...

Lexi stopped and perused this portion more intently. 'After eleven months of negotiation, Titus Blaylock convinced the Shenandoah Light and Power Company to string high-voltage electrical power along the State Route 250 corridor to the Highland County townships of McDowell and Monterey. On October 27, 1911, the project culminated with a grand illumination ceremony at the Blaylock's mountain estate in Monterey.'

Lexi snatched her notepad and rifled through to the notes she had taken after Paragon's quicksand incident. JB had told her Titus dug the ice pits in the summer of 1911.

She reread that portion of the article and set it aside again. If Titus knew electricity was coming to the valley in October, why would he bother digging another ice pit? If anyone in this part of the world could afford a refrigerator, it would be he and Andrea. Andrea would have insisted on it.

Lexi heard the heavy knocker on the front door rap three times. She stood, instinctively tidied her papers and looked around to make sure everything was presentable, and went to answer it.

There was a middle-aged woman standing on the door step; an older lady wearing a black scarf on her head was waiting two steps below her.

"Mrs. Willow, we're sorry to just drop in like this," the younger woman said. "But ..."

"No, please come in," Lexi replied.

"Thank you kindly."

The woman assisted the older lady over the threshold and down the foyer steps. "I'm Christina Baldwin and this is my mother, Millie. We're the welcoming committee for the Monterey First Pentecostal Holiness Church."

Millie—who had large, radiant eyes teeming with the vigor of

86

a woman half her age—handed Lexi a pie.

"Haven't seen you folks at Sunday preachin' yet. Figured it was time we paid you a visit. Reverend Eugene Booker says a wandering soul is the devil's tinder box."

"Amen, Sister," replied Christina.

Lexi showed them to the study.

"I've always wanted to come up here," Christina said. "It's even more beautiful than I could have possibly imagined."

"A might tidier than it was back when Deacon and Raymond were about," Millie added. "Thought you'd be interested to know, the church is giving Raymond a proper Christian burial on Wednesday at two-thirty, God rest his soul. Interment will be at the family plot, beside his mother and that derelict daddy of his. The pie's one of my world-famous brown sugar ones. They're all the rage down at the Maple Restaurant. You can eat it cold or heat a single slice in the oven for six minutes at 350. I prefer mine hot."

Lexi realized she needed to learn how to bake as pies seemed to the local calling card. "Thank you. It looks delicious. May I offer you ladies some coffee?"

"Thank you, Mrs. Willow," said Millie. "But dropper-inners shouldn't be a burden. Even if they are extending the Lord's hand."

"It's no trouble, really," Lexi said. "It's nice to have some company. JB's the only other local visitor we've had."

"On the eve of the second coming, breathless heathens shall tread a path onto the righteous," Millie blurted.

"Praise be to the Lord," Christina chimed in.

Lexi felt her cheeks blush slightly. She didn't know what these little rituals meant but, given the context of the conversation, they seemed rather humorous. She bit her lower lip to keep from letting it show.

Christina turned to Lexi. "Mother and Miss Janice have not

been cordial for several years."

"Janice?" Lexi quizzed.

"Janice Bandy," Millie said with total distain. "I'm probably the only one around here that still knows the godless harlot by her Christian name, dare I be damned to hell for calling it such. She shortened it to JB when she became a highfalutin' woman of commerce."

The connection clicked immediately: JB, Janice Bandy and Jandy were all one and the same...Gentry Willow's college sweetheart, *JANDY*.

The thought of it made Lexi's head swim. She had to get away from the Baldwin's and straighten out her thoughts. "If you will excuse me, I'll just go to the kitchen and put on the coffee."

Lexi navigated her way into the kitchen on autopilot as her head now had room for only one thought: *JB WAS JANDY! Why hadn't she seen it earlier?* Now she understood that glimmer in JB's eye the day they first met; JB had recognized Chet and knew he was Gentry's son. But why did she feel the need to hide it?

Lexi spilled the last tablespoons of Folgers on the floor trying to shovel it into the coffee maker, spooned in three extras without thinking, went to the sink to fill the carafe forgetting there wasn't any water, found some in a gallon jug Chet had brought back from JB's, sloshed it in the carafe without measuring, poured it in the top of the Bunn, flipped the power switch and hurried back to the study.

The conversation turned to church matters. Lexi listened as earnestly as possible, the whole time looking for a way to politely steer things back to JB.

The coffee maker alarm beeped and she excused herself again. As she opened the cabinet to get the cups, she spotted the remains of JB's maple pie on the counter. It was the perfect bridge she needed. Millie obviously had more than a run-of-the-mill dislike for JB. Lexi just needed to prod a little to get the whole feud out in the open. It was an inexcusable way to treat a guest, but nothing a trip or two to Sunday preachin' shouldn't fix.

She returned to the study with a tray of coffee and served Millie and Christine. "I can't wait to try your brown sugar pie. JB gave me a recipe for a maple pie but I haven't had the chance to bake one yet."

Millie's eyelids scrolled open like a pair of broken window shades. "She gave you the recipe for her maple pie?"

The fuse was lit. Lexi just needed to hold the match to it a moment longer. "She said it won a baking contest somewhere and made me promise not to share it with a single soul."

"Why that old witch!" Millie shrieked, the Christian highness in her voice was completely gone.

"Mother, please," Christina pleaded.

"I've been trying to decipher that recipe for five years now," Millie screeched. "Even packaged a slice of it off to Virginia Tech for analysis but those turnip-heads wouldn't know maple syrup from crow shit. Probably cashed the check I sent and bought a Coca-Cola to wash it all down with."

Millie looked as if she might burst apart at the seams. Lexi hesitated, but then decided to snip one more stitch. "Why, JB has been a wonderful help to Chet and me; it's such a change from New York. She even calls every day to let us know what her lunch specials are."

"You had best keep your husband away from that festering old crotch-grabber." Millie's voice was getting louder and shriller with each word. "She tried to steal my Harold, not two months shy of our wedding day. Found them down in the clearing behind the old schoolhouse. She was down on her knees in front of him, workin' his man horn like it was a hunk of summer sausage. She weren't but

89

sixteen years old then, either."

"Mother, that's enough!" Christina exclaimed.

Lexi's pent-up laughter was shaking her insides like a miniature earthquake. "Why, Mrs. Baldwin, I had no idea."

"Caught her red-handed, I did. Ruined Harold for our entire marriage. He's a always wantin' me to do this and do that for him, just like Janice did. Told him if'n he didn't stop gordin' me, I was going to cut it off and feed it to the hogs. Serves that godless Jezebel right to be straddled with that bastard son of hers. Carries the markings of the devil plain as day, he does. She probably got knocked up by one of Satan's strays slithering down the highway. Like that boy from VMI. Peckers with legs, the lot of 'em."

JB had never mentioned a son, Lexi thought. Then it hit her like a bolt of lightning. PORTER! Holy God, Porter was JB's son!!

Christina pulled her mother to her feet and practically dragged her to the front door.

"I apologize, Mrs. Willow. I don't know what's come over her. She's usually such a dear, sweet woman."

Lexi held the door open while Christina prodded Millie out. "Thank you so very much for the pie."

Christina was still mortified. "Oh, Mrs. Willow. I do hope you will please forgive Mother. This just isn't like her at all." Millie continued to spout hell and damnation as she hobbled down the steps to the sidewalk.

Lexi couldn't wait to share this with Chet...CHET! Oh my God, she couldn't tell him. Millie had said VMI so, if Jandy and Gentry Willow had a roll in the hay, that could make Porter Chet's half-brother!

"See you and Mr. Willow at Sunday preachin'," Millie bellowed. "I'll expect to see a nice fat envelope in the collection plate with your name on it, too."

Chapter 9

Lexi didn't know what to do with herself. She had to get her mind off JB and Porter. *JB WAS JANDY; PORTER COULD BE CHET'S HALF-BROTHER.* What can of worms had she just opened?

The water was still off so she couldn't relax in a bath; the track hammer was pounding away at the ice pit, shaking all the plates and glasses in the kitchen cabinets, so writing or watching television were out of the question. She decided to go to the barn and check on Paragon.

Lexi went outside; the tat-tat-tat of the track hammer was deafening. She returned to the house and found the headphones Chet wore when target shooting. They reduced the hammering to a dull thump. *It was going to be a long 8-10 days*, Lexi thought. Maybe this was a good time to do some research in Staunton and Harrisonburg.

All the topsoil from the drainage trench had been removed and piled by the base of the mountain. Lexi was surprised to see that, in some places, it was only two to three feet deep; beneath was solid rock. A twelve-foot section of the wall had been taken down, the stones numbered and stacked neatly off to one side.

The construction crew had made a temporary bridge out of pieces of lumber and placed it over the furrow where the road was. It bowed a little under her weight but seemed sturdy enough.

Paragon was prancing from side to side in his stall; all the new noises had him spooked. Then the hammering stopped and he calmed down. Lexi took a brush from the tack box and brushed the sides of his neck which seemed to help settle him even more.

While reapplying a new bandage, the hammering suddenly resumed. Paragon reared up and kicked his back hoof. Lexi braced herself against his leg and was pitched backward like a rag doll. Paragon kicked a second time, this time connecting with the right side of Lexi's head, and slamming the back of her head against the stall door.

Lying in a semi-conscious state, the lucid portion of her brain started screaming for her to get out of there. She opened her left eye and focused enough to see that Paragon was rearing back again. If she didn't move, she would be stomped to death.

Her muscles somehow mustered a coordinated response and she rolled out of the stall door just as Paragon's front hooves crashed down precisely where she had been. She pulled herself to her feet, latched the door and staggered out of the barn. When the sunlight hit her eyes, the world took a hundred-and-eighty degree spin and then everything went black.

It could have been minutes, an hour, or even days but the next thing Lexi felt was a floating sensation and tightness across her chest. A piercing noise ricocheted through her skull; the right side and back of her head throbbed to the rhythm of her heartbeats. Something was pressing against her face. She tried to touch it but her arm was pinned to her side. She felt a slight pressure on her hand, and then everything went black again.

Chapter 10

Chet checked his watch for the umpteenth time. It had taken longer at the airport to wash and wax his Mooney than he had expected and, thanks to the eighteen-wheeler lumbering up the road in front of him, he was now a full fifty-five minutes late. He had planned to surprise Lexi with dinner at The Crazy Greek in Harrisonburg and maybe a room at the Marriott—she would probably appreciate the hot bath more than the meal—but it had gotten so late, she might not feel up to it.

As he popped over the eastern ridge, his eyes were drawn to an ambulance racing toward the base of the mountain from the edge of town; Drexel's truck was right on its tail.

He downshifted, shot past the truck and slid through a pair of hairpin-turns. He continued down the mountain and pulled off on the shoulder at the spot where Sheriff Godsey usually hid to pluck off speeders.

From this vantage point, all of Monterey lay before him—no wonder Godsey spent so much time here. Everything on his and Lexi's side of the valley looked normal; the bulldozers were still working on the airstrip, gravel trucks were lined up waiting their turn to lay the pavement bed, Norman was at the ice pit, and there was no sign of fire anywhere. With a good pair of binoculars, Chet figured he could probably see right into his and Lexi's bedroom.

When the ambulance was within a hundred yards, Chet eased the BMW closer to the road and flashed his lights so Drexel would recognize him.

The ambulance flew past but Drexel screeched to a stop in the middle of the road, leaping out of his truck.

"Lexi's had an accident," he shouted. "We think the horse kicked her. She's out cold. JB's in the ambulance with her."

Chet felt his chest tighten; his heart jumped a beat. He threw the BMW in gear and punched the gas, catching up to the ambulance before it reached the crest of the mountain.

The darkness in Lexi's head began to lighten. Images appeared. She was riding a horse: Cherokee, a small Appaloosa mare her parents bought her for her seventh birthday. Mom and Dad were leaning on the corral gate watching her, both smiling.

Lexi kept riding and riding, around and around the corral, going faster and faster, growing more confident with each lap. As she rode, she began to notice subtle changes in herself. Her body took a more feminine shape and the pigtails were replaced by flowing blond hair that chased along behind her, dancing on the wind. Lexi felt the cool breeze on her face.

She was going faster now and the horse beneath her was a sleek, black stallion; tall and lean, with a powerful, pounding gate. His elegant tail stretched out behind him like an arrow...Paragon, her first true love.

The years passed as she rode. The faces at the corral gate grew a little more weathered, but still radiated a sense of warmth and love.

Around and around, faster and faster still. Suddenly the faces turned grim. The gate opened slightly and her father struggled to push it closed. Around and around and around she rode. The faces at the gate disappeared.

With one mighty leap, Paragon cleared the corral fence and cantered off across the pasture. The two of them were on their own now; she felt cold and alone. The scenery passed by in a complete blur. Up ahead, there was a misty white light; Paragon headed directly for it.

Lexi saw the face of Zachary Rhineman flash by, a literary agent friend that introduced her to Chet. She remembered him telling her about this handsome, maverick stockbroker who seemed to control the nerves of Wall Street.

She met Chet at a Christmas party the following month. He wasn't the slicked back, three-hundred-dollar shoes Manhattan type she expected. He was strong and rugged, with deep, brown eyes that coddled her in velvet. When she was with him, she felt like nothing on the planet mattered to him but her.

The misty light drew closer. Paragon broke into a flat-out run across a meadow nestled between two towering rows of mountains. Up an incline they rode; a rock face passed by her to the left. Paragon paused briefly to drink from a whispering brook flowing at the base of a cliff. He was breathing hard, blowing a heavy spray of water between swallows.

All of a sudden, he threw back his head and belted out an agonized cry. His legs began to churn furiously but he wasn't going anywhere. Lexi felt something ooze up between her toes and her heart pounded furiously. Something brushed her thigh; she looked down and saw a decayed hand reaching up from a bed of mud, grabbing for her leg. Paragon heaved forward, the hand latched onto her ankle;

Paragon lurched forward again, the hand grasped her tighter. A body rose up out of the mud; a shaft was protruding from its chest. Its eyes were shriveled and sunken; its mouth was slung wide open.

She kicked at the hand trying to free herself but it wouldn't let go. There was a viscid slurping sound as the hand crawled up to her hip; Paragon was slipping deeper and deeper into the mud. The shriveled eyes and wrenching mouth drew closer; the smell of rotted flesh invaded her nostrils. The pounding in her chest moved up to her head, slamming against the back of her skull like a hammer. She was paralyzed...couldn't move...everything faded again.

A scream rose from her gut and clawed through the back of her throat, exiting her mouth like a staccato from an air horn. Her whole body shuddered and light pierced the twilight in her head as if red-hot pokers had been rammed into her eye sockets. A pressure clamped her left hand like a vise then, just as quickly, released it.

A voice spoke to her from above, soft and reassuring. "There, there, sugar. You just lie back and relax."

The voice sounded vaguely familiar. She looked to see who was there. The image that formed in her mind was glazed, as though she was looking through a frosted window. She tried to speak but her words sounded garbled and remote. Something was pressing on her face again.

"Don't try to talk, darling," the voice said. "Just breathe deeply and conserve your strength."

Lexi did as she was told. After several deep breaths, the world around her slowly came into focus. She realized that she was moving. Panic gripped her again and her brain fired messages to her vocal cords in cold, erratic bursts. "Stop the car...I'm not going back to New York...Where's Paragon?...he can't get out again...quicksand...it's not safe out there...Jandy...Deacon Blaylock wants us off the mountain."

"Paragon's okay," said the soft voice. "He's in his stall all safe and sound. We're just going for a little ride. Everything's going to be just fine, sweetheart."

Lexi focused on a shape huddled beside her and saw a pair of gold-rimmed glasses. At first she thought it was her mother, but the voice wasn't quite right. She blinked her eyes several times despite the pain but still couldn't make out the face.

"Where am I?" Lexi asked, this time understanding most of her own words. She detected movement down around her feet and tried to determine what it was. It wasn't until then that she realized she was lying down. "Chet, is that you? Why is the bed moving?"

The soft voice spoke again. "Chet's right behind us in his car. He'll be with you shortly. Right now you're with me, JB. I will take care of you."

It took several more minutes before Lexi's surroundings made sense to her. Her sight returned and she clearly saw JB sitting next to her. "What happened to me?"

"Suppose you'll need to ask that big black stallion of yours. Looks like he clobbered you a good one. You're one tough cookie, I can tell ya that much."

Lexi searched her memory for any traces of where she had been. All she could remember was brown sugar pie. "How did I get here?"

"Drexel found you on his way up from the well. The right side of your head was covered with blood. Lord only knows how you managed to get out of that stall alive. The rescue squad had to carry you on a stretcher over that ditch by the ice pit. The cut's not very deep but that goose egg on the back of your noggin's a doozy."

"Could you free my hands?" Lexi asked the EMT. "And please, turn that siren off. It's ricocheting inside my head like a bullet."

JB rapped on the cab window with her knuckles. "Tommy, kill that racket. I can hardly hear myself think back here." JB's shrill pitch was almost as damaging as the siren.

The EMT loosened the belt around her chest then cinched it back after Lexi got her arms out. She touched the cut on her head; it was bandaged but the hair below was all matted. The back of her head hurt worse than the side and the ice pack did little to relieve the throbbing.

"I suspect you caught the edge of a horseshoe there," JB said. "If it was a direct blow, I doubt we'd be talking. It's going to leave ya a nice shiner, too."

When the ambulance reached the outskirts of Staunton, the siren lit off again and the driver gunned the engine, speeding his way through traffic to the hospital. He pulled into the Emergency Room entrance and a nurse with a stethoscope looped around her neck helped pull the stretcher out. As soon as the wheels were ratcheted down, she took Lexi's pulse, checked her pupils, and listened to her heart. A young black girl was walking alongside charting the numbers and all the other medical jargon.

Lexi heard heavy footsteps running up from behind. It had to be Chet but JB broke off to intercept him. Lexi raised her hand to let him know she was okay.

The EMTs rolled her through two sets of automatic doors and into an examination room. A doctor, in her early forties, pulled a privacy curtain around them. The young black girl handed the doctor the chart.

"I'm Dr. Buettner, Mrs. Willow," she said in a moderate German accent. "Your husband can join you in a few minutes." She flipped through the pages on the chart. "A riding accident? You should never ride a motorcycle without proper head protection," she said in a scolding tone.

Lexi grimaced slightly. For all she knew, it *could* have been a motorcycle accident.

Dr. Buettner examined the cuts and lumps, and then repeated the checks done earlier by the nurse. "There doesn't appear to be any fractures but that laceration will require sutures."

She turned to the nurse. "Call radiology to schedule a CAT scan. Prep the right temporal for closure, then get me Lidocaine and a suture tray with 3-0 nylon."

Dr. Buettner rolled a stool up to the side of the bed. "The CAT scan is routine for all serious blows to the head. We need to examine your brain for signs of excessive swelling. While we're waiting, I am going to sew up this cut."

"Can you give me something for the pounding?" Lexi pleaded.

"After the scan, I'll give you Tordol. It will reduce the swelling and ease the pain. That is the strongest thing I can give you for now. The next eight to ten hours are critical so you must remain awake and lucid for observation. Plan on spending the night. If you fall asleep, we'll need to wake you every hour. If everything's good in the morning, I'll write prescriptions for something stronger to take home with you."

Dr. Buettner gave her a pat on the shoulder and a reassuring smile. "You're going to be fine, Mrs. Willow." She stood, dimmed the lights and opened a gap in the curtain. "I'll go find your husband. If you'd like, I can have a cot delivered to your room." She paused and shook her index finger at Lexi. "No motorcycles for at least six weeks." Then she tapped the top of her head with the butt of a pen. "I never ride mine without a helmet and a full face shield."

"Thank you, Dr. Buettner. I'll remember next time."

A few moments later, Chet peeked through the curtain. "How's my girl?"

CHEAT MOUNATAIN

Lexi could see the worry in his eyes. "The doctor said I need to have all my meals served in bed for the next two weeks."

"Whatever you want, sweetheart." He knelt down and kissed her on the cheek. "That was the longest forty miles I've ever driven. I was prepared for the worst. Drexel told me what happened."

"I don't remember any of it," Lexi said. "Not even going to the barn. Speaking of which, where's JB?"

"She rode back to Monterey with the rescue squad. She told them that since they brought her here, they were damn well going to take her home."

Chet clasped Lexi's hand and pressed it to his lips. "Dr. Buettner said you may experience some short-term memory loss." He gave her a puzzled look. "She asked if you ride a Harley."

Lexi grinned and put her hand over her eyes. "Oh, please, don't make me laugh. My head feels like its big enough to have its own moon."

The nurse came in and placed a tray on a metal table and rolled it over next to the bed. "Mrs. Willow, we need to get you into this gown."

Lexi sat up slowly and began to unbutton her blouse; Chet removed her boots. As the nurse collected her clothing, Lexi detected the distinct odor of horse manure. She quickly found that it was smeared all over the seat of her pants. There was also a large, red handprint—nearly half again the size of Chet's hand—on the back of her shirt. It looked as though someone had grabbed her from behind. It must have happened when the EMTs put her on the stretcher.

Chet helped her into the gown while the nurse changed the sheets.

Chapter 11

The most taxing part of the CAT scan was the trip back to her room. Lexi had to wait for an available transporter--*beam me up, Scottie. I'm growing a second head.*

The transporter, obviously a politically correct title for an orderly, must have thought he was transporting a werewolf: he reeked of garlic. By the time Lexi got to her room, all she wanted was drugs. Red ones, green ones, illegal ones, ones never before tested on humans...any king of drugs.

Perhaps she was being oversensitive but every light, every smell, and every sound seemed grossly exaggerated—the gripping of rubber-soled nursing shoes on the tile floors sounded like drag racers warming up their tires.

Lexi desperately wanted to sleep. But the hospital torture matrons had ingeniously wired her pillow to a call bell with a built-in EEG sensor. Every time she drifted off, a pair of squealing tires raced through the door to roust her and shine a flashlight in her eyes. Her mattress was little more than a strip of foam rubber with a sheet thrown over it so the only way she could get even marginally comfortable was by propping herself on her left side...providing her a stellar view of the maintenance department parking lot. Irritable didn't begin to describe her mood.

Chet had gone out to buy her some clothes to wear home in the morning. She had to get this headache under control before he came back. She had put him through enough for one day.

Another tandem of tennis shoes squealed through the door; this time, they belonged to Dr. Buettner. Perhaps relief was at hand.

"Feeling better?" she asked.

Lexi suppressed the urge to growl. "No, but I'm still holding out hope."

"The CAT scan showed minor swelling in the parietal and occipital lobes of your brain. Those are the areas just above and below the crown. The rest of your brain has experienced significant insult as well. You might experience brief periods of forgetfulness the next couple days but it will pass. You may also be sensitive to bright lights and certain smells. If your vision blurs, or your headaches don't improve, I want you back here for more testing. I've ordered fifty units of Tordol which can be repeated again in eight hours. That will help with the discomfort. Prescriptions will be waiting for you in the morning which you can fill in the pharmacy before you leave."

Lexi was relieved. At least to the professional world, it appeared she would live. "Thank you, Dr. Buettner. If the Tordol gets rid of this headache, I'll name my firstborn after you. Doctor Buettner, just like that, be it boy or girl."

Dr. Buettner flashed an awkward smile. It was the first chink Lexi had seen in her armor.

"When you get home, you're to remain on bed rest for three of four days. No driving, no heavy lifting and no horses." Chet had apparently straightened out the motorcycle issue.

"After that you should be able to resume normal activity, if you feel up to it. I want to see you again in seven days. No more bumps to the head. You may not be so lucky next time."

Lexi was released at seven-thirty the next morning. After dispensing with the customary wheelchair ride, she and Chet had a quick bite in the hospital cafeteria while her prescriptions were being filled. When Lexi walked outside, Mr. Sun had risen forty-five degrees in the sky but she was ready for him this time.

The pleated khakis, spring floral blouse and open-toed flats Chet had bought for her fit perfectly. But the most important part was a pair of polarized Maui Jim sunglasses with side shields—tortoiseshell with a braided, purple neck strap. Without the shades, she would have needed a blindfold to venture outside.

The hammering between her ears was much improved, down to a manageable—albeit constant—dull thump.

Chet drove back to Monterey at a leisurely pace; it was an absolutely beautiful drive. All the wild rhododendrons were in full bloom; great expanses along the road and mountain side were swept in a blizzard of pale pink and white blossoms.

As they came over the eastern ridge, Lexi saw Sheriff Godsey parked in his usual spot at the side of the road. It suddenly dawned on her that no one had taken care of Paragon the night before. "Paragon is probably starving. I don't remember if he even had water."

"Already seen to it," Chet replied. "JB said he ripped his ankle open again. So I called Dr. Kimberly while I was out getting your clothes. She said she'd take care of it; Drexel was supposed to leave the gate open for her. Kim also volunteered to check on him every day until your stitches come out."

Lexi leaned over and kissed his cheek. "My knight in shining armor."

"Don't forget next Thursday. I have my monthly market

conference in New York and probably won't return until Saturday morning. I'm canceling if you're not one-hundred percent recovered."

"Oh, don't do that," Lexi said. "You need to keep your commitments. I'll be fine. If I need anything, I can call JB."

Lexi felt a flutter in the pit of her stomach when she spoke JB's name; almost sense of urgency. Maybe there was something she was supposed to tell JB. She searched her mind but, whatever it was, was gone. At least for now.

It was good to be home. Chet hurried into the kitchen and came back carrying a tray with a pitcher of ice water and a glass. He had that smug look on his face again and Lexi knew he was up to something.

She opened her bedroom door and was stunned. Inside, there was every kind of flower imaginable: orchids, roses, gardenias, lilies and daffodils. At the head of the bed, was a spray of carnations shaped like a horseshoe with a picture of Paragon tucked in the middle. There must have been thirty arrangements in all.

The mix of fragrances made her head swim yet it was the most beautiful thing she had ever seen. The smile on Chet's face and the love in his eyes made her forget all about the pain.

"When did you have time to do all this?" she exclaimed.

"I was hoping you didn't notice the delivery vans we passed on the way home."

Lexi ran and gave him a sweeping hug, and gingerly nestled her head into his chest. "Thank you. They are absolutely fabulous."

He curled his arms around her. "If you ever scare me like that again, the flowers will likely accompany a headstone. Either yours or mine!"

Chet removed the horseshoe and folded back the spread. "Now get some rest. I'll take the flowers into the spare bedroom so the fragrance doesn't bother you."

"You will do no such thing!" Lexi replied. She rattled a pill bottle full of Mepergan. "After two of these, it won't matter if I'm nose deep in poppies."

Chet pointed to the bed. "Rest. I'll be back in a minute." He closed the curtains and dimmed the lights.

Lexi undressed and slipped under the covers. Chet came back with two double-bagged ice packs wrapped in towels and a zip phone. He tucked one pack under her head and placed the other on the pillow next to her.

"The water will be back on by noon," he said. "I'd better make the rounds and check on everyone." Chet reached into his pocket and pulled out another phone. "If you need me, just punch one." He gave her a peck on the cheek.

Lexi awoke at three-thirty. As she lay in bed, she could hear the hum of heavy equipment down in the valley. Absent was the hammering at the ice pit. Chet had probably given the guys the day off. She reached for the zip and hit the one. Chet instantly picked up.

"Where are you?" Lexi asked. "It sounds like you're on a tractor."

"I'm down at the airstrip putting up a windsock. Norman said they should begin laying the topcoat by next Monday. When you're feeling up to it, I'd like to bring the Mooney over and practice my soft-field landings."

"When are you coming back to the house?"

"Be there in five minutes if you need me. Otherwise, about twenty."

"No hurry. If the water is on, I'd like to shower."

"The pipes are all flushed and ready to go," Chet replied. "The filter and water softener should be here tomorrow."

"Why aren't the guys going working on the ice pit?"

"Not until you can handle the pounding."

"Tomorrow. I want that thing gone as soon as possible."

Lexi returned the phone to the nightstand and caught herself thinking about Raymond Blaylock again. She decided to forego a bath for the time being and hit the notes and pictures again.

She eased herself to a sitting position—her head felt surprisingly better since the nap—and toddled down to the study. She gathered all of her materials, returned to the bedroom and arranged them on the bed around her.

Lexi examined the scrapbook page by page: the pictures, various clippings about family gatherings, the illumination, mill prosperity and modernization, the *Titanic*, Titus and Andrea's death notices, the mill fire...the mill fire! The night Raymond supposedly disappeared.

'The Blaylock Lumber Company, founded in 1874 by Horatio Thomas Blaylock, burned to the ground July 15, 1950 in a predawn fire that is believed to have been started by hot ash from a boiler in the mill's steam plant. Deacon Venerable Blaylock, son of Titus Blaylock and current owner of the mill, stated that he emptied the ashes from the boiler the evening before and suspects that gusting winds carried hot sparks from the ash pile to an adjacent shavings bin."

Lexi finished the article but there was no mention of Raymond.

Something just didn't flesh out. She tried to search the gray matter back to her conversation with JB but nothing turned up. She grabbed her notes and leafed through them attempting to refresh her memory and came across an entry stating that, in the days of the Blaylock empire, the only mill running was the old steam plant down behind the barn...the one Deacon later threw himself into.

"If only the small mill was in operation, why would there be a fire in the boiler down in the large mill?" Lexi asked herself out loud. The little voice inside her head immediately answered, "There wouldn't be a fire in the large mill boiler!"

Deacon had lied about the cause of the fire. Perhaps that's why the insurance company determined it was arson and denied payment.

The next three pages of the scrapbook were empty and the last few contained articles about various sales of the property. But nothing about Raymond's disappearance, or even Deacon's death for that matter.

That struck Lexi as odd. If any of the Blaylock family history was worthy of documentation, it would be the death of Deacon Blaylock which, according to JB, was a month after the fire; August of 1950. The papers would also have reported Raymond's disappearance.

For nearly seventy years, the mills had been the primary source of employment in this part of the state. The folks of Monterey would certainly know if it was in operation or not. So how did the paper get the story wrong?

She returned to Titus's obituary. 'Titus Blaylock is survived by his son, Deacon Venerable Blaylock, age 18.'

Lexi quickly did the math. Deacon was fifty-six at the time of the fire, and his death...

"Excuse me, young lady," said an agitated voice.

Lexi looked up and saw Chet leaning in the doorway.

"That is not rest and relaxation. How can you even stand to read?"

"Chet, this is fascinating," Lexi exclaimed. "Deacon Blaylock claimed the fire in the mill was caused by cinders from hot boiler ash. But JB said the only mill in operation at that time was the one behind the barn. If she's right, there's no way the mill fire could have been

107

caused by..."

"I don't care if Deacon Blaylock was the one who goosed Katie O'Leary's cow." Chet marched over to the bed and confiscated the scrapbook and tablet. "You are not to read, knit an Afghan, or make shadow puppets on the walls. If I have to sit by your bedside and watch you like a hawk, then so be it."

He pulled up a chair and plunked down.

"You don't expect me to just lie here like an invalid."

"Yes, I do. For now, at least, you are an invalid. If you feel better tomorrow—and behave yourself—we can negotiate reading privileges."

Lexi started to protest.

"Not another word. Drexel's bound to have a couple rolls of duct tape around here somewhere. I won't hesitate to make a silver mummy out of you."

"What if I have to go to the bathroom?"

"I know what a catheter is. I'm sure I could convince a couple of the boys to hold you down while I..."

"You wouldn't dare."

Chet's velvet brown eyes flashed the steely edge of a Marine Corps drill instructor. "Try me."

Lexi clutched a pillow to her chest and folded her arms around it.

"Now, what would you like for supper?" Chet asked. "The choices are frozen crab cakes, leftover London broil and duchess potatoes, or cheese eggs with bacon."

There were few things Lexi hated worse than not getting the last word. But the expression on Chet's face told her the topic was closed. "I bet Titus Blaylock never spoke to Andrea that way."

"No, he booked her passage on the *Titanic* instead."

Chet pivoted and headed for the door. "Pleasant dreams." He

dimmed the lights again and unscrewed the dimmer knob from the switch plate.

Lexi reached over, switched on her bedside lamp, and quickly turned it off again. "Cheese eggs and bacon."

Chapter 12

The next morning, Lexi awoke to the familiar tat-tat-tat of the track hammer. She glanced at the clock: nine-fifteen, and ran a quick systems check. The head actually felt pretty good, but she didn't know how much of that pounding she could tolerate - perhaps longer reprieve would have been a good idea after all.

Lexi rolled out of bed and headed for the bathroom. When she caught her reflection in the mirror her heart froze like a block of ice. There was a dark circle around her right eye that trailed off across the temple and disappeared under the bandage.

She wet a washcloth and tried patting it away. No luck. She examined it closer...it was going to be one hell of a shiner...*more great news.* Covering it with make-up was certain to provide her that battered wife in denial look.

She turned around and faced the tub: a bath. When the going gets tough, the tough take a nice, warm bath. Hopefully, Raymond had already bathed this morning.

Lexi dressed and went downstairs. Drexel was about finished

in the kitchen. All it needed was some wallpaper, a little paint and a few decorating touches. It was clearly going to be her favorite space in the house—a great place to conquer the world of baking...pies.

She made a cup of coffee and carried it into the breakfast room. Sun filtered through the windows and provided a picturesque view of the lower terrace, bordered on the right by the village of Monterey nestled in the valley below. The Blaylock itch came calling again. She wasn't sure how long she could stare at a computer screen but, now that she had a better idea what to search for, she could make better use of the time she had.

She marched into the study and powered up the computer. As the cyber chatter flashed across the screen, she got an idea and went back to the kitchen to get her sunglasses out of her purse—the track hammer was beginning to have an effect on her. On the table next to the back door, she spotted Chet's earphones.

Back at the computer desk, she slid the sunglasses up her nose and carefully cupped the headphones over her ears, cocking the strap around to the back so it didn't press against the stitches. It was cumbersome, but tolerable. She adjusted the screen brightness and voila! No glare and no tat-tat-tat.

Lexi had already searched for the Staunton and Harrisonburg newspapers but neither of them had online archives. The library at James Madison University permitted archive access for students but required an account for all others. She filled out the online application, entered her credit card number, and waited for approval. Once access was granted, she entered a pin number she was likely to remember—BEECHER—and tooled to the main menu.

A section titled 'Local History' was provided so she entered the year 1950. The only paper with archives that deep was the *Richmond Times Dispatch*. She narrowed her search to August and a section of the paper called *Rural Virginian*.

After trying several different keywords and browsing screen after screen of copy, she finally hit on an article tagged "Son of Monterey Industrialist Found Dead." BINGO!

'August 25, 1950. Deacon Blaylock, son of wealthy lumber and coal industrialist, Titus Alexander Blaylock, was found dead at the family estate in Monterey, Virginia. On the morning of August twenty-first, the body was discovered by an employee in an old, steam sawmill located on a terrace behind the main house, a portion of the greater mill spared by last month's devastating fire. Investigators from the Highland County Sheriff's Department concluded that a shoulder strap from Mr. Blaylock's coveralls became entangled in the saw blade stock, trapping and then drawing Deacon Blaylock into the blade, causing the fatality.

Richmond Times Dispatch staff reporter, Robert F. Nunnaly, interviewed nineteen-year-old Janice Bandy, proprietor of JB General Merchandise, a retail establishment previously owned by the Blaylock Lumber Company. Miss Bandy indicated declining mill revenues, the fire and a pending bank foreclosure may have played a role in Mr. Blaylock's tragic death.

Deacon Blaylock is survived by his son, Raymond Blaylock, age twenty-six. Raymond Blaylock was not available for interview.'

"Jandy, Jandy, Jandy," Lexi repeated. "That's what gave me that funny feeling yesterday. The church ladies told me JB's real name was Janice Bandy. JANDY."

Lexi scanned the article again; JB sure made it sound like Deacon had intentionally checked himself out.

"Proprietor," Lexi said out loud. Not manager, not employee, but proprietor. She grabbed her dictionary and looked it up just to be sure: one who owns and operates a business.

She leafed through her notes again, looking for two specific items which she found: JB had purchased the store the summer before

Deacon died. At that time, the store was the only thing making any money but obviously not nearly enough.

That part made sense. If the store was showing a profit, Deacon shouldn't have any problem selling it. Doing so before he squandered it was the smart thing to do. But how could JB afford it? This was 1950. A nineteen-year-old female didn't just traipse into a bank and get a loan—not even a capable woman like JB. She needed experience, a business plan, collateral...or at least a sugar daddy to co-sign. Little wonder JB had failed to include the clipping about Deacon's death.

There were three empty pages in the scrapbook. That meant there were two other articles JB didn't want her to see. Lexi clicked the printer icon, saved the article to a file folder and began searching the rest of August for a follow-up story.

A yellow sheet of legal paper suddenly descended between her face and the computer screen. I ADMIRE YOUR TENACITY!! was printed on it in black marker.

Lexi turned and discovered Chet standing behind her. He mouthed something to her and pointed to his ears. Lexi peeled off the headphones.

"I came to see if you needed anything. But you seem to have things well in hand. Are we writing something or just watching loud music?"

Lexi dipped the sunglasses and exposed her black eye.

"Oh, my." Chet crouched down for a closer look. "That's a dandy. Should I thaw a steak?"

Lexi wondered how long he had been watching over her shoulder. She eyed the article from the *Richmond Times Dispatch* sitting in the printer tray. "No. But you'd better cover all the mirrors."

"How's the headache?"

"Pretty good, actually." 'Good' was stretching it a bit but Lexi

113

didn't want him fussing at her. "I couldn't stay in bed any longer. Figured I might as well be productive."

"As long as you don't overdo it," he warned. "What's this?" Chet reached over and plucked the article out of the printer tray.

Lexi snatched it from his hand. "It's a work in progress. You can see it after it's finished."

Chet stood. "Okay, as long as I end up the hero. JB said she's going to Staunton today. Thought I would hitch a ride and fly the Mooney back. Can you spare me for a couple hours?"

JB! How was Lexi going to break the news to Chet about Jandy? Or worse, tell him about Porter? The thought of doing the latter made her want to pack up and move back to New York.

Chet certainly had a right to know, though maybe it was none of her business. Perhaps JB needed to find a way to tell him herself. She certainly didn't pose him any kind of physical threat.

"The two of you don't have a thing going, do you?"

"It's strictly platonic. Besides, I prefer the blond-headed raccoon type."

Lexi picked up an eraser and threw it at him. "If she ties you to a bed in the back room, don't say I didn't warn you."

"Can I get you anything before I leave? How about a bite to eat?"

"I'll fix a sandwich later. Just be careful. I always worry when you fly alone."

Chet bent down and kissed her on the side of the neck. "I'll take my lucky horseshoe."

"You might want to scrape my scalp off first." She kissed him back. "Where's Drexel working today?"

"At the barn. I told him to hold off on the bathrooms until you're feeling better."

Ten minutes after Chet left, the jack-hammering stopped.

114

Finally some peace and quiet. Lexi removed the earphones and continued searching the archives, not finding anything of significant interest.

At one o'clock sharp, the tat-tat-tat resumed and Lexi's head was beginning to throb again. She returned to the bedroom, took a Mepergan and flaked out.

The next thing she knew it was two-thirty. She rolled out of bed and nearly stepped on Beecher who looked a little rattled, too. Perhaps all the noise was getting to him as well. Lexi scratched him between the ears. "Just a few more days, buddy, and the confusion around her will all be over." She grabbed his ball and tossed it out the bedroom door and down the hall. He scrambled after it and brought it back for more.

"That's all for now, boy. When Daddy gets home, maybe we can all go for a walk."

In the kitchen, Lexi poured a glass of Diet Pepsi, returned to the study, sat down in front of her computer and pulled the Deacon article out of her notepad.

Like JB said, something sinister happened that night. But there was more to it than just Deacon and Raymond.

Lexi considered returning to the archives at the *Times Dispatch* but the Mepergan still controlled a majority of her neurons. Being glued to a computer screen for the rest of the afternoon probably wasn't such a good idea. She opened a desk drawer, pulled out a fresh legal pad and decided to start blocking-out the novel.

She reached for the earphones but, at that moment, the tat-tat-tat didn't seem quite as loud. In fact, it wasn't much more than a hard vibration—a pattern of concentric circles played on the surface of her Pepsi. The vibration must be emanating through the bedrock and up into the foundation of the house, she thought.

Lexi rummaged around her desk for a pen, tossed the

earphones aside and curled up on the sofa. All of a sudden, she heard a muffled crash coming from under the floor near the corner beneath the computer desk.

She got off the sofa, stepped over and listened for it again. Nothing happened. She was certain she hadn't imagined it but there wasn't anything under the floorboards but a shallow crawlspace. Pulling the chair out, Lexi got down on her hands and knees, crawled under the desk and placed her ear against the hardwood floor. She felt the vibration against her cheek but there was something else there, too...a faint rattling sound. She knocked on the floor with her knuckles. It sounded solid enough.

The back door slammed and Lexi figured Chet had returned. She got to her feet, went into the kitchen, and found Drexel measuring the wall behind the sink.

"Drexel, is there someone under the house?" she asked.

"No ma'am." He stared at her black eye. "I've only got one crew today and they're down at the barn. I just slipped up here to measure the backsplash for the granite countertops. If I'm disturbing anything, I can..."

"I swear I just heard a crash under the floor in the study," Lexi interrupted. "Like something fell."

Drexel arched his eyebrows. "Show me."

Lexi led him back into the study and pointed to the spot under the computer desk. "It came from right under there," she said.

"Let's take a look."

Drexel squeezed between the desk and the wall and pushed until the power cord on the lamp pulled tight.

"Wait a minute," Lexi said. She logged off the computer, waited for it to power down, then switched off the lamp.

Drexel unplugged the cords, put his shoulder against the desk and pushed it another three feet: he caught JB's photo album and

Lexi's notebook as they landslide off the back of the desk. Then, he rapped on the flooring with butt of his hammer.

He glanced at Lexi, excitement filled his eyes. "I think I know what this is." He tried to pry off the shoe molding at the base of the wall with his fingers but it wouldn't budge. He grabbed his hammer again. "Do you mind?" Lexi consented without hesitation.

Drexel tapped on the molding from the corner out to the computer desk, then from the corner along the adjacent wall to the trim around the archway leading to the foyer. He pried on it again, and it popped it right off.

There was a gap in the flooring along the foyer wall, slightly narrower than the width of the thick shoe molding. He put his fingers inside the gap and slid them toward the corner, then braced his right knee and jerked at the flooring with all his strength. Several of the floorboards lifted a fraction of an inch.

"I'll bet this thing hasn't been opened in fifty years." He sprang to his feet. "I need to get some tools. Be right back."

Drexel returned in three minutes. In one hand, he had a long crowbar; in the other, he held a flat piece of steel with a ninety-degree bend to it. He inserted the short end of the crowbar into the gap under the baseboard and pried the floorboards up a little more.

"There must be ten coats of polyurethane on these."

He pried on the floor again and it gave a little more. "Pull back on this while I use the flat bar to break the rest of them free."

Lexi did as instructed. Drexel inserted the flat bar under the end and carefully worked his way along the edge of the wall; the floorboards popped up at irregular lengths.

As each one gave, Lexi was able to apply a little more leverage to the crowbar. The pressure she was exerting made her head start throbbing again but a pattern was developing along the floor so there was no way was she stopping.

117

Drexel yanked the last board free; set the crowbar aside, placed his fingers in the gap, and jerked a second time. There was a loud crack as the last of the poly stubbornly relented and a hinged three-by-five-foot section of the floor lifted. It was a hidden trap door meshed so perfectly with the other flooring that nobody would have ever known it was there.

"I came across one of these in an old house in Harrisonburg about five years ago," he said. "But the craftsmanship was nothing like this."

"Let's see where it leads," Lexi urged.

The strain on Drexel's face told her that the door was extremely heavy.

"I think we need to oil the hinges," Drexel groaned.

A long wooden stick was hanging from a dry leather strap on the underside of the door. Drexel grasped the stick, fitted it into a carved slot under the bottom and propped the other end on the first step leading down. It was pitch black inside.

"Chet keeps his Mag-Lite on the shelf by the back door," Lexi said.

"I've got a halogen in my truck." Drexel tested the prop with his hand. "I'd better get a couple two-by-fours. If this trap door falls, it could cut one of us in half."

Lexi found the flashlight and hurried back to the study. Standing at the front edge of the opening, far enough back so that if the prop snapped the door wouldn't brain her, she shined the light into the hole.

There were eight steps leading down into a large cavity. The whole thing was chiseled from solid rock; it resembled a crypt.

The side walls reached all the way up to the bottom of the floor joists. In fact, the joists were actually setting on them, banded on the ends to seal off the hole from the rest of the crawlspace. Whatever the Blaylocks stored down here was intended to remain private stock. Lexi knelt down and swept her light across the bottom. It passed over something that reflected the beam back like a mirror, but she couldn't tell what it was from the glare. She placed her hands on the first step and lowered her upper torso, reverse pushup style. As her head broke the plane of the opening, her elbow nudged the wooden prop. The cellulose fibers in it made a distinct crackling sound and every nerve in her body immediately contracted. She hauled herself back up just as the prop snapped in half and the door slammed like the jaws of a starving animal.

The percussion from the slam nearly gave Lexi an out of body experience: *the stars looked familiar but the galaxy was completely foreign.*

After the initial wave of pain passed, Lexi inventoried her parts to make sure everything was accounted for. She rolled onto her stomach and saw a fan of blond hair protruding from between the re-approximated floorboards.

Drexel rushed in from the foyer and dropped to her side. The whites of his eyes were the size of billiard balls. "Are you alright?" he asked in that half-panicked way men speak when they are deeply shaken. He helped Lexi to her feet and guided her over to the sofa.

She glanced back at the trap door. "If I lose any more hair, I'm going to run for governor of Minnesota."

"That was too close. You just stay here; I'll take care of the door."

Drexel pulled it open again, put a two-by-four under it, tacked a smaller piece to the bottom, and then nailed the prop to it. Then he took a third piece of wood and hammered it in place along the first step, wedging the base of the prop to the rock wall.

He pushed against it with his hand. "That should hold it."

Lexi walked over to the opening and Drexel plugged the

119

halogen light into the wall socket. "You want to go first or shall I?"

"I saw a reflection off something down there," Lexi said. "Like a mirror." She grasped the light. "I hope it wasn't a giant eye."

Lexi switched on the light, climbed down the first four steps, and peeked in. It wasn't one set of eyes...it was more like a hundred, maybe two hundred. She had never seen so much silver in her entire life. There were shelves stacked four high lining the exterior walls of the vault; each one was packed full. There were platters, tea and coffee services, three- and five-branch candelabrums and individual candlesticks. There was a British soup tureen similar to one her grandmother had; goblets, jewelry boxes, brush and comb sets. There were several wood boxes—Lexi guessed they contained flatware. Many of the items were badly tarnished, others wrapped in cloth. The vibration from the track hammer had displaced a rather large serving tray. Had she not been in the study at the time, she would never have heard it hit the floor.

Lexi navigated the last four steps without looking; Drexel was right behind her.

"Holy Mother of Jesus!" gasped Drexel.

"Have you ever seen anything to beat this?" Lexi exclaimed.

It took Drexel a few moments to respond. "I don't think anyone's ever seen anything like this."

Lexi retrieved the serving tray and examined the hallmark on the bottom—double stars. She was no silver expert but had once seen a collection of Sheffield plate on display in a museum in New York. The markings were identical.

"JB mentioned Andrea collected silver but Titus couldn't have made this kind of money selling lumber."

"Maybe he was a cat burglar." Drexel's lips twitched as though he was making mental calculations. "What do you want to do now?" he asked.

"I need to get my video camera and record it just like we found it. Then let's take it upstairs and see what we have." Lexi thought for a moment. "No, wait. I want Chet to see it first. Let's just get some of the larger pieces."

Lexi got her digital recorder and Drexel took shots with cell phone. Afterwards, Lexi put a blanket on the study floor and selected a dozen or so pieces to bring up, including the British tureen and a French jardinière.

There was a knock at the front door. Lexi rushed over and cracked it open; it was Dr. Kimberly.

"Good afternoon, Mrs. Willow. I'm surprised to see you up and around. Glad to see you're feeling better."

"A lot better than I look." She took Kimberly by the hand. "There's something I've got to show you."

She led Kimberly into the study and showed her the silver. "And if you think that's something, look down there."

When Kimberly reached the bottom of the stairs, her jaw dropped. "Oh my goodness!" She walked over to a large silver tankard. "Do you mind if I touch it?"

"Do you know anything about it?" Lexi asked.

"A little. My mother had a collection, but nothing anywhere near this." She turned the tankard over and examined the bottom in the light. "It's Russian. My mother had a book that identified stampings."

Lexi looked at the two oval eights and what appeared to be the profile of a woman's head.

"Later, Russian silver had an oval stamped on the bottom. The direction the head is facing indicates the period it was made, and the Cyrillic to the left is the silversmith's stamp."

Lexi picked up a wine flagon with a gadrooned base that was sitting on the shelf next to the tankard. It had an HB stamped on the bottom. "What's this one?" Drexel came over for a look, too.

"I remember this one from college art history," Kimberly said. "That's Hester Bateman's hallmark. She was a famous eighteenth-century British silversmith. You could say she was the Gloria Steinem of the early precious metals industry."

Kimberly examined several other markings but couldn't identify any of them. "You can probably research all of these on the Internet," she said as she gazed at all the shelves. "No telling what all this is worth."

"We need to get it out of here, that's for sure," Lexi added.

"You're going to need a keg of silver polish," Kimberly said. Lexi followed Kimberly and Drexel back up to the study.

"I wish I could give you a hand but I need to get back to the clinic," Kimberly said. "Paragon's foot is looking great but we should continue the sedative for a couple more days. The noise from the digging is still liable to set him off."

Lexi agreed and walked Kimberly to the door.

"Either Terry or I will be back tomorrow. Congratulations on your silver. If I can be of any help later, don't hesitate to give me a call."

"I'd best get back to work, too," Drexel said. He looked at the clock on the computer desk. "The boys probably think I cut out on them." He surveyed the silver again. "There are a lot of people around here that would like to get their hands on this. You can keep the light but, if I were you, I'd find a safe place for this stuff as soon as possible."

Chapter 13

Chet was completely overwhelmed. "At this rate, Cheat Mountain will pay for itself before the ink dries on the bank draft."

"Where are we going to put all of it?" Lexi asked.

"I don't know, but Drexel's right. We need to get it out of here before people start tearing the walls down looking for more. Let's first inventory everything. Tomorrow morning, I'll find an armored car service and see if they can recommend a place to store it."

"Do you suppose there's more hidden around here?"

"Who knows," Chet replied. "We just might find Fort Knox hidden under the barn. JB mentioned something about gold, too, didn't she?"

The thought of having a fortune in antique silver lying around the house made Lexi extremely uncomfortable. "I think we should contact the state police," she said. "Maybe they have some off-duty officers that can camp-out here for a couple days."

"The only ones who know about this are Drexel and Kimberly, right?" Chet asked.

"And Drexel's men, probably Norman's people, and half of Staunton and Harrisonburg by the time the supper dishes are cleared."

"How about Sheriff Godsey?" Chet asked. "He already knows all the stories. It would prevent us from involving more people."

Lexi had reservations and said, "That's like inviting the fox in the hen house."

"I'll start hauling stuff up while you give him a call," Chet said, ignoring her remark. He grabbed a flashlight and climbed through the trap door. "This is absolutely amazing."

Lexi figured she and Chet needed some help. So she decided to call JB first; she wouldn't mention anything about the silver.

JB said she would be over after she closed the store.

Fifteen minutes after she called him, Sheriff Godsey was ringing the buzzer down at the gate. Chet went to the control panel and let him in.

The study looked like a silver auction at Sotheby's. Tea services must have been Andrea's favorite; there were at least thirty in all shapes and sizes. Ten times that many pitchers, platters and goblets, and five sets of engraved flatware. Lexi was making a list and marking the counted items with a grease pencil.

Chet was still bringing things up when Sheriff Godsey knocked at the door. Beecher ran to it barking.

"Thank you for coming over," Lexi said. "I guess the easiest way to explain why we called is to show you."

When Godsey saw the silver, he rocked back on his stumpy legs like one of those clown-faced punching bags. Chet came through the trap door with another armful of loot.

"All that was down there?" Godsey gasped.

Chet grinned. "That's just a little over half of it."

The sheriff waddled over to the trap door and stepped down. "Well, I'll be damned. Titus Blaylock's treasure."

Lexi heard him shuffling his feet around in the crawlspace. In a couple minutes, he squeezed himself back through the opening. "Folks have searched every inch of this mountain looking for this and it's been right under their feet the whole time."

"Our contractor saw the raised section of stone when he pulled up the kitchen floor," Lexi said. "He thought it was a support pier."

"I'd bet my retirement there's over a million dollars sitting here. Is it all silver or is there gold, too?"

Lexi thought Godsey's question sounded a little too eager.

"No gold," said Chet. "We'll let our grandchildren find that. We were hoping you could help us with security until we figure out what to do with it. Too many people already know about it."

A thin smile creased Godsey's lips. "I can assign you two deputies and a car. Have to charge you for the overtime though."

"We'll need them through the night and probably most of tomorrow," Chet said.

"Two shifts with two men tonight, two men during the day tomorrow." He placed his hand on his protruding stomach and tapped his fingers. "Fifteen hundred dollars should cover it."

He careened himself to the left and patted Beecher on the head. "If you can leave this little fellow inside, I'll bring over a pair of bloodhounds. If anyone sets foot on the place, they'll be on 'em like stink on a mess of boiled Ramps."

Lexi liked the bloodhound idea. But she also figured Godsey would pocket at least five hundred of the fee for himself. She, of course, would ask for a receipt...any of the larger candelabrums was easily worth three times that.

"Three shifts, two men on the first two, one on the third and both the dogs for a thousand," Lexi said. She wasn't going to be horse-traded by a greedy sheriff. "And if the night shift manages to stay awake all night, I'll throw in breakfast tomorrow morning."

"Who's cooking?" Godsey asked.

"Me," Lexi replied.

"Make it hotcakes with scrambled eggs and crackling, and I'll see what I can do."

"When can they get here?" Chet asked.

"Give me about an hour to get my dogs. I'll swing over and pick up Randy, then buzz you from the gate."

"You'll be coming too, then?" Lexi asked as if there was any doubt. *If she had enough time to bake a pie, she could have probably gotten the whole sheriff's department for eight hundred.*

"My hounds won't work for anyone but me," Godsey replied. "Besides, I know this mountain like the back of my hand." He turned and waddled in the direction of the front door.

As the sheriff departed, Lexi wondered how many times he had searched the property for Titus's treasure himself.

"I'll bet you another fifteen hundred bucks he has a pillow and a Teddy bear in the back of his patrol car," Lexi said, not even attempting to conceal her dislike for him.

"Just having him here should keep people away." Chet walked back to the vault. "By the way, how's your headache? I got so caught up with this I forgot to ask."

"I'd almost forgotten about it, too." Lexi walked over and hugged him. "How does it feel having your airplane in your own front yard?"

Chet glanced around at all the silver and grinned. "Make that two airplanes."

"You've got a half-a-million dollar Mooney and a new, or soon to be new, Pierce Arrow. All this is going to a charity. Besides,

126

we can use the tax deduction." Lexi returned to her inventory list.

The gate buzzer sounded again and she heard JB fussing over the intercom. "Come on up JB."

"That lard-ass Sheriff Godsey wouldn't let me in the gate until I had proper clearance," JB squawked. "Pulled his blue lights on me like I was still runnin' shine."

When Lexi opened the front door, JB was still fuming. "Before I got that boy elected, he didn't know the difference between a night stick and a night crawler," she cursed. "Evening, Lexi, hope everything's okay up here." She zeroed in on Lexi's black eye. "Land a Goshen, child. You need a green mushroom poultice and a shot of chilled mineral oil."

"It doesn't hurt, really," Lexi said. She couldn't wait to get JB's reaction to the silver.

This time, JB was completely speechless. She stood there, rigid as a wooden Indian, taking it all in. Only her head and eyes moved; she placed a trembling hand upon her chin.

Chet came out of the hole carrying a box full of file folders. "Evening, JB. Looks like Santa came a bit early this year, doesn't it?"

"Or late. Depending upon how you look at it."

JB walked over and ran her finger along the scallops on the top edge of the jardinière. "Andrea Blaylock's silver. I never thought I'd live to see it."

Lexi detected a solemn edge in JB's voice.

"You folks are making quick work of the mountain's secrets. Before long, I won't have anything left to tell the tourists."

Lexi felt a need to console her. "There's still the gold." She put her hand on JB's shoulder. "It's beautiful, isn't it?"

"I've seen pictures of these but never one up close."

Lexi placed the jardinière in JB's hands. "It's yours. I think the local Blaylock historian deserves a fitting piece of Blaylock

127

history."

"Oh, no. I couldn't," JB balked. "It must be worth five thousand dollars."

"I insist. You've been an invaluable friend to Chet and me since we arrived. It's a fitting way to say thanks. Besides, we were hoping you might help us inventory all of it."

JB's eyes started to tear up. "Thank you, Mrs. Willow. Truly, thank you." She set the jardinière back on the coffee table, wiped her eyes, and then rubbed her hands together.

"Alright then, let's get down to business. Do you want to do this by the Dewey decimal system or the oxymoron?"

"Oxymoron?" Lexi asked.

"The oxymoron system it shall be," exclaimed JB. "Let's throw everything in the middle of the floor and hope someone else cleans it up."

With JB on board, the work went much faster. Like with most things, she had a surprising knowledge of silver and was able to identify many of the pieces.

Sheriff Godsey and Randy checked in at quarter past seven. They concealed the patrol car behind the garage as if doing so gave then the element of surprise. JB called it a Barney Fife stakeout.

Lexi broke off to make sandwiches and, by midnight, the inventory was complete: three hundred seventy-seven individual pieces, not counting five twelve-place settings of flatware, fifty-three assorted serving utensils and a shoebox full of meat skewers.

Lexi was exhausted and her hands were filthy from all the tarnish. After she and JB washed up, JB told her how to cook crackling and said she would have Porter run a two-pound bag over in the morning. She then said goodbye and Randy escorted her down to the gate.

Chet made certain all the doors and window were locked, set

the alarm system, and flopped into bed; Lexi downed a six-hundred milligram ibuprofen, kissed him on the lips goodnight and followed suit.

Sleep came fast.

Lexi was bounced awake when Chet abruptly sat up in bed and then jumped to the floor.

"What's wrong?" she asked.

"Godsey's dogs," Chet replied. "They're after something."

Downstairs, Beecher ran to the foyer and began scratching at the front door. There were two or three loud whoops, more barking, and then either Sheriff Godsey or Randy crossed the front lawn yelling, "GET 'EM, BOY!"

Lexi glanced at the clock; it was almost two-thirty. She and Chet had barely been asleep two hours.

"They're headed for the barn," Chet said. He started getting dressed.

"Where are you going?" Lexi asked.

"To see what's going on." He switched on all the outside lights. "You stay here."

"Like hell I am." She nearly jumped into her robe. "You're not leaving me in this house all alone."

Chet stepped out of the closet, took down a brushed aluminum gun, pulled out his 45-caliber Colt automatic, chambered a round and tucked it into the back of his jeans.

"Please don't shoot anyone," Lexi pleaded. She had a good working knowledge of guns; but they were one of the psychological triggers Dr. Fontenberry helped her overcome after her parent's murder.

"I'd rather have it and not use it than need it and not have it. Let's go."

Chet deactivated the security system. They went downstairs and—holding Beecher back—slipped through the front door into the darkness.

The night air clutched Lexi in a damp, cool embrace. Beecher started barking and growling again. There was a loud thud and a muffled scream. Lexi rushed back into the house and found Beecher scratching at the floor under the computer table. There was another thud under the floor, some cussing and then a voice yelled out, "STAY AWAY FROM ME!"

She ran back to get Chet. "Someone's under the house."

"Lock the front door," Chet ordered.

Lexi did as requested and hurried back.

Chet took her by the hand and rushed around to the side of the house to where there was an outside access to the crawlspace. He crouched and peeked around the corner. "The crawlspace is open," he whispered. He reached behind his back, pulled out his pistol an eased around the corner.

There was a light thrashing about inside the crawlspace, getting closer and closer to the opening. Lexi heard heavy breathing and what sounded like pleading. "KEEP BACK! PLEASE DON'T LET IT GET ME! DEAR JESUS, DON'T LET IT GET ME!"

The light broached the opening and a pair of hands clawed at the access. A dark-clad figure with a blackened face extruded himself from the opening, jumped to his feet and took off across the side yard.

"HALT!" Chet shouted.

The robber screamed again but gave no sign of slowing down. Chet shot his pistol into the air and took off after him. Both of them disappeared into the darkness between the house and the outbuildings.

Lexi felt a burst of cold wind brush past her like a blast from an air conditioner. The burglar had accidentally dropped his flashlight; she grabbed it and went after Chet.

Down near the barn there were three different voices yelling and the dogs sounded like they were about to rip something to shreds. Somewhat closer, near the ice pit Lexi estimated, there was another loud scream.

"IT'S BROKE, IT'S BROKE, IT'S BROKE. GOOD GOD ALMIGHTY! THE GHOST OF RAYMOND BLAYLOCK DONE BROKE MY LEG!"

Lexi recognized the next voice as Chet's. "Just lay still. Over here Lexi, hurry! Bring the light." She rushed toward the sound of his voice.

"Be careful, honey," Chet called to her. "The drainage ditch runs to the right and left of where I am standing."

Lexi caught up and shone her light on the ground. "Jimmy, what are you doing here?"

"Jimmy," repeated Chet. "Drexel's Jimmy?"

"Sorry, Mr. and Mrs. Willow. I didn't want to do it. I swear. You folks have been nothing but good to me. Cedric said, if I didn't, he'd turn me in for them other jobs. If I'd known that ghost talk was true, I'd 'ave never come. It had huge red eyes. Ya gotta believe me. I swear to God, it was gonna take my head off."

"What ghost, and what other jobs?" Lexi asked.

"Raymond Blaylock," Jimmy said his eyes wide with fear. "He's under that house, protectin' the rest of his treasure. He attacked me just as I got near the hole with the silver."

Jimmy grabbed at his leg. "Oh, God, it hurts something fierce. I ain't never gonna walk again. I just know it."

Chet intercepted his hand and forced him to lie back down. "It's broken pretty bad, Jimmy, but you'll live. I need to make a tourniquet. Give me your belt."

"Who's Cedric?" Chet asked while Lexi examined Jimmy's

131

leg. A splintered end of the right fibula was protruding through his pants, four inches below the knee; his foot was rotated counterclockwise ninety degrees. Lexi had to turn her head to keep from retching.

"I owe Cedric some money," Jimmy said. "He said he'd call it square if we snagged some of the silver. Ain't no amount of money gonna' get me under that house again."

Chet wrapped the belt just above Jimmy's knee and used the flashlight to tighten it.

"Tell me about the ghost, Jimmy," Lexi asked. "How do you know it was Raymond Blaylock?"

"'Cause it looked just like that thing we pulled out of the ice pit. Except its eyes was red."

"Was there a pitchfork in his chest?"

"Can't say for sure, Mrs. Willow. It came at me face to face, on its belly, just like I was. Then it circled around me until I got back to the door. I heard Mr. Willow shoot but I couldn't make my feet stop. Forgot all about the ditch here. Oh, God, my leg hurts. Didn't you see it?"

"No," Lexi replied.

"You've got to believe me. It breathed on me, breath as cold as the wind off a blizzard. I can still feel it on my face."

Lexi recalled the burst of cool air she felt after Jimmy ran by her.

Two lights came bouncing up the road from the barn. "Sheriff Godsey," Lexi shouted. "We need an ambulance."

The lights separated; one crossed over the ditch and headed for the house—Lexi assumed by the speed it was moving that it must have been Randy; the other followed the ditch over to where she and Chet were holding Jimmy.

"Try anything funny, boy, and I'll fill your ass with number four buckshot," Godsey growled. He pushed another young man, wearing handcuffs, into the light next to Jimmy. "Get on the ground next to your partner there."

Godsey removed the tape from a flashlight he'd attached to the end of his shotgun. "Mighty sharp piece of shooting there, Mr. Willow. Hitting a man's leg like that in the dark and all."

"I shot in the air," Chet said. "He broke his leg tripping over the ditch. His name is Jimmy Grubbs. He works for our contractor."

"This one's Cedric Ritter," Godsey said. He tapped the radio transmitter hanging from the breast pocket of his jacket. "Flash your lights, Tommy." Across the valley, a set of headlights blinked.

"Tommy's been running the plates of every car that's come west ever since you reported finding the silver. Grubbs came over a little after six. He must have seen me and Randy come up with the dogs and decided to call for reinforcements. Ritter crossed the mountain about eight-thirty in that beat-up, old red rattle truck of his. I've got a unit searching for their vehicles now."

Lexi now recognized Ritter as the driver of the red truck which had tailgated her and Chet up the mountain; the one that ran over the ghost of Shepherd Blaylock leading the wounded horse.

"What prompted you to run plates?" Chet asked.

"Just a hunch," Godsey replied. "Everyone who left here this afternoon drove east, toward Staunton. When news of the silver broke, I figured any attempt to steal it will come from that direction. Running plates gave me a list of suspects...I'd rather have two hundred possibilities than none.

"They needed to make a run at the silver tonight, before you moved it. With the gates closed, the only way in is down from the top or up the terrace from the rear. That's why I brought my dogs. They didn't pick up Grubbs' scent because it's probably all over the place to begin with but they knew Ritter's didn't belong."

133

Chet elbowed Lexi. "Excellent work, Sheriff," he said.

"It's called the dumb-end hook-n-run. The dumb end, that's Ritter here, acts as a decoy while the smart end hooks the valuables and runs. If they know what they've come for, the whole thing takes only a couple minutes. If Ritter gets caught, he plays dumb. The only thing we can arrest him for is trespassing—Virginia doesn't convict for accessory to theft."

Randy drove up in the patrol car and left the headlights on. "The squad will be here in five minutes," he said.

"Tell 'em to take their time," Godsey said. "Me and the boys here have a little talking to do."

"You're not going to deny an injured person medical attention on my property," Lexi protested.

"No, ma'am," Godsey replied. "The thought never crossed my mind. But there's been a rash of break-ins in Staunton and Harrisonburg the past few years. I'm just curious if these fellows know anything about them, is all."

"Jimmy claims he saw a ghost under the house," Chet said.

"Where he's going, he'd best get used to it,' Godsey said. He gave Jimmy a hard look. "There's always things going bump in the night around a cell block. You boys make sure an' keep your drawers pulled-up good and tight. Ya hear me, Jimmy?"

"You can't intimidate someone like that," Lexi said angrily. "He's got a broken leg, for Pete's sake."

"It was a real ghost, Sheriff. I swear to God," Jimmy cried. "It came at me under the house, its mouth hanging open. It was comin' to collect my soul."

Lexi believed Jimmy was telling the truth. Every time he mentioned the ghost, there was genuine fear in his eyes.

"Did ya see ghosts under them other houses you broke in, too?" Godsey asked.

"There weren't no other houses," Jimmy whimpered. "And I ain't broken in to this one. The crawlspace door wasn't even locked."

Chet weighed in. "Jimmy told us Cedric was going to turn him in for some other jobs if he didn't help steal the silver. I suspect the truth lies somewhere in between."

"You said what!?" Cedric shouted. He slammed an elbow into Jimmy's ribs. "I ought to break your other leg, you lying son-of-a..."

"That's enough out of you," Godsey said. "We'll let Judge Spencer sort it out. B&E should get each of you five years, minimum."

"Jimmy broke into all them other houses, Sheriff," Cedric spouted. "He told me so himself. Check it out. Drexel Yeatts and Shenandoah Restorations worked at every one of them. Jimmy knew everything they had, and where they kept it. He woulda come back later and done this house, too, if all that silver hadn't shown up when it did."

A call came over Godsey's car-radio and Randy went to answer it. "Sheriff, the squad's down at the Willow's gate but can't get through.

"Tell them to punch zero, nine, nine, zero, five on the key pad," Chet said.

Randy relayed the instructions, repeating the number sequence twice. "That did it. They'll be here in two minutes."

The rescue squad loaded Jimmy into the ambulance and drove away. Randy tied the sheriff's dogs to a tree, and then put Cedric into the back of his patrol car. Godsey returned to his security detail.

Lexi's head began to throb again. She took Chet by the hand and led him back toward the house.

"I thought the crawlspace door was wired into the security

system," she said.

"It is," Chet replied. "Jimmy must have jumpered it." Chet closed and latched it.

Lexi continued around to the front door. "I hope you have a key."

"No, I don't."

Lexi twisted the knob and opened it. "I know I locked this right after you told me to."

Chet pushed the door, pulled his pistol again and looked around in the foyer. "Where's Beech?"

Lexi inched in behind him; everything looked normal. She peeked into the study and immediately noticed all three of the five-tier candelabrums were missing.

"Chet, someone's been in here."

The British soup tureen was also gone as were two boxes of flatware and the largest Argyle pitcher.

A raspy chill passed through Lexi's body. "We've been robbed!"

Chapter 14

This robbery wasn't perpetrated by a pair of drunken stable hands; it had taken intelligence and split-second timing.

The silver pieces were not the only things missing. The minitower from Lexi's computer and all of the notes from her conversation with JB and the photo album were missing, too. The computer contained some of Chet's portfolio strategies and stock market forecasts, all of which was fortunately backed up on a remote drive. That and the silver had tangible value—if Chet's forecasts proved right; they could easily be worth millions. Perhaps the album and her notes were mistaken for something else.

Godsey searched the study and foyer evidence, doing his best to look official while trying to hide the fact that he'd been duped just like everyone else.

"I know where the dumb end was this time," Lexi said, staring directly at Godsey. "But who was the hook? The only one not accounted for was Randy when he went to get the patrol car."

Godsey waddled back into the study. "Randy didn't do it. That boy's so straight he irons his dollar bills before putting them in the collection plate. Whoever it was got in and out while we were at the pit." He paced across the foyer again to the front door. "If the door was locked like you say, then the robber either used a pick or had a key. Since there are no scratch marks around the key hole or signs of forced entry, my guess is it was a key."

Chet came down the stairs carrying Beecher, a white scarf and a tennis ball. "Here's one mystery solved. I found him in the tub in the north bathroom, wrapped in a towel." He put Beecher on the floor and bounced the ball to Lexi. Beecher started to get up and then fell over. "He's been drugged. When I found him, he was just coming to. The ball was in his mouth, and his mouth was tied shut with this scarf. His feet were wrapped with duct tape. Whoever did this wanted to make certain he stayed put."

Lexi grabbed Beecher and hugged him. "Who could do such a terrible thing to my baby?"

"Someone he knew," Chet said firmly.

"That should narrow the suspects," Godsey proclaimed. "Can you make me a list of everyone that's been up here in the last month or so? Particularly those who have displayed an interest in the dog."

"There's been as many as twenty-five to thirty people here a day," Chet said. "Most work for Drexel or one of his subcontractors."

"Plus the movers, UPS people, the church ladies and an assortment of delivery drivers," Lexi added. "Beecher greets everyone who drives up. Usually with his ball in his mouth."

"What about Dr. Kimberly?" Chet asked. "She knew about the silver, and can certainly sedate an animal."

"So can half the people in this valley," Godsey replied. "Most keep a supply of drugs on hand to treat their livestock. It's just a matter of adjusting the dosage according to weight."

"And Kimberly would be too obvious," Lexi added.

"I'll have a forensic team here at first light to scour the

grounds for evidence," Godsey said. "Our collector may have dropped something we can pull a print off." He turned to Chet. "Randy will finish out the shift when he gets back. Nobody else is going to bother you tonight. I'll check back in the morning."

Godsey toddled toward the door. "This is an official crime scene now. I'll only charge you half of our private security fee. Eight hundred dollars."

Lexi figured Godsey had some serious damage control to attend to. She could just imagine the newspaper headline: WILLOW ESTATE HOOKED WHILE DUMB SHERIFF TORTURES WOUNDED SUSPECT. The thought of that almost made her laugh out loud—*ten bucks says he's back in time for crackling and pancakes.*

"Four hundred," Lexi replied.

Godsey frowned and showed himself to the door.

It was nearly 5:00 AM when Lexi finally crawled back in bed. "Why the ghost of Raymond?" she asked. "Why not Deacon or Titus?"

"One Blaylock's as good as another," answered Chet. "Any one of them had cause to haunt this mountain."

"But until we discovered Raymond's body, nobody seemed interested in his disappearance. Given the family's wealth and stature, I find that odd."

"It was fifty years ago. Besides, without Raymond to inherit everything, it was open season on Titus's treasure."

Lexi propped her chin in her hand. "JB said Raymond was a good man. It must have driven him crazy to be part of such a screwed-up family."

"He didn't pitchfork and chain himself, if that's what you're thinking."

"No, but there might be something to this ghost idea. I've never been totally against the notion. After all, Christianity is practically based on ghosts."

Chet rolled onto his side and faced her. "Look, Jimmy was spooked by a light shining through a crack in the floor, or a beam from a flashlight sweeping across a foundation vent. Nothing more."

Lexi noted the irritation in Chet's voice. "That boy was frightened to death."

"He certainly was. And I believe Cedric forced him to go under the house. Jimmy got unnerved by the ghost stories he'd heard and by seeing Raymond's body. His imagination filled in the rest. He probably had enough adrenalin flowing under there to mistake a caterpillar for an anaconda."

Lexi knew she would never get Chet to admit to having a ghost. "Okay, let's forget about Raymond. Who would have known Jimmy was going to break into our house tonight?"

"Coincidence," said Chet. "Robber Number Two simply capitalized on Robber Number One's blunders."

"Okay, a professional hit. But why take the computer?"

"Maybe someone came for the computer but couldn't resist the silver. Many stock brokers are desperate these days. When the markets get hammered like they have been for the past eighteen months, people start looking to other investments. Funds dry up, fund managers get fired and commissions plummet. Some guys will do anything for an edge. It's no secret that I'm not in New York anymore. But only my working files are here. All my matrices are on the secure LAN at Price-Lynch. Nothing I have here would make sense to anybody."

Lexi was thinking along a different line. "What if it had nothing to do with your work? JB said something tonight that got me thinking. She said that we were making quick work of the mountain's secrets. Suppose there are secrets somebody doesn't want us to uncover?"

"Secrets like...?"

"The truths behind four murders: Titus, Andrea, Deacon and Raymond," Lexi answered.

"This wouldn't happen to have anything to do with your new book would it?

"No. I'm serious. I can't prove anything yet, but I'll bet there's a link."

"If you feel that strongly maybe we should stop work on the house and barn until we figure out what's going on."

"No way," Lexi said eagerly. "Let's see who shows up for work tomorrow and who doesn't. If one or two don't show, we'll see if Sheriff Godsey ran their plates."

Chet kissed her cheek and turned out the lamp. "He can run plates all he wants, sweetheart. But if the Cheat Mountain Royal Mounted Police don't have their man by next Thursday morning, Trooper Lexi Willow is going on furlough with me to New York City."

At eight o'clock am, Tat-Tat and Scoop commenced again—*hell hath no fury like the tat-tat-tat of a track hammer,* Lexi thought.

She rolled over to discover Chet was already gone. Between sets of tats, she heard voices outside her window; she got dressed and went downstairs.

Sheriff Godsey was standing under the front portico, apparently dusting the landing area for fingerprints. Two deputies were on their hands and knees combing the grass and shrubbery under the front windows.

"Finding anything?" Lexi asked.

"The perpetrator was wearing gloves," Godsey replied. "The

door handle was all but wiped clean. Only one set of prints; probably yours or Mr. Willow's. Same with the duct tape used to tie Beecher's feet. The scarf may give us something but we'll need to send it to Quantico for analysis."

Lexi smelled hair burning and cut him short, racing for the kitchen. She found Chet bent over the stove surrounded by a cloud of smoke, the exhaust fan running wide open. On the counter next to him was a plate full of little brown BBs floating in a sea of oil. The whole top of the stove was splattered with grease.

She tapped him on the shoulder. "Breakfast smells like...well, it definitely smells. But Beecher prefers his cholesterol medium-rare. Shouldn't you have a fire extinguisher handy?"

Chet was digging at the frying pan with a spatula. He had both front burners on high; the other was roasting a pan full of butter. Next to that was a bowl of pancake batter with little craters sprinkled across the surface of it from impacting grease meteorites.

"This crap is like trying to fry firecrackers," he barked, loud enough to be heard over the roar of the exhaust fan. "Human beings don't actually eat this stuff, do they?"

She reached over, turned off the flames, and silenced the fan. "Six-thousand degrees is a bit much to cook eggs and pancakes." She removed the frying pans and placed them in a dry sink. "Find me two more. Once I get this oil slick under control, we will try it again together."

Lexi could see she'd wounded Chet's ego. "Cheer up, sweetie. Chef Ramsey couldn't have put more heart into it. JB said the trick is to cook it on low and slow."

"I say we give them what I've cooked and toss in a bowl of Sugar Pops. Raymond could have robbed us just as easily without them. We probably would have gotten more sleep too."

CHEAT MOUNATAIN

Lexi's batch of crackling didn't smell any more appetizing than Chet's, but at least it wasn't burned.

Randy ate two stacks of pancakes and a glass of milk. He thanked them for breakfast and left. Godsey devoured nearly half the bag of crackling, four eggs and ten pancakes. The whole house reeked. Lexi opened all the windows downstairs to air it out.

Then she located her earphones and herded Chet toward the back door. "We're going for a walk," she announced.

"What about the silver?" he asked.

"If they can handle the stench, they're welcome to it.

The sky was a wonderful powder blue, trimmed with a thin wisp of high cirrus. The pain in Lexi's head was a three on a scale of ten—comparatively speaking, that was almost no headache at all. She didn't need the sunglasses anymore except to conceal the black eye. In any case, she wanted to see how the trench was progressing in the daylight.

The angular, yellow track hammer was beating out its steady rhythm of tats, a plume of dust rising up around the digging end. The excavator was dutifully crawling along behind, scooping out the shattered rubble in precise, mechanical sweeps of its inverted arm, and depositing it's catch in a giant dump truck behind it.

Lexi was pleased with the progress. The methodical duet of tat-tat and scoop had dug down ten feet at the terrace end of the trench and almost five feet next to the dam at the ice pit. At this rate, the pit would likely be drained before Chet left for New York.

They climbed aboard the Gator. The next stop was the barn; Lexi had not laid eyes on Paragon since the accident. Chet instructed the track hammer operator to take a break until he and Lexi finished their tour. Drexel's crew had not arrived yet—hopefully, they weren't still back at the office waiting for Jimmy Grubbs to show up.

Most of the stalls inside the barn had been demolished. The plan was to build new rows of smaller enclosures along each of the exterior walls, allowing for a row of larger stalls for mares with nursing foals to be built down the middle.

A strange feeling gripped Lexi as she entered the barn: an imbalance, almost a sense of foreboding. She paused and felt Chet's arms cradle her from behind.

"Are you okay?" he asked.

"I'm fine." Lexi put her other hand to her forehead. "Just a little dizzy."

Chet sat her on a stack of feed bags. "Let's go back to the house and lie down. You've been exerting yourself too much."

"Please, I'm ok," Lexi objected. She stood and walked over to Paragon's stall. As she touched the latch, a bolt of lightning passed through her brain. Immediately following it was a black-and-white image of a man, like an old, out-of-focus photograph. He was standing on the other side of Paragon's stall holding a pitchfork. Lexi felt herself recoil.

The image disappeared as quickly as it had come; she felt Chet's hand on her shoulder again.

"You paused again," he said. "Is something happening?"

"No. I just got a strange mental image. Like a vision."

She pulled the stall door open and stepped inside. The bolt of lightning bleached her thoughts again. The picture that followed this one was of two people and much better focused. A young woman was leaning back on a bale of hay; her legs were naked and splayed apart. Another man, not the one in the first picture, was positioned between them. It was obvious he and the woman were having intercourse. The vision suddenly disappeared again.

"What's going on, Lexi?" Chet asked. "Your face is completely white."

"There was a couple making love somewhere here in the barn, a large man and a young woman."

Chet softly gripped her arm. "Did you see their faces?"

"No. The man had his back to me and the woman's head was turned."

"Come on; let's get back to the house."

"Chet, I'm alright!" snapped Lexi. "Stop worrying, will ya?"

Paragon walked up to her and gently nuzzled her hand.

"Hey, buddy," Lexi said. She patted him on the side of the neck. "Do you see the same things I'm seeing? Is that what spooked you the other day?"

Chet grasped Paragon's halter and Lexi saw the muscles in his forearm flex, prepared to jerk the horse's head down if he attempted to rear.

"That's a good boy," Lexi said in a calming voice. She ran her hand along Paragon's back, and then bent down to look at his injured ankle. The bandage was snug and there was no sign of blood. "I see Dr. Kimberly is taking good care of you. You and I'll be running through that valley together in no time. I promise."

As she turned to leave the stall, there was a third lightning bolt...the strongest so far. So much so that Lexi had to steady herself against the door. The picture of the man with the pitchfork flashed before her again, larger and better focused. Had she known who he was, she was certain to have recognized him. But there was no mistaking the look on his face—brows furrowed, eyes narrowed, jaw clenched and mouth drawn.

"There's the first man again," said Lexi. "The one with the pitchfork." She described every detail of him to Chet. "He walked in on the couple making love, but they don't know he's there." The picture faded and then vanished again.

"Could the older guy have been having sex with the stable

hand's girlfriend?" Chet asked.

"I don't know. Maybe. There's nothing about the pictures that I can date to anything." Then Lexi remembered the photo of Titus Blaylock from JB's scrapbook; he was a large-framed man.

"No. I think the man with the girl is Titus," Lexi stated. "JB said Deacon loved his stepmother even though she treated him like a slave. Maybe Deacon walked in on his father cheating on Andrea with one of the saw mill people."

"That may have angered him but what's the significance of it? People cheat every day. Why would you be seeing it?"

Lexi suddenly had a wild thought. "Maybe Deacon killed Titus. It makes perfect sense. Only Deacon knew Titus and Andrea had gone on a voyage. A man who owns an empire of coal mines and lumber mills doesn't just up and leave for England in the middle of the night. He would at least tell his key executives. In a fit of rage, Deacon killed Titus, hid the Pierce Arrow and Andrea's steamer trunk in the lower ice pit to make it appear as though they were gone. When he learned that the *Titanic* had sunk, he had the perfect cover story."

"Then what happened to Andrea?" Chet asked.

"Deacon gave her a chunk of money and she moved back to Richmond. JB said she never liked it here anyway."

"In the middle of the night, and no one ever hears from her again?" Chet shook his head. "That won't work. If Titus was dead, she stood to inherit the whole damn valley. Why settle for just a small piece of it? And why leave all the silver?"

Chet closed and latched the stall and made Lexi sit on the bags of feed again. "Are you sure you're okay?"

"If it wasn't Deacon that caught Titus, who was it?" Lexi asked.

"Raymond was the one with the pitchfork in his chest. Maybe he was caught raping one of the mill worker's daughters."

146

Lexi did not see any resemblance between Raymond's remains and the image of the man holding the pitch fork. "Maybe he caught someone else. Deacon was the womanizer. What if Raymond caught him forcing himself on a young girl and they got into a fight? That would tie in with Deacon burning the mill to hide Raymond's body. Except the evidence was never in the mill because Raymond was in the ice pit. A place no one would have thought of because it was believed to have dried up years earlier."

"What if Deacon killed the girl and burned her body in the mill?"

Lexi was not sure if Chet was really interested or just playing along. Either way, he was being quite helpful. She also knew that, at some point, she would have to broach the Porter issue with him. She had hoped JB would have already addressed it but Chet would have certainly told her if she had.

"JB would have mentioned that she was missing. That's too important a detail to leave out. And there would have been an investigation."

"What if nobody knew about her?"

"Possible. But JB knows everything that's happened around here."

"So where does that leave us?" Chet asked. "We have the Pierce Arrow in ice pit number one and Raymond Blaylock with a pitchfork through his chest in ice pit number two. Right back where we started."

"We also have a mill girl being raped." Lexi climbed back aboard the Gator.

"Your evidence on that score may work in the court of Willow, but I doubt it would get very far anywhere else." Chet slipped into the seat next to her. "Are you certain you're not overdoing things?" he asked. "I think we should tell Dr. Buettner about the visions."

"They're nothing." Lexi managed a tentative smile. "Maybe getting kicked in the head put me in touch with my extrasensory perception." Lexi reviewed the images in her mind one more time. "Everything that happened to the Blaylocks and everything that's happening to us here now is all related. I'm certain of it. We just need to find the connections."

"If they can be found, I'm confident you will discover them." Chet put the earphones over Lexi's ears and honked the horn to get the track hammer operator's attention. He waved his hand and the tat-tat-tat resumed again.

Chet drove toward the back of the terrace, past the old steam mill and down into the valley to the air strip. He stopped the Gator next to his Mooney.

As far as machinery goes, it truly was a beautiful piece of human engineering: top of the line, turbocharged, single-engine private aircraft; cobalt-blue over metallic gray with the trademark forward-canted tail section and every piece of avionic gadgetry imaginable.

Chet ran his hand over the starboard wing. "Soon as you can handle a subtle change in pressure, you've got to see this place from the air. The whole valley looks like an endless river of green. From a thousand feet, you can even see the breeze ripple across it."

"I should be ready in a day or two."

"Then let's fly to Roanoke on Saturday," Chet said. "I'll rent a car and treat you to shopping at the Orvis warehouse and catch a late lunch at Montano's."

"As long you don't mind being seen with a woman with a bag over her head."

"Wear something clingy. Show a little cleavage and nobody

will think twice about the black eye."

Chet's gaze had that velvety texture again. As far as Lexi was concerned, that was one of the most beautiful feelings in the world. She would follow him anywhere. And if the paving crew wasn't around, she would spread a blanket on the grass and demonstrate her love here and now.

"Have I told you lately how much I love you?" Lexi asked.

"When you look at me that way, words aren't necessary."

Lexi combed her fingers through his thick brown hair. "When did you first know I loved you?"

"The first time I saw you without make-up."

Lexi gasped. "Without make-up? That's not very romantic. I thought it would have been the first time we kissed, or the first time we made love."

A wry smile slowly worked its way across Chet's mouth. "I had you between the sheets two weeks after we met. We were dating nearly a year before I saw you without make-up. Kisses are candy; letting your true color show, that's love."

"It was not two weeks!" Lexi exclaimed. "It was more like five or six months."

"Come on. I could have had you that first night, right after the Christmas party. I just didn't want you to think you were being too easy."

"Easy! Why you pompous, arrogant..."

"But if I could do it all over again, I wouldn't wait. Those were two more weeks that I could have spent holding you in my arms."

Lexi angled her head and cut her eyes at him. "Was that a compliment? Because if it was and I ignore it, I might say something I'll really regret."

Chet put his arms around her, pulled her from the cart and

kissed her on the lips. "That was a compliment. When you were in that ambulance, I would have traded everything I own for just two more weeks."

Lexi ran her foot up the back of his leg and then entwined her leg between his, drawing him to her—at that moment she wanted every square inch of her body touching his.

A gold pickup rounded the end of the runway and bounced over to the Gator. Drexel poked his head out the window. "If I didn't know better, I'd swear you kids were newlyweds."

"Drexel Yeatts, you have an uncanny knack for showing up at the most inopportune times," said Lexi.

Drexel flashed his impish smile. "I'm practicing for when my daughters become teenagers. I heard about your unwelcome visitors last night. I'll take full responsibility for any damages. Jimmy called me from the hospital this morning and filled me in."

"No damages, Drex, just concerns," Chet said.

Like who was their third partner and what's coming next, Lexi thought.

"Jimmy's a good boy, Mr. Willow. He just got a little sloppy picking his friends. I'll restore the alarm system so it won't happen again."

"We're not going to press charges," Lexi said. "But we have to give signed statements to the sheriff. Jimmy implicated himself with some other break-ins."

"Whatever that was he saw under your house scared him so bad he would have confessed to just about anything."

Lexi found that statement a little overly-defensive. It hinted at duress and implied she and Chet may have forced Jimmy to talk against his will. Not even Godsey had done that, though he probably would have given a chance. "I hope he knows a good attorney."

Drexel nodded his head and glanced back across the runway.

"Another day or two of paving should take care of it, Mr. Willow. Soon as they're finished, we can start on the hangar and the horse arena. I estimate we'll be completely out of your hair in three months."

"It will be too quiet around here without you," Chet said. "All the noise reminds me of New York."

"The way things looked when I drove up, it won't stay quiet around here for long. You guys might need bunk beds in the nursery."

A second truck drove up. "Here's the rest of my crew," Drexel said. "We'll be putting in a little overtime today and Friday to get back on schedule. A third crew will be joining us on Monday."

"Hey, that reminds me," Chet said. "Sheriff Godsey wants a list of all the men you've brought to the job, including Norman's people and all subcontractors. Bring it to the house as soon as you can."

Chapter 15

When Lexi and Chet returned to the house, Sheriff Godsey and his crack team of forensic scientists had finished collecting evidence. The results of their investigation amounted to approximately thirty-five thousand dollars in missing silver (Lexi's own estimate), a partial casting of a footprint (which was an exact duplicate of the tread on Chet's Dexters), smudges of graphite residue from Godsey's Dick Tracy fingerprinting kit, everywhere, and a house that still smelled like roasted animal intestines.

The only evidence worth keeping was the white scarf, the tennis ball and Jimmy's flashlight that resembled every other Mag-Lite, right down to the missing rubber bubble over the thumb switch...all of which Chet had found the night before.

Chet examined the evidence bag that contained the Mag-Lite.

"We pulled a couple good prints off it," exclaimed Godsey. "I'll run them through the lab but I'll bet my retirement we'll have three matches: Ritter's, Mrs. Willow's and yours."

"What about the batteries and bulb? Neither Lexi or I touched either of those."

Godsey's eyes widened. "Why, you'd make a right smart deputy, Mr. Willow. Yes, sir, right smart indeed." Godsey took the bag from Chet. "I'll dust them soon as we get back to headquarters."

Lexi could see the wheels in Chet's head turning. "What are you thinking?" she asked.

"Nothing really. But if this is Jimmy's flashlight, only his prints should be on the batteries."

Lexi cleared everything off the coffee table in her study; it was time to examine the box of files Chet had found in Titus's vault.

The box was actually a drawer of a wooden filing cabinet. The study may have at one time been Titus's personal office. When he went away for an extended period of time, he simply removed the drawer and put it down below for safekeeping. Deacon obviously never knew about it.

The file folders, seventeen in all, were the copper-colored accordion-type with a string tied around the outside. Three of them were over an inch-thick with the subject matter neatly notated on the top left-hand corner.

Lexi thumbed through the titles: Birth Certificates, Licenses, Blaylock Imports, Blaylock Timber Company, Blaylock Mining and Minerals, Cedar Mountain Timber Company, First National Bank...Norfolk and Western Railroad, Silver Receipts, Titles and Deeds...the last one was labeled West Virginia Mail Pouch Tobacco.

Since it was the thickest one, she examined the Silver Receipts files first. Enclosed were six manila folders, each one with a different name. She opened one for Tetley Mercantile, London, England.

Inside was a stack of receipts. As Lexi leafed through them she came across one for the Sheffield Plate soup tureen. Titus paid ^103 for it on August 21, 1909. Depending upon the exchange rate,

153

^103 could have been as much as four to five hundred dollars - a substantial amount of money in 1909.

Lexi examined the other folders; each one contained more receipts. It appeared as though she may be able to document Titus and Andrea's purchases of most of the silver—she would compare with the inventory list later.

She returned the folders to the accordion file and set it aside. The next one she examined was marked First National Bank which was curious because she remembered JB saying Titus had little use for banks. Inside, there was a series of letters to Titus from Jerome T. Wilson, President, First National Bank, Richmond, Virginia. Paper-clipped to each was yet another receipt. Some were dated as early as March 15, 1894. The later ones—March of 1908 through November of 1911—were typewritten.

The first letter was the confirmation of a request from Titus to exchange $10,000 cash for four hundred thirty, twenty-dollar U.S. gold coins, each valued at twenty-three dollars, plus a hundred-ten dollar handling fee. It also indicated the date when the gold would be available. The document attached to the back of it was the actual receipt for the gold, signed and dated by Titus Alexander Blaylock on the day of delivery.

Lexi quickly scanned the receipts; they varied from ten thousand to one hundred seventy-five thousand dollars. Incredible amounts of money back in those days. She snatched the calculator off her computer desk and added up all the receipts.

By the time of his death, Titus had exchanged $1,160,000 for 50,435 gold coins. If each coin was one ounce of pure gold, their worth today would be about $1200 per ounce, give or take fifty bucks. The value of the gold alone, say nothing of numismatic value, would be $60,522,000!

Lexi's mouth went dry. She rechecked her figures; they came

154

out the same. Third-world dictators have been overthrown for less.

"Chet," she shouted, though her voice came out little more than a croak. "Chet, are you in here?"

There was no answer. She checked the kitchen and then the bedroom: no Chet. As she was about to leave, she noticed his pager on the nightstand and grabbed it; he answered on the second ring.

"Chet, where are you?"

"Beech and I went to JB's to get some boxes. Why? Is something wrong?"

"Come to the house as soon as you can. I've got something to show you."

"What is it?" Chet asked.

"The rest of Titus Blaylock's fortune."

"You found the gold?"

"Just hurry, will you?"

Chet didn't reply but Lexi heard the engine of the Expedition ratchet up a couple notches. She returned the phone to the nightstand and headed for the study again. Halfway down the steps, she stopped. "50,435 ounces..." She did some rough division. "That's more than a ton-and-a-half of gold." When she got to the study, she ran it through the calculator—3,152 pounds of gold, to be precise.

"That's ridiculous. Nobody's going to stash three thousand pounds of gold around their house, or a million dollars in silver for that matter."

Titus was bound to have spent some of it. He leveled the terrace, built a stone mansion, vacationed in Europe, had to keep his Jezebel in caviar and silk stockings, and bought toys for himself like the Pierce Arrow. Those things had to cost a wad for the times.

Still, 1.2 million dollars in the 1900s was a lot of logs. Certainly more than one mountain full by the time you subtracted expenses and labor. Titus must have had another source of income.

She returned to the files again: Blaylock Mines and Minerals—his coal inheritance.

Lexi started at the rear of the file. On June 1, 1885, after the death of Thomas Horatio Blaylock, Titus inherited three parcels of land in West Virginia totaling one thousand two hundred and fifty-three acres. Included in the bequest were five active mine shafts, all equipment, and structures.

She jumped to the front of the file. Three pages back, she found a contract dated September 12, 1908 for the sale of Blaylock Mine and Mineral Company to John D. Rockefeller and Henry Flagler, Standard Oil Company. The amount of the sale was $2,600,000.

Chet rushed into the study. He seemed disappointed to find Lexi sitting amongst the opened files but she filled him in on what she had discovered.

After an hour of deciphering handwriting and transcribing numbers, she and Chet had a good feel for Titus's financial empire; it was considerable. By the time of his death, he had divested of everything but the two lumber companies—Blaylock Lumber and Cedar Mountain Timber Company—and ten thousand shares of the Mail Pouch Tobacco Company. His most lucrative deal was selling off his interest in the Norfolk and Western Railroad to the tune of $7,246,000, stemming from a twenty-five thousand dollar investment by Simian Blaylock of Atlanta, Georgia in 1837 when Norfolk and Western was chartered. Simian must have seen it as a stable way of getting West Virginia coal to market: *buy IPO and sell high, as Chet always bragged.*

"The Sixteenth Amendment to the Constitution was passed in 1913," Chet said. "It gave Congress the authority to levy income taxes. But rumors of the legislation had been around for years. Titus must have seen the handwriting on the wall and cashed out before

Uncle Sam could find out how much he was really worth. Yet I thought there was a government recall on tangible gold holdings in the early 1900s. The Fed would certainly audit the bank's records and discover Titus's transactions. They were bound to have gotten their hands on part of it."

"Maybe he held onto the lumber companies just to keep people around," Lexi said. "People with daughters who like to hang out in horse barns."

"No, he kept the lumber companies because he still wanted to make money," Chet replied. "I've known dozens of people like him. It's in their blood. Titus just had the sense to realize he didn't need to make so much of it anymore. What puzzles me is—if Titus didn't believe in banks—what could he have done with all his money? Other than the gold, this estate and the silver, he doesn't list very much in personal expenditures. He was bound to have a mountain of additional wealth somewhere."

"Could he have laundered it through the mills?"

"He couldn't have laundered that much if he owned the entire detergent industry."

There was a knock at the front door. Lexi opened it and found a young black man dressed in a blue uniform and wearing a gun.

"I'm Martin Stucky with Wells Fargo Armored, ma'am. I have orders to transport a shipment of silver to our secure facility in Charlottesville."

Chet joined Lexi at the door. "That's why I went to JB's, to get boxes. I guess I forgot to tell you."

Lexi showed the guard into the study. "As you can see, we're not quite ready."

Stucky gazed around and then rocked back on his heels. "Well, either I can wait for you to box it up or I can come back later today. I'll still have to charge you for the second trip though."

Lexi wanted the silver out today. "Go get your hand truck, we'll pack."

Chet went to the Expedition and brought back a stack of collapsed boxes; Lexi rounded up spare towels, sheets and blankets, anything to use as packing. She wrapped while Chet stuffed, labeled and sealed. It took nearly three hours to finish—minus a tea service, a Sheffield vase and a Hester Bateman water jug Lexi wanted to keep on display.

Once the truck was loaded, the guard came back with the forms for Chet to sign.

"That's one problem off our backs," Lexi said after he left.

"Now we know why there's so much interest in Titus Blaylock's fortune. What we just carted out of here doesn't even put a dent in it. I'll bet Andrea and Deacon never had a clue what the old goat was really worth."

"Which brings us back to the *Titanic*," Lexi said. "You don't kill someone, even in a fit of rage, and then hope to stumble upon his fortune later. You kill him after you know where it is."

Chet winked at her. "The plot thickens."

Chapter 16

Friday was the first day in several weeks that something weird didn't happen. Lexi spent the afternoon working on her novel. With most of the research complete, it was time to put it in the hopper and plant two thousand words per day.

Chet served supper to her in the study; Lexi didn't finish her 2000-word quota until quarter to eleven. She still couldn't decide who the bad guy was going to be; that was gumming up the whole process. She took a 600-mg ibuprofen, went upstairs, and dropped into bed. Chet was already snoring.

When Lexi awoke Saturday morning, she found herself completely headache-free for the first time since the accident. She felt like leaping out of bed but feared the consequences.

She reached for Chet, *it was time to finish what they started down at the airstrip yesterday,* but he wasn't there again. Their body clocks seemed to be running on completely different schedules these days.

Suddenly, she remembered he was going to fly her to Roanoke today if she felt up to it. It probably wasn't such a good idea—the change in altitude could send her head reeling if the cabin pressure fluctuated too much—but Chet wanted so much to show her their mountain from the air. He was most likely down in the valley right now spread-eagle across a wing digging dried wax out of rivet heads. Everything had to be perfect. The only thing he enjoyed more than his Mooney was flying it with Lexi riding right seat. It was one of those "me Tarzan, you Jane" sort of things, but she was still flattered by his need to impress her.

She had to admit, though, when it came to flying an airplane—at least a single-engine—his skills were truly exceptional. Lexi guessed as long as he flew straight and level with no maximum performance takeoffs or wing stalls, no simulated engine emergencies and pretend crop dusting, everything should be fine.

She switched on the bathroom light and found a note taped to the mirror. At the bottom of it, there was a heavy black arrow pointing to her pager resting on the vanity: ROANOKE TODAY?? Press #1 if by land (next to a line drawing of a small car); or #2 if by air (next to a drawing of an open-cockpit airplane with the copilot wearing dark glasses and earphones).

It took Chet three rings to answer. "Cheat Mountain Airlines, may I have your reservation number please?"

"Lexi Willow, party of two. Preferably something in the Mile High Club."

"I'm sorry, Mrs. Willow, heavy petting is already booked for this flight. But I do have an opening in tail gunner."

Lexi smiled. "Oh my, that sounds delightful. I'll take it. Make it noonish? What's the in-flight meal?"

"Fried crackling and hog jowls."

"Cancel room service. I'll wait for Montano's."

Lexi sank into the Mooney's thick, leather-upholstered right seat as Chet ran through the last steps of his pre-flight checklist; she thought it peculiar that he always cracked open the window and yelled CLEAR PROP! before starting the engine, especially when it was obvious that nobody but the two of them were within a country mile of the propeller.

Chet touched the ignition switch and the twin turbocharged Lycoming engine instantly fired-up. He gave Lexi a smug smile. "Mooney Acclaim Type S: The Lamborghini of personal flying machines."

The wind was blowing down the valley from the north. Chet taxied onto the south end of the runway, set the parking brake and powered up to complete the engine pre-takeoff checks: flaps, magnetos, guesstimate the altimeter setting...seats locked in place.

Because the runway was only partially paved—and still ridged where it was paved—Chet elected do to a soft-field takeoff to prevent damaging the landing gear on one of the bumps. He applied power smoothly and quickly, and then pulled back on the elevators, taking the weight off the front tire as the plane accelerated. The front tire lifted off the ground and Chet maintained back pressure, keeping the nose up until the Mooney was airborne. He then quickly leveled off, flying just feet above the ground until the airspeed was high enough to clear the power lines along the road. Lexi heard an electric whirl beneath her feet, felt the landing gear retract, and the fairing doors lock closed.

The view of world beneath them was nothing short of magnificent; forests and valley wrapped in every imaginable shade of green; beauty which exceeded the descriptive elements of the language required to describe it.

Chet flew north past Monterey and then circled around, following the valley back south. The houses and buildings of Monterey looked like a rift of bony teeth protruding from an emerald sea.

As they approached Cheat Mountain, Chet configured the Mooney for slow flight by reducing power and adding twenty degrees of flaps. The house and outbuildings were nestled into the side of the mountain under a canopy of oak and pine. It was the picture of complete serenity, even with the two mechanical monstrosities at the ice pit, each with its long neck curled in upon itself like a sleeping, yellow swan.

Lexi thought the barn seemed to be missing something; a word or some catchy phrase needed to be painted on the white gable facing the valley, like Longview Stables or maybe Willow Mountain Thoroughbreds. That was definitely something she intended to fix

Further beyond the barn, was the old sawmill with its rusted tin roof. Forlorn, not meticulously maintained like the rest of the estate; no longer an integral part of anything.

Chet increased power and retracted the flaps ten degrees at a time until they were once again straight and level. "That was the appetizer. Now it's time for the main course," he said.

He nudged the throttle forward, pulled back on the yoke and began to climb, slowly, so as not to risk a pressure imbalance that might cause Lexi discomfort. Her eyes were glued to the expanding view of the valley until the plane rose above the lateral peaks of mountains; more than 3500 feet above sea level and two to three hundred feet below the scattered fluffy clouds. The whole panorama of Highland County and eastern West Virginia came into view. Lexi found it hard to believe that her and Chet's little farm was a part of such majesty. A kingdom ruled by mountains and green.

Chet leveled off at four thousand feet and slowed to 110 knots. He flew east and circled Jack Mountain, one of the highest peaks in the area, yet soft and tree-covered like most of the Appalachians. He circled to a heading of 240-degrees to cut over to

Highway 220 which he intended to follow south straight into Roanoke.

He punched a series of buttons on the stack of avionics. Colored maps flashed by on the one of the navigational gear screens and a string of numbers raced across another small computer readout.

"This slight tail wind's giving our fuel efficiency a nice boost," Chet said. "I thought we might have to stop at Hot Springs and fill up. Looks like we have enough to get to Roanoke."

"We may have another brewing problem, though," Lexi said.

"What's that?"

Lexi was embarrassed to even mention it but it wasn't like she could excuse herself and walk down the hall to the ladies room. "I forgot to use the bathroom before we left home. It's not immediate or anything yet, but we shouldn't get too carried away with sightseeing."

"Roger, that," Chet replied. He gave the engine a little more throttle and checked his computer again. "Estimated wee-wee time is forty-five minutes. How's the head doing?"

"Like a champ," Lexi replied and kissed him on the right cheek.

Chet had an aviation sectional map which encompassed Virginia neatly folded and clipped to a kneeboard on his lap; Lexi picked it up and examined it to get her bearings.

"We're right here," Chet said pointing to a radio tower symbol on the sectional, and then pointing to the actual tower through the windshield. Then he traced Highway 220 with his finger to where it intersected with Interstate 64. "We're about fifteen minutes from here. When we get to Covington, we'll break away and fly directly south to Roanoke." He handed her the map. "You get to be navigator."

Lexi pointed out each of the major ground references shown on the map as they flew past them. She was always amazed at the

163

detail of an aviation sectional—there was even a cute little fan-shaped symbol for a drive-in theater. Playing navigator helped keep her mind off the pressure mounting in her lower abdomen.

When they were twenty miles from Roanoke, Chet tuned the radio to the frequency of the control tower at Roanoke Regional Airport.

"Roanoke Approach Control, this is Mooney Acclaim. Call letters, November, niner, niner, zero, five, niner, requesting approach and landing instructions. Over."

"Mooney, zero, five, niner, this is Roanoke Approach Control. Confirm your position. Over."

Chet pushed the red button on his radio transmitter so the control tower at Roanoke could identify him on their radar display.

"Affirmative, Mooney zero, fife, niner. Come to heading two-seven-zero and descend to two thousand feet. Enter crosswind at one-five-zero, runway twenty-four. Altimeter setting is twenty-nine point eight-seven; wind is out of the west at eight to ten knots. Tune your radio to one two six point niner for further instructions, and enjoy your stay in Roanoke."

Chet circled the airport for entry into the pattern. He pointed to a mountain just to the west that had a big white star on it.

From the air, Roanoke looked like any other medium-sized city: a downtown business district in the center adjacent to rows of older homes. Outward from that was a scattering of factories, a railroad yard, shopping centers and then suburbia.

The tower instructed Chet to turn to heading one-five-zero, descend to one thousand feet and enter number four in the landing pattern behind a larger twin-engine plane.

He reduced power and went through the usual landing checklist; he made a ninety-degree turn, flying parallel to the runway, and entered the pattern on the downwind leg. After turning onto the base leg, he further reduced power and pushed the toggle switch to lower the landing gear.

Lexi heard the familiar whirl of the electric motor that extended the gear. Suddenly, there was a dull thump and a loud click inside the cabin followed by a piercing alarm.

Chet quickly silenced the landing warning horn. "That's not supposed to happen," he said. He ran his hand across the breaker panel and reseated a tripped breaker. He tried to lower the gear again but the same thing happened.

Lexi's muscles tensed. She looked at Chet; his attention was focused on his instruments. The pressure in her bladder immediately reached critical mass.

"Roanoke Control, this is Mooney zero, fife, niner turning downwind onto base. We've got a little problem here. Request permission abort landing and continue in the pattern for another pass."

"Permission granted, Mooney zero, fife, niner. What's your situation?"

"We're having trouble extending our landing gear. Could you give us a visual?"

Five seconds later, the tower responded. "Negative, Mooney zero, fife, niner. Your doors are open but your gear is not extended. I repeat. Your gear is not extended. Do you copy?"

"Approach Control, this is Mooney zero, fife, niner. I copy," Chet replied. "Coming ninety degrees to final and switching gear to manual. When I have down lock, will ask you to confirm. Over."

"Roger, Mooney zero, fife, niner. I have a spotter assigned. Will wait to confirm."

Chet switched the landing gear from electric to manual and tried to ratchet down the wheels. The handle took half a turn and stiffened. Lexi kept her eyes pasted to the landing gear indicator. Chet applied more force to the handle, but could not make it advance.

"Roanoke Control, this is Mooney zero, fife, niner. I still do not have down lock. Requesting a second visual."

"Mooney zero, fife, niner, the gear has traversed the plain of your fuselage but is not fully extended."

Chet looked directly at Lexi; his pupils were constricted, his face completely expressionless. "Roanoke Control, we've got a small problem here. Request wheels up, emergency landing instructions."

"Mooney zero, fife, niner, what is your fuel situation? Can you divert?"

Chet pushed the buttons on the computer again. "Negative, Roanoke. We've got ten minutes left."

The pressure in Lexi's bladder, now just shy of excruciating, took a back seat to the pounding in her chest.

"Mooney zero, fife, niner, we're going to move you out to clear other traffic. When we bring you back in, you'll be the only aircraft in the pattern. Emergency units are being dispatched. Proceed left to heading three three zero and await further instructions. Do you copy?"

The voice on the radio tried to remain calm, but Lexi immediately picked up on the higher pitch and the faster pace of his words.

"Affirmative, Roanoke Control," Chet replied, still as calm as a rowboat in a sheltered cove. He looked at Lexi. "Lexi, you've got to do exactly as I say. Okay?"

Lexi focused her anxieties on containing her desire to urinate. "Chet, I love and trust you more than anything God has ever placed on this earth. But how do you plan to land an airplane with no landing gear?"

"That's what I want to explain to you. First, promise me you'll remain calm. We can do this. Just take it one step at a time?"

"Okay, okay," Lexi said; her heart was pounding even harder than before. She wondered what Dr. Fontenberry would recommend she do now. The fear was definitely not from within. "Is there going to be fire? Because I really hate the thought of being roasted like a chicken."

"I don't think so. If they foam the runway, probably not. Besides, we will be almost out of fuel by then."

"Okay. But, if there is, don't worry. I've got to pee so bad I could extinguish Mt. Vesuvius."

Chet smiled. "See, you've already taken care of two problems. Now, here's what is going to happen. When we get back into the pattern, we'll have only enough fuel for one attempt. First thing I want you to do is take all the slack out of your seat belt and shoulder strap. Make them as tight as you can stand, then make certain your seat is latched."

Lexi tightened her belt and then rocked her seat. It didn't budge.

"Great. Now I want you to put your hand on your safety belt latch again, and then look where your hand is. After we touch down and the plane comes to a stop, you need to pop the latch and get out of the plane. Fire trucks will be sweeping the fuselage with hoses, so it should be safe to get out. Once you are, get as far away from the aircraft as you can.

"As we cross the end of the runway, I will be at full flaps and flying as slowly as possible. At ten feet above the pavement, I will start the round-out and do a complete wing stall just as we're about to touch the ground. I'll make the impact as soft as I can to minimize the chances of head whip but be prepared for a good jolt just the same. Just before we touch down, I want you to unlatch your door."

"Unlatch the door?" Lexi objected. "We could be thrown out."

167

"No, you won't. Remember, you are firmly belted in place. If there's a fire, we don't want to be trapped inside by a damaged door or latch. I know it sounds stupid. Just trust me."

"Mooney zero, fife, niner, this is Roanoke Approach Control. Do you copy? Over."

Chet pressed the microphone button on the steering yoke. "Roger, Roanoke Control."

"The pattern is clear. Come left to heading zero-niner-zero. We will bring you around on final, runway two-four. Wind is still out of the west at eight knots. Make your approach at low speed and full flaps, and keep your wings level to the runway through touchdown. Fire and rescue units are in position. Good Luck."

"What's the worst that can happen?" Lexi asked.

Chet looked surprised like he hadn't considered the possibilities. "Nothing is going to..."

"Just humor me," Lexi said. "I'm a writer. I thrive on conflict."

"We could run out of fuel before completing our final approach and crash into one of these office buildings. We could come in hot and nose down, spear the ground and tumble end over end. Or we could drop a wing tip and do cartwheels down the runway."

"I am so sorry," Lexi said.

"Sorry for what?"

"We're going to destroy your beautiful new airplane."

Chet placed his hand on top of hers. "The airplane I can replace."

The picture of the angry-faced man holding the pitchfork materialized in Lexi's mind again. She saw something this time that she had not seen before. There was a gold chain looped around his belt...a pocket watch chain.

"RAYMOND BLAYLOCK!" she shouted. "The man in the

barn holding the pitchfork is Raymond Blaylock. I can see his pocket watch."

"Raymond Blaylock," repeated Chet.

The image of Raymond remained in Lexi's thoughts; it was like her eyes had turned inward, looking into her brain. Suddenly, Raymond pointed the pitchfork at something and Lexi wasn't certain what it meant. Raymond pointed a second time. She didn't know why, but she reached her right hand toward the dashboard. Her index finger came in contact with the tripped breaker; she instinctively punched it back in place. The moment she did, Raymond disappeared. There was a brief whirling of the electric landing gear motor beneath her feet, then the click and warning horn again.

Chet silenced the horn. "Do that again," he said calmly.

Lexi reset the breaker again; Chet toggled the landing gear switch: whirl, click, horn.

"Mooney zero, fife, niner, this is Roanoke Control. Turn right to heading two-four-zero. Be advised, your landing gear doors have fully opened. Are you able to extend your gear?"

Chet came around as directed. Lexi could see the runway about a mile and a half up ahead.

"That's affirmative, Roanoke," Chet replied. "We're running it out one turn at a time. Over."

"If you cannot fully extend, I strongly recommend you stop trying. A partial extension of your landing gear could cause your aircraft to skid out of control upon contact with the runway."

"Roger that, Roanoke Control. Make that blanket of foam soft. Mooney zero, fife, niner, out."

Chet returned his left hand to the landing gear switch. "Again." Whirl, click, horn. "Again." Whirl, click, horn. "Again."

The sound of the warning horn was beginning to echo through Lexi's head.

Chet reduced engine power and fully extended the flaps. Lexi saw that the glide slope indicator at the end of the runway was pink, indicating Chet was perfectly aligned for landing. As the ground got closer, the aircraft was buffeted laterally by a crosswind. Chet maintained firm control and kept toggling the landing gear switch.

"Again." Whirl, click, horn. "Again."

The altitude indicator was passing under eighty feet, and the needle on the fuel gauge had passed into the barren wasteland to the left of E.

The pressure in Lexi's bladder went supercritical.

"Again." Whirl, click, horn. "Again." Whirl, click, horn.

The tower had said landing on partially extended gear could cause them to skid out of control. Like a twenty-five hundred pound aircraft doing a belly flop was on solid asphalt was controlled. Lexi checked her seatbelt again. Why had Raymond come to her?

The airport was certain to have had enough time to contact a local television station, Lexi thought. The entire eastern United States would see footage of her urine-soaked body being pulled from the wreckage.

"Again!" Chet shouted.

Lexi reset the breaker again; the sound of the horn was like symbols clashing in her head and she braced herself for it each time.

"Again."

The nose of the airplane crossed the threshold of the runway, not twenty feet above the ground. A picture of Raymond flashed in Lexi's head a second time. There was a smile upon his lips.

"Again."

Chet cut the throttle and applied back pressure to the elevators; the Mooney started to flair. Beads of sweat broke across his forehead and rolled down the sides of his face; he was obviously trying to glide as far as possible before making contact. Lexi could see the coarse grain of the blacktop passing under them.

"Again."

Lexi obeyed and braced herself for the crash.

The landing gear motor whirled but, this time, there was no breaker click and siren.

"DOWNLOCK!" Chet shouted.

Lexi cut her eyes to the indicator light; it was glowing bright green. At the exact moment, she felt the rear wheels contact the ground. She held her breath as the plane slowly leveled off and the nose wheel lightly touched the ground. All of the gear had safely extended.

Chet hit the brakes and the airplane came to a controlled stop, perfectly centered in the runway. He goosed the throttle to get it rolling again and taxi over to the tarmac. But the engine was dead. He hit the starter; the prop turned but the engine did not crank-up. Both fuel tanks were completely empty.

Rescue vehicles raced up on both sides of the airplane.

Lexi looked out at the flashing lights. Raymond had saved her and Chet. There was no doubt about it. Lexi realized her legs were bouncing but the pain in her bladder was so intense that she couldn't feel it. "Do you think any of those trucks has a porta potty?"

It took a second, but then Chet burst out laughing. It was a nervous but hearty rumble straight from the pit of his stomach.

Lexi started, too. "Chet Willow, don't you dare make me laugh. I haven't wet my pants since I was three years old. I don't have another pair to change into."

"Sweetheart," he exclaimed, "you can have mine. I don't care if I walk down Main Street in nothing but my boxers."

Lexi popped her seat belt and pushed the door open. "I've got to go right now."

She climbed out onto the wing and a fireman helped her to

the ground; she ran toward the rescue vehicle stooped like a hunchback.

Chet deplaned behind her. Lexi heard him call to one of the other firemen, "You'll have to tow her to the FBO. Both fuel tanks are dryer than a skeleton's pecker."

Chapter 17

Lexi didn't think she would make it to the ladies room, almost stopping to squat on one of those pedestal-style ashtrays next to the rear door of the FBO—Fixed Base Operator was the aeronautical equivalent of a full-service truck stop but, right now, it stood for Find Bathroom Orelse...

Never before had one of Mother Nature's most basic functions delivered such relief, every passing droplet as vital to her continued longevity as brain oxygenation.

Before she flushed, Lexi glanced at the water in the toilet. It had a slight reddish tint to it and there was a thin smear of blood on the tissue. Spotting; no real surprise there. The female bladder wasn't designed to stretch ten sizes, times two.

When she found Chet, he was already on the telephone with the Mooney dealership in Leesburg, Virginia which had already authorized a technician from the Roanoke FBO to begin troubleshooting the problem. Any findings were to be videotaped in case the FAA decided an investigation was in order. A Mooney representative—armed with a new set of landing gear switches, circuit board, and a wiring harness—would arrive in two hours and take over.

The rep assured Chet that simultaneous failures of the primary and backup landing gear systems had never happened before. "Highly unlikely," he said, as if trying to make the fact that it had occurred somehow easier to swallow.

"Where do we pick up the rental car?" Lexi asked. "By the time we get to Montano's my digestive tract may have relaxed enough to eat something."

"The rental car counters are on the first floor of the main terminal," said Tucker Boyd, the FBO Duty Officer. "My car's just outside. I'll give you a lift."

"Thanks," Chet said. "Give me a minute to get my cell phone out of the cockpit."

After Chet left, Tucker turned to Lexi. "That was a pretty gutsy piece of flying. We were listening on the tower frequency. Your mains weren't down two seconds before you touched the ground. I'm surprised the struts locked."

Lexi couldn't tell if he was trying to give her a retro-scare or just making conversation. She answered with the first thing that popped into mind. "*Semper fidelis.*"

"The Corps," he said with a funny look. "Are you the marine or is Mr. Willow?"

Lexi had been called many things, but never a marine. Then she remembered her black eye. It had faded some but, as close as Tucker was standing, she figured he could see the slight discoloration in the white area. "No, I'm just a groupie. Olive drab makes me look fat."

"Did he fly?"

"Jumped."

"Well, that explains the nerve. I probably would have done

174

what the tower recommended and trashed the Mooney."

"Maybe our insurance company will send us a free set of steak knives."

Tucker smiled. "You've got grit too, lady." He pointed to the back door. "I'm parked out there."

Chet rented a red Camaro SS convertible—the wind on his face made him feel like he was flying. Under the circumstances, Lexi preferred to think of it as a stiff ocean breeze. Like on a beach somewhere.

Montano's was a cozy bistro with a pickled-vegetable bottle decor; the food was Italian-American and the place was packed.

Lexi still wasn't hungry. She kept mulling over the landing in her mind. The Mooney representative said failure of both landing systems was highly unlikely. Just like a two-ton vehicle whacking a tree without damage was highly unlikely; like unearthing an antique car in your pasture was highly unlikely; like finding a body sunk in your backyard and solving a fifty-year-old missing persons case was unlikely; like nearly getting stomped to death by a horse you've owned for ten years was unlikely; like discovering a fortune in silver under your living room floor was unlikely. And the most unlikely thing was all of that happening within a span of two months!

And why did Raymond come to her rescue on the airplane like that? Why now was she shown the pocket watch chain?

Lexi glanced over at Chet who was now gazing at her with concern.

"Either you're asleep with your eyes open, or your mind is somewhere between the Roanoke Regional Airport and the ice pits of Monterey," he said. "You've been staring at the same spot on your menu for five minutes."

"If we were run out of Monterey, who would stand to gain the most?" she asked.

"The realtors," Chet immediately replied. "Audrey Pepper's people have made a fortune in sales commissions selling the place."

"I hadn't even considered them," said Lexi. "What about Porter?"

"It wouldn't be for money. Porter wouldn't get off the sofa to pick up a hundred-dollar bill. You obviously think what happened today was no accident either."

"Too much has happened the past two months for it all to be coincidence."

"Maybe there really is a ghost," Chet said.

"Ghosts don't need silver or gold," Lexi said quickly. "We solved half the mystery with the silver, and now someone doesn't want us beating them to the gold."

"Tampering with landing gear would be construed as pre-meditated murder," Chet said. "That's a pretty hefty allegation."

"Raymond had a pitchfork through his chest, didn't he?"

"There's no evidence linking that to Titus's money."

"Not yet. But who knows what we might find next."

Chet leaned back and crossed his arms. "What made you think of resetting the landing gear breaker? Don't get me wrong, I'm glad you did. I'm just curious."

If Lexi told Chet that Raymond had told her to, he'd drive her straight to Dr. Buettner and demand shock therapy. "It was a lucky shot. I was just slapping the dashboard out of frustration." Chet appeared to buy it.

"I've got my meetings in New York at the end of the week," Chet said. "Why don't you come with me? We could leave Wednesday. Maybe stay an extra week. Godsey's people can watch the house."

"Yeah, right. He'll give each of his men a shovel and an

eighty-twenty split. Our yard will have more craters than a minefield at rush-hour. No, you're going to New York but I'm staying here."

"Sorry, Cat Woman. But you and Batman are a team. If you stay, I stay."

"You can't let them know we suspect something."

"I'm not leaving my wife behind as bait," Chet snapped.

Lexi passed her hand across Chet's cheek. "You won't be. Besides, only a handful of people even know you're leaving. That should narrow the field of suspects."

"News travels fast in these parts. You've already been witness to that." Chet looked around the restaurant. "Unless, of course, you need a waiter." He caught one's attention and motioned him over. "I don't like the thought of leaving you alone. If this was an attempt on our lives, then next time we might not be so lucky."

Lexi felt warm, like she was running a low grade temperature. "I don't think anyone was trying to kill us. Shake us up, maybe, but not kill. Chances are nothing will happen while you're gone anyway. Titus's gold has been hidden for ninety years. We're not just going to trip over it. Besides, I won't be alone. I've got Beech, your target pistols and four days to get ready."

"Maybe JB or Kimberly could spend a couple nights."

"Drexel will be around during the days," Lexi added.

"I can't tell you what to do, but the decision whether I go or not is mine. I'll think about it," Chet said.

Lexi knew that whenever Chet said, "I'll think about it," she stood an eighty-percent chance of getting her way. He patted her knee under the table; she stopped his hand and slowly guided it along the inside of her thigh.

"Using feminine charms to get what we want, are we?" Chet asked.

The velvet in his eyes, his hand on her thigh, the latent buzz from her brush with disaster, and a slightly elevated body temperature caused Lexi to become immensely aroused. She guided Chet's hand to the crux of her slacks and manipulated his fingers until they were pressing on just the perfect spot. The stimulation was so immediate that she had to concentrate to keep from moaning. Suddenly, Chet's cell phone rang.

Lexi was nearly panting. "If that's Drexel Yeatts, tell him he's fired."

Chet attempted to pull his hand away. Lexi squeezed it tighter.

"Sweetheart, in a coat closet at the opera or a cab on Fifth Avenue during rush hour, gladly. But I have to draw a line where people are trying to eat. French maybe, if I'm properly inspired, but definitely not Italian. Though feel free to continue without me."

Lexi pinched his finger and allowed him to pull away. "You're a heartless man, Chet Willow."

Chet answered the call; his expression hardened.

"I understand. Did you find both bolts?...No, I do not want the police involved. When the Mooney tech gets there, have him double-check the cables and pulleys and replace the harness and switch. I'll be there in about an hour."

He flipped the cell phone closed and dropped it on the table.

"What did he say?" Lexi asked.

Chet gave her a long look before he answered. "You may be right. There was a hunk of solder on the back of the landing gear switch that caused it to short. It couldn't have come from the factory that way or the gear would have failed months ago. It probably wouldn't even have gotten through initial flight testing. Technically, the gear shouldn't have retracted when we left Monterey."

"Once in the air, it wouldn't have made any difference. We'd still have to fly to Roanoke for a controlled crash."

178

Chet nodded. "It gets even more interesting. Two locknuts on a cable guide for the manual system had backed off. Those bolts are mechanically distorted and then torqued into place at the factory, one on top of the other. The chances of both backing off are less than one in ten million."

Chapter 18

Chet's Mooney was up on jacks in the maintenance hangar. The wheels were down, two mechanics were under the plane, and a third was inside. Seeing the airplane suspended like that made Lexi realize just how fragile it really was.

"We've replaced the toggle switch and tested the action half-a-dozen times," Tucker Boyd said. "The gear retracts and extends perfectly. We also replaced all the hardware, guides and reinstalled all new locknuts. When the guys finish with the wiring harness and control module, we'll run a few more checks, put it all back together and take it for a test flight. There's a private airstrip just outside of town that we use for touch-and-goes. The whole thing shouldn't take more than another two to three hours."

"Do you think it's been tampered with?" Chet asked.

"I'm not in a position to say," Tucker replied. "I'll file a report and keep the old parts on hand in case the FAA wants to examine them. Unless other Mooney's have experienced similar problems, there shouldn't be any questions. On the other hand, they might impound it and take it apart piece by piece. You never can tell with the Feds. We'll get you home one way or another."

Chet drove Lexi to the Orvis store. Neither she nor Chet spoke much. Lexi bought a pair of sandals she had seen in the catalog, a cedar bed for Beecher, and several other items that she neither needed nor particularly wanted. But spending a little money made her feel better. She also bought Chet a leather working tool that had everything from a set of pliers to a spy code descrambler. He pretended to be appreciative, nodding his head and saying 'thank you' when appropriate.

Taxiing back out to the runway, Lexi was more than a little nervous. Chet was stone-faced so she knew he felt the same way; he offered to let her drive the rental car home but she declined. If he didn't think it was safe, he wouldn't have allowed her to set foot on the plane.

The takeoff was smooth and the gear retracted like clockwork. The tower gave permission to remain in the pattern for a touch-and-go. Half way through the downwind leg, Chet lowered the gear and the down lock indicator illuminated a crisp green. He completed the touch-and-go, powered back up, went airborne again, retracted the gear, thanked the tower and turned north for home.

At two-hundred fifteen miles an hour, the return flight to Monterey took less than forty minutes. There was no sightseeing this time. By 6:30 PM, the sun was already stretching jagged shadows to the east. The beauty of the valley was still spectacular but its effects were diminished by thoughts of actions perpetrated by greed. This was no longer about some old skinflint's gold. It was about intrusion, and an attempt on their lives. It was about not being afraid to stay at home, and not being afraid to go outside. Lexi felt fatigue catching up with her.

"Let's not say a word to anyone about what happened," Lexi

said. "If it was rigged, whoever did it will think their plan failed. I suggest we take the Mooney back to the Staunton airport where it will be safe. If someone wants to tamper with something, let it be something that can't fall ten-thousand feet to the ground. I'll get the car and pick you up. Make several slow circles over town so everyone gets a good look. Ham it up a little, but nothing too drastic. Deacon may have pulled your wings off and reattached them with Elmer's."

When the runway was in sight, Chet dialed a new frequency into the radio and took the microphone in his right hand. The windsock was pointing a crooked finger south away from the road and power lines, indicating about six-knots worth of wind.

"Watch this." He pointed out the windshield and clicked the transmit button on the microphone two times. Lights on each side of the partially-paved runway lit up in running linear succession. "I can deliver presents to the kiddies even on the murkiest of nights, with or without Rudolph." He gave her a wink. "When the lights come on, you have about ten minutes to get your boyfriends out of the house." Chet clicked the transmitter again and the lights extinguished.

After a perfect landing, Chet turned around and taxied back to the Gator. Lexi unbelted, popped open the door and gave Chet a kiss. "I'll wait for you in JB's parking lot and follow you out."

Chet taxied back onto the runway, did a soft-field takeoff, boosted power and did a maximum-performance climb. Then he banked a hard one-eighty, made a simulated bombing run on one of the bulldozers and headed off for Monterey, waving his wings.

Chapter 19

Sunday had all the makings of a completely uneventful day.
Thank God. Lexi took advantage of the calm to work on her book.

Beecher was a more nervous than usual. He kept grabbing his
ball and running to the front door, whining to be let out. But as soon
as Lexi did, he began pawing to be let back in. She had once read that
dogs can sense changes in weather long before they occur. Maybe
another storm was brewing.

At eight o'clock Monday morning, Tat-Tat and Scoop came
back to life down at the ice pit. By nine, the stench of fresh asphalt
was wafting up from the valley floor. At nine-oh-five, Tat-Tat
stopped.

Lexi straightened the kitchen after breakfast and returned to
her book. A few minutes into it, she heard Chet come in the back
door.

"Honey, what's happened to Tat-Tat?" she called.

"A mudslide," Chet replied.

"You don't have a mudslide when you're digging in solid
rock."

Chet walked into the study. "Not in the trench, in the fuel tank. Red mud to be exact. Norman has to drain the tank, flush out the mud, replace the filters and purge the fuel lines. Tat-Tat and Scoop have left the building, at least for the rest of today. Friday it was a broken track, now this."

"Okay. So why don't our ghosts want us to finish draining the ice pit?"

"Ghosts? So it's plural now, is it?" Chet plopped down on the sofa. "Maybe they're afraid we'll find Jimmy Hoffa."

Lexi watched Chet to determine if he was trying to be funny. He wasn't.

"To drain, or not to drain? That is the question," said Chet. "This is becoming more convoluted than a murder at a soap opera convention."

"Good comparison. It just goes to prove everybody really is out to screw their neighbors," Lexi replied. "But isn't that a violation of the Third Commandment? Thou shalt not muddy thy neighbor's track hammer."

"I believe the word is covet. Thou shalt not covet thy neighbor's track hammer."

"We're getting a bit testy, aren't we? What does Norman think?"

"He wants to pack up his toys and go home. Are you sure you don't need me to cancel Thursday?"

"Not on your life."

"Then you've talked to Kimberly or JB?"

"Not yet."

Chet began searching around the top of her desk.

"What are you looking for?" Lexi asked.

"The number for Wells Fargo. I'm going to see if they can recommend a good security company."

"We don't need a security company, Chet. I'll be fine. If there's a problem, I'll hit the panic button on the alarm system. Sheriff Godsey will be here before the Krispy Kreme glaze dries at the corners of his mouth."

Chet reached for the phone. "Not good enough."

"Okay. I'll talk to Kimberly when she comes to check on Paragon this afternoon. I promise."

"If she can't make it, you'll talk to JB, right?"

"And if JB can't, I'll call the Baldwin ladies. They can tell me all about Harold's summer sausage again."

"Harold?" Chet asked. "Who's Harold?"

"Didn't I tell you about my visit from the Baldwin ladies? They're the welcoming committee for the Pentecostal Holiness Church."

"No. When was that?"

"The morning Paragon kicked me. They brought the brown sugar pie."

"I recall the pie. Figured you'd bought it at JB's."

Lexi had to be careful. If she let slip anything about Porter or JB now, there would be a FOR SALE sign on the front lawn before dark. "Harold is Millie Baldwin's deceased husband. She claims to have snatched him from the jaws of sin not two months before of their wedding day." Lexi was amused by her extemporaneous summary of the Baldwin's visit—Chet didn't need to know the jaws actually belonged to JB.

"They sound like delightful company. Why don't you invite them over anyway? Turn it into a slumber party. You can pop Jiffy Pop, play Twister and read from the scriptures."

"I've got a better idea," Lexi said sarcastically. "Why don't I invite all of Monterey and hold a séance down at the ice pit. Sheriff Godsey can arrest any ghost who acts suspicious."

Chet's eyes narrowed. "Quit blowing smoke, Lexi. You assure me somebody's going to be here with you or I'm calling Camp Lejeune and will have a marine guard posted here by tomorrow morning. I bought General Shanaberger a thousand shares of Amazon the first day they went public. He'll put an M-1 tank on this mountain if I need one."

Lexi knew the conversation just hit the wall. It wasn't that she didn't want someone with her; she just didn't know at this point who to trust. "Would you feel better if I called Kimberly now?"

"You can call her after we get back."

"Get back from where?"

"Target practice. You haven't shot a weapon in over a year."

Lexi saved her work to the hard drive and then a second time to a CD-ROM. "Do I get the Glock or the Colt?"

"Your choice."

Chapter 20

Thanks to Chet's insistence, Kimberly Buchanan was on board for both Thursday and Friday night. Norman's men completed paving the airstrip late Monday evening and, at eight-thirty Tuesday morning, Tat-Tat and Scoop resumed their droning medley. For the first time in several weeks, things seemed to be moving along as scheduled.

Lexi showered, dressed and went down to the kitchen. Chet had already made a pot of coffee and placed a cup on the counter for her.

He had begun spending large chunks of time at his computer in preparation for his meetings in New York. Ever since the Laws of Newtonian Physics finally caught up with the "new economy" markets (A: what goes up based upon reckless speculation must come down, and B: a stock in the Crapper shall remain in the Crapper until acted upon by a stimulated earnings forecast) the three-hundred-dollar shoe types were clamoring for Chet's advice.

Lexi decided she needed to pay the editor of *The Staunton News Leader* a visit. She walked into the study to tell Chet her plans and found him sitting at the computer with her headphones on. She eased up behind him and kissed him on the cheek. Chet wheeled back and pulled off the phones.

"You need the sunglasses to get the full effect," she said.

"I figured as deep as they're working, the noise wouldn't be a bother. Maybe I should have them stop."

"Just let them finish," Lexi replied. "The sooner that ice pit is gone, the better. They'll probably break down before lunch anyway. I'm heading into Staunton. Can I get you anything?"

"See if Sam's Club has a display of peace and quiet. Get me the industrial-size box."

Lexi kissed him. "I'll see what I can do."

She telephoned the *Staunton News Leader* and was surprised to learn the editor, Kirby Caruso, was familiar with her old column at the *Times*. He even invited her to meet him for lunch.

The forty-three mile trek east through the mountains was still new enough to be a pleasurable experience. As she passed through the village of McDowell, her thoughts reached back to her conversation with JB and the description of the Civil War battle fought here, specifically the struggles of Major Shepherd Blaylock. It must have been a terrorizing way to die; death by latitude. How many of America's sons have been killed over some stupid, invisible line, she wondered?

Lexi pulled off the road to examine a monument dedicated to the battle; it seemed selfishly small considering the number of lives sacrificed there. There was Major Blaylock's name, along with the rest of the Georgia Twelfth. The battlefield itself was several hundred yards up the mountain and was still mostly preserved, or so JB had said. At least until the government or some developer decided differently.

Lexi returned to her car and continued on toward Staunton.

188

When she came to the wide spot where the red truck almost ran her and Chet off the mountain, the image of Major Blaylock leading his horse returned to her—in particular, the red splotches on his uniform. He was like a messenger bringing word of danger. It was more than a coincidence that the spot was halfway between McDowell and the Confederate Breastworks at Fort Johnson. Perhaps Major Blaylock was trying to prepare her for a battle of her own.

With the last of the hairpins behind her, Lexi coasted through the foothills. Finally, the outskirts of Staunton came into view. It was a charming little city, full of eighteenth-century stonework, tidy neighborhoods with beautiful flower gardens and a lot of country charm. Staunton was the birthplace of Woodrow Wilson, a subject of great pride to JB.

Lexi shoehorned the BMW into a parking space on the street right in front of *The Staunton News Leader,* waited for a delivery truck to pass, squeezed out the door, and hurried inside. She was greeted—if "yes" uttered in a flat, monotone voice can be construed as a formal greeting—by a pale-faced receptionist dressed in a sleeveless black blouse and a mini-skirt with silver fringe around the bottom. She had streaky, purple hair and a pair of darkened deadpan eyes that looked as if they had been dragged across a stretch of broken beer bottles. The nameplate on her desk, quite fittingly, read Zelda Haggard.

Lexi handed Zelda a calling card. "I'm Alexis Willow. Here to meet with Mr. Caruso."

Zelda picked up the phone and placed a call to Caruso, Editor-in-Chief, then snaked her hand out toward a worn leather chair next to a table piled with old newsprint. She didn't blink her eyes once and Lexi figured, if she did, that brief moment of darkness might cause her to fall into a deep, prolonged sleep. One she might not awake from until she had grown a long, streaky, purple beard that matched her hair.

Kirby Caruso was more the husky, ex-jock, television sports anchor type than a newspaper editor. He was around six-foot-two, smoky Italian looks, and a quick pearly smile. When he walked by the reception desk, Zelda noticeably perked up and even almost smiled.

"Lexi Willow," said Caruso, extending his hand. "This is indeed a pleasure." His accent was definitely New York.

Lexi shook his hand and returned the smile. "You make me sound important."

"Columnist for the *Times*, wife of Chet Willow—the Wizard of Wall Street—and new owner of the infamous Blaylock estate. Around here, that makes you a celebrity."

Lexi jumped on that with both feet. "Does that mean I get preferred parking?"

Caruso smiled again. He directed her to the front doors and held one open for her. "Down the street, there's a little spot called Walker's Diner. It looks a bit rough on the outside, but they prepare a lasagna that would make my grandmother burn her apron."

"Sounds great," Lexi said.

Once outside, the exhaust fumes made Lexi's head swim and her right eye began to water. She reached into her purse, removed a handkerchief, and stopped.

"You'll have to excuse me," she said. "I got kicked by a horse a couple weeks ago and it seems to have made me sensitive to strong smells."

Kirby cut his eyes at her in a rather suspicious manner. "That might be a good angle for an article on Multiple Chemical sensitivity. Six to eight hundred words should cover it."

Lexi stared at him and stuffed the handkerchief back in her bag. "If that's why you invited me to lunch, the answer is 'no'. I don't do deadlines anymore."

The expression on Kirby's face was that of a thirteen-year-old who'd got caught peeking at his sister in the bathroom.

"Just thinking out loud," he said. "I've got one or two staffers who are more than capable." He turned and walked away. Lexi followed. "So what's this about needing access to my archives?"

Lexi could see exactly where this was heading. "You can take the editor out of New York, but you can't take New York out of the editor."

"Mrs. Willow, my job is to sell newspapers. And I sell a lot of newspapers. When I leave Staunton, I intend it to be for a senior position at either the *Post* or the *Globe,* or maybe even back at the *Times.* To do that, I need quality writers that can stir public interest. Writers like you. When Bert Saratosa of the *Times* finds out you're writing for the *News Leader*, he'll want to know how *I* managed to get you."

"So you intend to use me to make a name for yourself," Lexi said, trying to sound disapproving.

"I assure you, I've earned my shot. It's no worse than using my paper to fill the holes in your novel. You probably won't even mention me in the acknowledgments."

"Not unless you give me something I can use," Lexi said.

"How about Janice Bandy and Deacon or Raymond Blaylock? The summer of 1950 seems to have been particularly hot. Hot enough for Raymond to go for a fifty-year swim in a muddy ice pit."

"I see you have contacts in Monterey," Lexi replied. "Sheriff Godsey would be my guess. Did he tell you about finding Andrea Blaylock's silver?"

"Didn't have to. I know the surgeon who pinned Jimmy Grubbs' leg. Though I would like to know more about this ghost he saw under your house. Oh, and I found an interesting bit on Porter

191

Bandy, too. I understand he has a half-brother."

"Half-brother?" Lexi asked. "On his mother's side or his father's?"

"I don't have all the facts yet, but you'll be the first to know when I do."

Lexi's heart was pounding in her throat. A third Bandy could put a whole new spin on things. "What's your source?"

"Do we have a deal?"

Kirby obviously knew how to play the game but so did Lexi. "I'll give you two articles a month, six hundred words apiece. Three hundred dollars each for starters, you own all rights. No deadlines and I pick the topic. Editorial corrections are welcomed, content changes are not. A contract is fine if you want one but not necessary. I can't start until all the renovations on the house are completed and Chet and I get settled in. In the meantime, I get full access to your archives."

"One article a week for six months, no written contract," he replied. "You can stay longer if you develop a taste for it. Deadline is noon on Thursday for the Friday edition. I want you when advertisers are loosening their purse strings for the weekend sales. Six hundred words will do fine, five hundred bucks a month and generous advertising space for each of your published novels, starting with the Blaylock tale. Human interest stories are fine, but I want upscale. People around here can get the hog report at noon on just about any radio station. My archives are all yours. If you need more information than what we've already pulled, I'll give you a research assistant."

Kirby stopped and put his hand on the door of a quaint little restaurant which resembled an old railroad car. "The editorial part is fine with me as long as what I read is all pop and no poop. Do we have a deal?"

"Just two more things," Lexi said.

"Name them," Kirby replied.

"Zelda goes to an ophthalmologist to have her eyelids unglued, followed by a week off to catch up on her sleep. Just looking at her makes me want to pull a Rip Van Winkle. If she returns from "zombie land" before my six months are up, I'll give you a seventh month for free."

Kirby's brow furrowed as he examined the remains of Lexi's blackened right eye.

"The two of you seem to have a few things in common," he said. He flashed his bright white smile again. A Cover Girl model would kill for teeth like those, Lexi thought. "Multiple Chemical Sensitivity and the physiological hazards of repetitive exposure to the *Rocky Horror Picture Show*. See, your first two articles are almost written and you haven't even had to center your byline."

Lexi's insides were jumping up and down. A third Bandy and a research assistant; her venture had worked out better than she could have possibly hoped. A regular column would help her maintain her writing discipline and give her the opportunity to experiment with a variety of different topics. It was like freelancing with the luxury of a regular paycheck.

"Noon I can live with," Lexi said. "I use MS Word 2010 and deliver copy via e-mail. You get to worry about byline justification."

Kirby offered her his hand again. Lexi accepted.

Walker's lasagna was respectable but not nearly as good as Montano's—if that's the best Kirby's grandmother could do, her apron should top the New York City Fire Marshall's most wanted list.

Excited to get started, Lexi ate faster than she normally would have. Kirby didn't reciprocate. In fact, he ate painfully slow; too slow for an ex-jock turned newspaper editor unless he was already attempting to exercise his editorial control. Nor did he elaborate on the missing Bandy brother, only that he would let her know if he heard anything more. Lexi figured she could worm it out of him later.

Back at the newspaper, he led her down two sets of stairs to the microfiche archives: the walls vibrated from the rolling of the press and the slapping sound of papers being folded and placed on a conveyor belt.

"We're not very sophisticated around here," Kirby said. He gazed at a row of four-drawer filing cabinets. About twenty in all; some were wooden and some were grayish metal. "The microfiche is filed by year, starting in January of 1920. A fire during Christmas of 1919 destroyed everything prior to that. What little we have predating the fire was recovered from private collections."

So much for any new information on the disappearance of Titus and Andrea, Lexi thought. But that was okay. Deacon and Raymond were the ones she was really interested in.

Lexi picked up one of a dozen or so manila folders stacked on a table between two microfiche machines.

"That's what I've gathered for you so far," Kirby said. "From what you said on the phone, it should be enough to get you started. When you've finished, give me a call. The number's on the wall next to the phone. I'll send Zelda down to give you a hand."

"Zelda?" Lexi objected.

"She may have a slight identity problem, but she's not stupid," Kirby replied. "Who knows, you could be the perfect role model for her. Before her stint with *Rocky Horror,* she came to work looking like Hillary Clinton. Personally, I prefer this Zelda better."

It suddenly dawned on Lexi where she had seen the name Haggard before...one of the shops in Monterey was called Haggard's Attic. "Does she have any family in Monterey?"

"Very good, Lexi Willow. You've earned a secret decoder ring to go with your press pass." Kirby cocked his head and cut his eyes at her. "Like I said, the two of you may have more in common than make-up secrets."

Lexi touched her black eye and began to leaf through the first file. "Maybe my first article should be about people who push their ambitions ahead of their manners."

Kirby grinned, threw his hands up and backed toward the door.

"When Zelda goes to lunch, I'm sending her out to buy a pair of slacks," Lexi said. "Deduct the cost from my first paycheck if you want to. But we can't have her bending over in filing cabinets wearing a mini-skirt or your press operators might bust all their leader sheets."

Chapter 21

Lexi switched on the microfiche machine, loaded one labeled July 1950, dimmed the overhead lights and kicked off her shoes. It was going to be a long afternoon. She retrieved her purse, pulled out a bottle of mountain spring water and downed a 600-mg headache eraser just as a precaution.

After scanning two complete editions, she figured out how the fiche was subdivided. The paper had a section titled *Area News* that included stories from surrounding towns: Harrisonburg, Lexington, McDowell, Monterey, Warm Springs and Waynesboro. Something from each town was included in every edition (births, deaths, and who had gone where to visit who mostly—people just loved to see their names in print).

"My job is to sell newspaper," Kirby had told her. *"And I intend to sell a lot of newspapers."* He'd probably stand on the street corner barking "EXTRA, EXTRA, READ ALL ABOUT IT" himself if it would land him at the *Times*, Lexi thought.

Nothing in June was of any interest to her. She moved on to

July. There she found the article on the mill fire. It was the same as the one in JB's scrapbook. She continued looking.

In the first August edition, Lexi came across an article titled *New Monterey Business Owner is County's First.*

'Miss Janice Evelyn Bandy, nineteen years of age, recently became the sole proprietor of Blaylock Lumber General Merchandise, officially making her the first female storefront business owner in the history of Highland County. Miss Bandy said she had been running the store for most of the past two years anyway and has several ideas how to make it turn a better profit.

'Deacon Blaylock, son of the late lumber tycoon Titus Blaylock, deeded the store to Miss Bandy at noon on July thirtieth of this year. Terms of the sale were not disclosed, but it is generally assumed that Mr. Blaylock financed the deal himself.

'Millicent Baldwin—Monterey resident and part-time secretary of the United Methodist Church—claims the transfer of ownership is the result of shameful behavior on the part of both parties.'

Lexi pushed the copy button. The microfiche machine whirled a few times, and then a negative image of the print on the view screen scrolled out and dropped in front of her.

Millie Baldwin, she thought. The Hell and Damnation church lady with a distain for oral satisfaction. Perhaps young Harold's sausage wasn't the only one Jandy was caught working on. Judging from the prize Deacon awarded her, she must have had a pretty good knack for it—in his fondest reminiscing, Gentry Willow failed to mention that aspect of Jandy's congeniality.

After the second page dropped out of the copier, Lexi returned the microfiche to the August folder and opened the file labeled PORTER BLAYLOCK. The first fiche had a sticky note adhered to it giving the coordinates of the article, and the words

197

PORTER GOES TO HOLLYWOOD printed in a man's handwriting. She placed the fiche in the glass tray, slid the position indicator to the coordinates listed on the note and read: June 8, 1976—**Highland County Man Found Guilty of Sexual Assault.**

'By a unanimous vote, a Highland County District Court jury found twenty-three-year-old Porter C. Howard Bandy of Monterey, Virginia guilty of the March 14 beating and sexual assault of eighteen-year-old Treena Patricia Aupperly.'

There it was in black and white. "Porter Bandy is a convicted rapist!" Lexi shouted. She sprang from her chair. "Why that greasy, chicken-wrapping, one-eyeball, Cheat Mountain skinflint calling sonofabitch. I knew I didn't like him the moment I saw him."

She remembered Audrey Pepper saying Porter was the caretaker of the property before she and Chet bought it. "No telling what that bastard has done inside my house."

The door opened and Zelda Haggard walked in. "Mr. Caruso said you wanted me," she said in her monotone, deadpan voice. This time her eyes moved, but they didn't blink.

"Zelda, do you know Porter Bandy?" Lexi asked.

"Yes, ma'am," Zelda replied, her face completely expressionless.

"Did you know he was convicted of rape in June of 1976?"

Zelda continued the blank stare. "Yes, ma'am," she droned again.

"Do you know this Treena Aupperly?" Lexi quickly read the rest of the article and didn't hear Zelda's reply. When she looked up, Zelda was still standing by the door. "I'm sorry. What did you say?"

"Yes, ma'am."

"Do you think she would be willing to talk to me?"

Zelda's voice was as featureless as a winter sky. "No, ma'am."

"Could you tell me where she lives so I can at least ask her?"

Again that blank stare. The same look Lexi had seen in pictures of starving Ethiopian children...the look of patient hopelessness, a look that didn't belong in the eyes of such a young woman.

"She's dead, Mrs. Willow. She shot herself in the head when I was sixteen."

Lexi's lungs stopped mid-breath; all the thoughts that were flying through her head crashed to a stop. There was a thin trail of tears on Zelda's cheeks. The full force of the truth struck Lexi like a speeding freight train. Treena Aupperly was this child's mother, Porter Bandy was her *father*.

"Oh, Zelda. I am so sorry." Lexi rushed over and wrapped her arms around the girl who stood like stone. "Please forgive me."

Zelda's reply was purely mechanical. "It's not your fault, Mrs. Willow. You couldn't have known."

Lexi pulled a tissue from her purse and handed it to Zelda; she wiped her eyes and, in so doing, finally blinked.

"Haggard took us in when I was five," Zelda droned. "He made it legal with a wedding and an adoption, but all he wanted was someone to take care of his urges and cook for him. Momma was the cook and, just after my thirteenth birthday, I became the recipient of his urges. He'd sneak into my room, when he was still sober enough to walk, holding his crotch with one hand and a bottle in the other. He called it "getting appreciation.""

Zelda wiped her eyes again. No wonder she looked like she never slept, Lexi thought. After three years of that, how could anyone sleep?

"I didn't tell Momma about it. Figured it was the price I had to pay for a roof and food. She knew though. One night, she confronted Haggard as he was leaving my bedroom. They yelled at each other for a while, Haggard stormed out the door and Momma slept on the floor next to my bed, clutching one of Haggard's pistols. When I came home from school the next day, I found her in the bathroom, dead. The sheriff found Haggard in the barn, at least most of him." A faint and fleeting smile played at the corners of her mouth. "His penis and testicles were missing. I suspect a buzzard or maybe a barn rat made off with them."

Now it was Lexi's turn to smile though she had to part her own tears to do so. "What did you do after that? Where did you go?"

"Miss JB took care of me."

That struck Lexi as odd. The mother of her mother's rapist came to her rescue. But then, JB was the type that did what needed doing. Zelda could have fared a lot worse.

"She sold the farm, rented me a house, set up a trust and made me graduate high school," Zelda said.

Talking seemed to loosen Zelda up—downloading to a complete stranger can be the emotional equivalent of hanging your soul over the clothesline and beating all the spiders out of it.

"Did Porter ever bother you?"

Zelda wiggled her head a smidgeon. "Miss JB watched me like a hawk. I was to tell her if he ever came near me. After he got out of prison, he stayed drunk most of the time."

"Do you still have contact with JB?"

"No ma'am. I waitressed at the Maple for a while then moved to Staunton four years ago. I'm beholding to her, but I still can't come to terms with things. Mr. Caruso ran an ad for a nanny, and later gave me a job here at the paper."

Lexi noticed that little *brightness* in Zelda's face when she said Caruso's name. That was all she needed to lighten the conversation. "Kirby Caruso must be a pretty special guy."

Zelda nodded. "He's practically the only man I've known that didn't introduce himself by first unzipping his pants."

"Let's not be too hasty now," Lexi said and grinned. "It may be worth just a little peek."

This time, Zelda's face stretched into a genuine smile. Lexi could see that beneath that glum façade resided a very attractive young woman.

"Why don't you go freshen up," Lexi said. "I need to run upstairs and talk to Kirby. Let's meet back here in fifteen minutes and I'll show you what all this is about."

Lexi marched up the stairs and down the hall until she found Caruso's office. He was sitting at his desk marking copy with a red pen. It was the perfect ambush.

"You've either got the world's most disgusting sense of humor or you are the most uncompassionate jerk God ever created."

Kirby gazed at her for a couple seconds and then calmly put down his pen. "I didn't think the lasagna was all that bad."

"You knew Zelda was Porter Bandy's daughter, didn't you?"

"Porter Bandy's daughter? What are you talking...?"

"Come on, you pulled the fiche yourself. You called the Porter Bandy piece an interesting tidbit. Well, it just so happens the woman he raped, Treena Aupperly, was Zelda's mother."

Kirby's eyebrows shot upward and his complexion turned to ash. "Who told you that?"

Lexi crossed her arms. "Zelda did."

Kirby stared blankly at his desk before he replied. "Well, that explains a few things." He cut his eyes at her. "Lexi, I wouldn't hurt Zelda if my life depended upon it. She's one of the most kindhearted people I know. And my kids are absolutely crazy about her."

His reaction was genuine. "Good," Lexi chirped, dropping the daggers from her tone. "I just wanted to make sure you're being straight with me. So, what did you mean when you said Zelda and I may have some things in common?"

Some of the color returned to his face. "Do you take prisoners before you torch the village or just wait to see if anyone's left standing?"

Lexi felt herself blush. Maybe she should have given him the benefit of the doubt. "Sorry. When I taste blood, I tend to go for the kill."

"That's admirable in this profession. But I'm on your side, remember?" Kirby retrieved his pen and returned to his copy. "Zelda cleaned house for the previous owners of your mansion, Mrs. Madison. I was simply alluding to the fact that she has spent a lot of time in your home. She may even have bumped into your ghost a time or two."

Chapter 22

Thursday morning: Lexi's alarm erupted at six o'clock. She coaxed herself out of bed and finished packing Chet's suitcase while he showered and got dressed. Chet's flight to New York departed Roanoke at nine forty-five.

By the time the coffee maker had stopped drizzling, the sun had begun lifting over the eastern rise. Lexi filled Chet's special spill-proof aviator's cup and packed two granola bars and an apple in a small, Tupperware lunchbox.

Chet breezed into the kitchen and kissed her on the back of the neck. He took a sip of coffee. "I bet this is exactly how the Wright Brothers envisioned life in the twenty-first century, men and women flying off to work each morning in their own airplanes."

"And we think rush hour is frightening now."

Lexi slipped into the laundry room, pulled on a pair of jeans, and opened the back door. "You'd better get hopping, Orville, or you'll be stuck taking the bus." Chet collected his bags and followed her out.

Around the boss house, Tat-Tat and Scoop came into view,

their long, yellow necks tucked underneath them. Scoop was sleeping but Tat-Tat, resting in a pool of his own hydraulic fluid, was dead. It had simultaneously ruptured five—not one, but five—hydraulic hoses the day before. That had to be some kind of mechanical-monster breakdown record. Norman was threatening to quit and hire a subcontractor to finish the job.

Lexi stood at the edge of the trench. The opening was roughly ten feet wide with jagged walls narrowing to about three feet at the bottom forming a crude vee. And it was deep: twenty-two feet toward the pit, dropping to twenty-five at the terrace end. Only five feet of undisturbed rock remained at the pit side. Major Blaylock's troops had cut a mile of trenches at the Confederate Breastworks using only picks and shovels in less time than it had taken Norman's two behemoths to dig ninety-five feet.

"So close, and yet so far." Lexi sighed.

"Don't let all the good stuff happen while I'm gone," Chet said. "I'm as eager to see what's at the bottom of this as anyone else. I should be home by noon on Saturday. Earlier, if my meetings go well."

"You don't need to rush." Lexi glanced at Tat-Tat. "The way things are going, we'd better plan on having Norman's men for Thanksgiving dinner."

She sauntered over to the Gator and slid behind the wheel. "The meter's running, mister. Next stop, Willow International Airport. Ghosts and muddy corpses to the rear, women with small children to the front."

Chet arched his eyebrows and placed his bags in the back. "Women with small children?" he asked.

"It's just an expression. Besides, I was late last month too." Lexi started the engine and pulled off with a jolt. Her head snapped backward, a slight wave of pain rippled through her brain. "It's from all the stress."

"So, how late are we?" Chet asked.

Lexi refused to get excited about it. There had been too many disappointments. "Two days, and stop looking at me like that. I'm no more pregnant than you are."

"Well, I have been feeling a little bloated lately..."

"It's nothing two Gas-X won't fix."

Lexi zipped past the barn and saw Paragon grazing in the corral. She missed spending time with him but wasn't ready to go riding yet. The image of Raymond and the others were still quite vivid; she wasn't afraid of them, just preferred not to be alone in the barn with them. And she hadn't yet resolved the muddy handprint on the back of her blouse from the day of the accident. It could have come from one of the guys in the rescue squad, but where they have found red mud? Unless one was on the upper terrace or down below at the runway before responding to the call. Neither was likely. Lexi felt a firm pressure on her arm.

"Still with me, baby?"

"Of course, I'm with you," Lexi said, though not really knowing at that precise moment just where *with me* was.

"Then what did I just ask you?"

"You asked me if I was still with you."

Chet smiled. "Before that?"

Lexi was vaguely aware that he'd said something, but had no clue what it was. "You said you would be home around noon on Saturday."

"Nice try. I asked you what time Kimberly Buchanan was coming over. You had this intense expression on your face, like you were eavesdropping on a distant conversation."

Lexi couldn't remember if she had told Chet about the handprint. If not, now was not the time. "She'll be over following the afternoon surgeries. She's got a K-9 gastric bypass, two spays and three castrations scheduled. Should be around five or so."

"Keep Beecher by your bedside and the door locked tonight in case Kimberly has a penchant for sleepwalking."

A light mist still clung to the grass in the valley. Lexi parked the Gator behind the Mooney's right wing, and switched off the engine.

"Do you have everything you need?" Lexi asked. "Notes, credit cards, insider trading briefs?"

"Plus an Ouija Board and my rabbit's foot."

Chet loaded his bags into the cargo compartment behind the rear seats. "You know, I really could postpone..."

"Stop worrying, will you? I've got a security system; Kimberly, Beecher and two six-foot black lions. How much more protection could a girl ask for?"

Chet took her in his arms and gave her a loving kiss. "Just call me three hours before anything looks suspicious."

Lexi sat in the Gator as the plane rolled down the runway and grabbed a slice of air. Chet flew out over Monterey, did a hundred-eighty degree turn and headed for Roanoke. When he was directly overhead, he increased power and banked the plane again, initiating a tight, climbing spiral. Lexi had no idea what he was doing.

Chet continued his upward spiral. Somewhere between three and four thousand feet, he reduced power and leveled off. Suddenly, the sound of the engine totally disappeared. The Mooney assumed a slight nose-down attitude and began to make wide, spiraling circles back toward the ground.

Lexi felt her heart somersault...something was wrong. Chet was attempting a dead-stick landing.

Every muscle in her body tensed. She had flown with Chet a

206

time or two when he had practiced power-off landings. With the runway right below him, all he had to do was reduce altitude and line himself up for a safe landing.

"LANDING GEAR!" Lexi shouted. She squinted and examined the bottom of the plane. The gear was still up!

Chet's descent steepened. The Mooney was literally falling from the sky.

Lexi covered her eyes. "Chet's a skilled pilot,' she said out loud. "He's just bleeding off altitude."

She peeked through her fingers. "Extend your landing gear this instant, Chet Willow!"

The plane leveled off again. Lexi calculated the distance between it and the ground was roughly two hundred feet. There was still no landing gear. She covered her eyes again. "Please, God, extend that gear." The words sounded as if she was being choked.

Suddenly, there was a great rush of horsepower. Lexi looked up. Chet cycled his gear down and then up again, and flashed his landing lights twice. He had been under power the entire time. The whole charade was nothing more than a little aeronautical target practice. Lexi placed her hands over her heart. "Chet Willow, when I get my hands on you, I'm going to flatten your rudder!" she shouted.

Chet laid into the throttle again and the Mooney powered back into the sky.

Chapter 23

Lexi spent the remainder of the morning at *The Staunton News Leader*. On her way home that afternoon, she listened to an old Keith Bryant hit playing on the only radio station that didn't fade out through the mountains. The song was *Drivers in Heaven* and the phrase 'black number three' reminded her of the hat Porter wore the first day she and Chet met him.

The rapist, Porter Bandy. If there was any justice in the world, he'd have pulled time for Zelda's mother's suicide, too. Maybe even find himself on the losing end of a little late night prison block pokey pokey. Wouldn't that be justice?

And Zelda, what a metamorphosis. Yesterday, she looked like a refugee from a Metallica concert; today she appeared ready to ship off to Vassar. She'd even dyed her hair platinum blond.

Kimberly arrived at five-thirty. Lexi showed her to one of the guest bedrooms on the north wing. Once she was settled, Lexi drove her down to the Maple Restaurant for a cold plate and a slice of pie. She was finding it increasingly difficult to ignore her sweet tooth, ordering a large slice of the brown sugar, baked by the loving,

Christian hands of old Millie Baldwin herself, no less.

The dinner conversation mostly consisted of veterinary shoptalk. Kimberly said Paragon's leg had sufficiently healed for Lexi to start riding him again. Kimberly kept yawning, apologizing each time she did. Saying the anesthesia they used in surgery always made her sleepy.

They left the Maple and walked across the street to the Expedition. The air was thick and humid and the sky was turning dark. The rain would be along at any moment.

As Lexi drove up the driveway, a flash of lightning struck somewhere behind the barn and the lights along Chet's airstrip blinked on. There was another quick strike and the lights went out again. It seemed Mother Nature had stumbled onto the correct frequency for Chet's state-of-the-art radio-controlled runway lighting system.

Lexi managed to get Kimberly into the house before the deluge arrived. She made a pot of coffee and carried it to the breakfast nook to watch the storm. Lightning flashed, thunder boomed and rain fell in buckets. The kitchen lights flickered a few times before the generator kicked in.

Down below, all of Monterey went black.

At first, the sound seemed like it was part of a dream...a vagrant, distant rumbling. When it came a second time, Lexi was closer to full consciousness and re-categorized it as a low growl. Not distant, but right next to her.

She opened her left eye and scanned the bedroom—a bolt of lightning bleached the sky and painted her walls with a regiment of crooked shadows.

The growling sound came again. This time, Lexi was able to hone directly on the source. It was Beecher, crouched on the floor beneath the window adjacent to the foot of the bed. The hair on his back was flared like porcupine quills.

There was a light thud outside the window followed by a series of faint scratching sounds; Beecher's growl raised a click in volume. Lexi rolled away from the windows and off the other side of the bed. She opened the drawer on her nightstand, reached inside and tightened her hand around the butt of the 9mm Colt, exactly where Chet had put it before leaving that morning. She arranged the pillows to appear like she was still sleeping, tossed the sheet over them and then eased down and kneeled at the foot of the bed. She raised the pistol, jacked a round into the chamber and laid her hand on the bed with the sights level with the center of the lower window.

Beecher's growls grew more impatient, yet he stood motionless.

A head—or rather a hat—appeared at the bottom of the window, rising upward. Another bolt of lightning blanched the darkness. The hat dipped as if startled.

Lexi tightened her grip on the pistol; the muscles in her abdomen tightened as well. But the sights on the 9mm remained glued to the window.

Slowly the hat reappeared and then a face below it. It had ashen-white skin with large black eyes and a round mouth. The face moved closer to the glass. A large hand, probably gloved, came up and cupped around the left side of it.

Lightning flashed again providing Lexi a better look at her guest. The face was actually a white cloth bag with a rope wrapped around the neck. The hole for the mouth was bordered with red paint, the eye sockets bordered in black.

Lexi felt the curved steel of the trigger pressing against the tip of her right index finger. She estimated that she was dangerously close to the pressure needed to pull it and relaxed her hand. Holding the gun made her nervous.

The face and hat disappeared again. Lexi heard a muffled curse, then more scratching and rattling sounds. Thirty seconds later, the hat reappeared at the window opposite the head of the bed. Some ghost. It had apparently floated up to the wrong window and needed to float back down to reposition the ladder.

Suddenly it struck her. "Porter," she said out loud. The left eye slit was larger than the right one; Porter was blind in his right eye.

The Porter-ghost began making low wailing sounds. Thunder rolled in the distance, masking Beecher's growling which was getting louder, too.

The ghost raised a pitchfork. Three tines—just like the one stuck in Raymond Blaylock's chest—and began to screech the tips across the glass.

Beecher could no longer contain himself and burst out barking. Startled, Lexi pinched the trigger and fire spat from the muzzle. The old glass in the window fragmented.

The ghost screamed. A fully audible, pared to the bone, scream of terror; almost a loud as the one Lexi belted out.

The gunshot and broken glass set off the security system and a loud, siren-style alarm accosted her from all directions. The head and hat had disappeared again.

Lexi gasped and raced to the windows. "Oh my God, I killed him!" she cried.

She saw Porter hit the ground; the ladder rattled down behind him. He bolted through the front yard, across the driveway and leapt over the cut-stone wall. She relaxed as the bedroom door flew open and Kimberly rushed in.

"Lexi, are you alright?" she shouted.

Lexi raced over to the alarm panel, silenced it, and then switched on the ceiling light. "I'm okay. Everything's fine."

Kimberly's eyes jumped from the broken window to the gun lying in the middle of the bed. Her skin was almost as white as Porter's scarecrow face.

"There was somebody at my window."

Lexi reached for the telephone on her bedside table; the security alarm company would be calling. It rang just as she picked it up. "This is Alexis Willow, code work "Bestseller." We had an intruder, but I'll call the sheriff myself." She hung up before getting a reply.

Kimberly went to the window. "Did you shoot him?"

"I don't know. If so, it didn't hurt him very badly. He flew over the terrace wall like an Olympic hurdler."

Lexi started shaking and sat down on the bed. Beecher jumped up beside her. "Thanks for the warning, buddy." She scratched his back and then kissed him on the top of the head.

Three patrol cars roared up the driveway with sirens blaring and lights flashing. It looks like Godsey mobilized the whole department for this one.

Lexi intercepted Godsey and Randy on the front portico. Randy was fully dressed in black like some Ninja SWAT team commando, and the pistol he was holding was one of the largest handguns she'd ever seen. When Godsey realized she was safe he dispatched Randy to help the other deputies secure the perimeter.

Lexi took the sheriff upstairs and began to describe what happened. Godsey inspected the broken window, then pulled a handkerchief from his back pocket and collected the pistol and spent shell casing.

"Sheriff!" shouted a voice from the foyer. "We've got something out here!"

Lexi hurried downstairs; Godsey waggled along behind like a bowling pin on legs. She found Randy in the foyer holding a pitchfork and the straw hat.

"We found these on the lawn." He raised the working end of the pitchfork and examined the tines. "There's blood on this one. Deputy Chatham found a blood stain on the stone wall, too. It looks like a partial handprint, likely from a glove. Whoever left it is bleeding pretty good. Chatham's tracking it now."

Godsey examined the straw hat. "Mrs. Willow, your ghost had best count his blessings he wasn't another three inches taller." He poked his index finger through a bullet hole two inches above the brim. "If he was, I'd say you'd a tagged him about center forehead."

He gave the pitchfork back to Randy. "Get a blood sample off this and another one off the wall. Specimen bottles are in the trunk of my car. Bag this and anything else you find. Put on some gloves and round up that ladder. We'll need to check it for prints."

Randy nodded and hurried out the front door. Godsey yelled after him. "Keep tabs on Chatham. Our ghost may not be trick-or-treating alone tonight." He looked at Lexi as if expecting praise for his little pun. Receiving none, he focused his attention on the 9mm.

"You say you only fired once?" Lexi nodded.

"One shot is all I heard," said Kimberly from the couch in the study.

"Where were you when this happened?" Godsey asked.

"In the bedroom down the other hall," replied Kimberly.

"Did you hear anything else? An engine, a dog barking, somebody toting a ladder across the yard?"

"Only the shot, until I got to Lexi's bedroom."

Godsey sniffed the barrel of the pistol and depressed the magazine release. He examined the peep holes in the side of it and then pushed down on the top bullet. Only one round was missing.

He jotted the pistol's serial number on a piece of paper, returned the magazine and placed it on the foyer table. "I believe you.

213

The blood-wound was probably caused by the pitchfork during the fall. We'll know for sure when we find him." Godsey examined the hat again. "He might have a permanent part in his hair though."

Godsey cut an eye at Lexi. "What makes you think it was Porter Bandy?"

"From the way Beecher was barking. It was exactly the way he acted toward Porter the day we found Raymond. Growling and barking."

"Ain't much to Porter worth liking, but what's your dog got against him?"

"I don't know," Lexi replied. But, of course, she did...she was certain Porter had been poking around the barn the night before Paragon got trapped in the quicksand. He had to be the one who unlatched Paragon's stall. Beecher recognized the scent and sounded the alarm, just like he did tonight.

Lexi wasn't going to tell Godsey that, though. For all she knew, he might have been steadying Porter's ladder.

"Keep that gun handy," Godsey said. "We might need it later. I'll talk to Porter in the mornin' if he shows up at JB's for work. If he doesn't, we'll have to wait until he comes down. We'd never find him in these mountains. Not even with my dogs."

"Can't you run a DNA test on the blood sample?" Lexi asked.

"Could, I guess, if we had a hunk of Porter's hide to compare it to. Trust me, Mrs. Willow. I've got ways of telling."

The sheriff tugged at his collar. "Say, you wouldn't happen to have a glass of water or a cold Pepsi-Cola handy, would ya? My throat seems to have gotten a tad parched."

Oh, brother, Lexi thought. If he stays here much longer, he'll be asking for crackling and scrambled eggs. "I believe I still have a sliver of JB's maple pie, if you're interested."

"Why, thank you kindly, Mrs. Willow. Turning down a slice

of JB's pie would be like slamming the door on Ed McMahon."

"Would you mind if I give Terry a quick call?" Kimberly asked. "Someone's liable to tell him there was a double homicide up here before I see him in the morning."

"Of course. Use the phone on the computer desk."

Lexi headed for the kitchen; Godsey padded along behind her, breathing so hard through his mouth she could almost hear it manufacturing saliva.

"When the boys get back, I'll leave Randy here with a cruiser for the rest of the night," Godsey said. "We'll both rest a little easier knowing he's here. No charge this time, of course. Official police business. With Mr. Willow in the Big Apple, you'd best have Drexel fix that window first thing in the morning. The mosquitoes this time of year are more vicious than a pack of widows on an unwed preacher."

Lexi dished up Godsey's pie. She didn't remember mentioning anything to him about Chet traveling in New York.

Chapter 24

Lexi lay in bed wondering if she should call Chet and tell him about the peeping Porter. But, if she did, he'd catch a red-eye and be home in time for breakfast.

She was certain the answers to everything were at the bottom of that ice pit. Tat-Tat and Scoop needed one more day to finish. Norman said he would hit it at eight sharp, providing his machinery was working. Lexi felt sure that whatever was going to happen would happen just before the pit was empty. She needed Chet to stay away at least another thirty-six hours. She decided not to call.

She rolled onto her side and gazed at the slab of cardboard she had duct-taped over the window. Porter was out there somewhere, bleeding. For all she knew, he might even be dead. If so, who was going to step forward and pick up where he left off?

Chapter 25

The clock on the nightstand read 8:00 AM but the hammering in Lexi's ears was already thirty minutes old. Norman must be chomping at the bit, she thought. Who could blame him?

Thanks to an absolutely miserable night's sleep, Lexi's eye felt like she had been using them to play marbles in a sandbox. It's hard to turn off one's brain after a visit from a full-bodied, albeit not-so-vaporous, nocturnal aberration...even it was a bumbling Porter Bandy. The most troubling part was that her sinuses were clogged and her feet felt like someone had inflated them with an air hose; maybe she was having an allergic reaction to something. It had all the makings of a Motrin morning, 800 mg if she still had that much—the first time she had needed it in over a week.

She suddenly remembered Kimberly had promised to fix breakfast. Lexi kicked off the covers, peeled herself from the mattress and hurried into the bathroom to brush her hair. When she arrived at the bottom of the stairs, a voice called to her from the study. "Lexi, you never told me you had a cat."

Lexi pivoted to her right and stopped. Kimberly was sitting

on the sofa. A fluffy white Persian was parked in the middle of her lap; Beecher was perched on the sofa next to them.

"I loathe cats." Lexi answered flatly. "They make my nose run and my feet swell."

"Oh, no," gasped Kimberly. "My purse is on the kitchen table. At the bottom of the larger compartment, there's a blister pack of Benadryl. Take two of them with a full glass of water."

Lexi rushed into the kitchen and dug into Kimberly's purse, removing the contents until she found the allergy meds. She dumped two capsules into her hand and swallowed them with bottled spring water from the refrigerator.

"A cat," Lexi spat. "A ghost wasn't enough. They had to throw a cat into the house, too." She put the water back in the fridge and slammed the door. Beecher clicked up to her. She patted the top of his head. "Benedict Arnold."

As Lexi was returning Kimberly's wallet to the purse, a picture valet fell onto the table. She retrieved it and instinctively examined the top photograph. It was a wedding picture of Kimberly and Terry. The third person, oddly enough, was Drexel; the fourth person was a woman Lexi didn't recognize. She had never noticed the striking resemblance between Kimberly and Drexel before.

Kimberly entered the kitchen carrying the cat. "Lexi, this Persian is identical to those Mrs. Madison had. It even has the same teal-green collar." She halted when she saw what Lexi was holding.

"This fell out of your purse when I was looking for the Benadryl," Lexi said. "You never told me you and Drexel were related. He could pass for your father. An uncle, maybe?"

"More like a father," Kimberly replied, her eyes still fixed on the picture. "He's my mother's brother. My real father disappeared when I was six. Uncle Drex more or less adopted me. He gave me away when Terry and I were married."

"Well he's certainly won our hearts. We couldn't have turned this place into a home without him. Is this woman your mother?"

"Yes, it is. Dear, old Mom. She lives just outside of Harrisonburg."

Kimberly certainly didn't speak of her mother with much compassion. Her "dear old Mom" sounded like she was talking about some stranger on the street.

Lexi returned the pictures to Kimberly's purse. "Thanks for the Benadryl."

"I've got to be getting to the clinic," Kimberly said. "If you don't mind, I'll take Miss Whiskers here with me. I still have the Madison's medical records. It shouldn't be hard to see if they match."

"You seriously don't think it's the one she lost, do you? Not after all this time."

"I spayed the two females." Kimberly held the cat in front of her and examined its stomach. "I don't see any scars, but no one else around here keeps white Persians. At least, none that visit me."

Lexi sneezed again. "It looks like someone's been taking good care of it." What she really wanted to know was why they dumped it here.

Kimberly squeezed one its front paws. "Declawed. Just like Mrs. Madison's. Not many people do that anymore."

Chapter 26

"Mornin', Mrs. Willow," crowed JB from behind the meat counter. "Haven't seen that fine-looking man of yours yet today. He's usually sugared his Joe and out the door by seven-thirty."

"Chet's attending his monthly business meetings in New York." Lexi glanced around the store as she spoke. There were six other people there, but no sign of Porter. "I don't expect him back until tomorrow afternoon."

"Just give me a call if'n you get lonely up there. Got the last two weeks' worth of *General Hospital* on the VCR, if you follow it. I'll even bring a box of Orville Redenbacher's, theater style."

Lexi smiled. "Thanks. If Kimberly doesn't get to come back, I'll take you up on it." She waited for JB's reaction.

"Kimberly? As in, Kimberly Buchanan?" JB asked.

The notion of Kimberly staying at the house appeared to wound her. "She's been looking in on Paragon for me since my accident," Lexi replied. "When she learned Chet was going away, she volunteered to keep me company."

JB appeared to buy the excuse. "You young girls probably

have more to talk about anyway," she said. "Dead folks and pie can get a tad boring after a while."

Lexi smiled. "Is Porter around this morning?" she asked.

JB put three trays of chicken in the meat case and slid the rear door closed. "No, he ain't," she spat. "He lit out of here yesterday evening with two twelve-packs of Budweiser and a fresh carton of Canadian night crawlers. When he does that, I usually don't see him again for two or three days. Left me eighty pounds of chicken to cut up, too." JB stomped over to the sink and washed her hands. "You're the second person that's asked for him this morning. What's he done this time?"

Lexi knew JB already had the answer to that question.

"I was wondering if he'd be interested in maintaining our lawn for the rest of the summer. Audrey Pepper said what a good job he did for the Madison's. Chet and I don't have a lawnmower yet and things are starting to look a bit shaggy."

"I suspect he'd be glad to," JB said. "Cutting grass and yanking weeds is one of the few things that boy shines at. When I see him, I'll tell him to give ya a call."

Lexi clicked through her mental checklist. By noon, everyone in Monterey would know that Chet was away. The bad guys probably already did but she might as well leave the welcome mat out for anyone else who might be interested.

Now, for the second reason she'd come to JB's; to plant a little suspicion.

"JB, something you told me a few weeks back has been gnawing at me." She looked JB straight in the eyes. "Why did Deacon Blaylock sell *you* the store? If he was as broke as you indicated, the only way he would have benefited from the sale was to get the cash up front. But a nineteen-year-old woman didn't just get a business loan in those days. And with a pending foreclosure, his credit couldn't have been good enough to cosign for you. That means he had to finance the deal himself but, by doing so, he forfeited the up-front cash. So there must have been another reason he did it."

JB bristled at that last statement. Lexi had intended to be blunt for effect, but she also wanted to come off sounding more inquisitive than accusing.

JB wiped her hands on the front of her overalls before answering. "That's an honest question and, if I've answered it once, I've answered it a thousand times. I'd worked the store for three years, two years full-time since graduating high school. I asked him to sell it and he agreed. It's that simple. Times were slack back then and there weren't any other offers. And since our agreement predated the foreclosure proceedings, the bank couldn't stop it. I paid him seventy-five dollars a month. Still got the receipts somewhere."

Lexi knew better than that. The bank would have placed a lien on all Deacon's owned property long before they actually foreclosed on those which were indebted. Any revenues paid Deacon would have been attached. He wouldn't have seen a penny of whatever JB could afford to pay him.

"Deacon wasn't the smartest businessman," said JB, "but he wasn't about to let the bank take everything. It gave him enough to buy his whiskey, I suppose."

"It must have been terrible for him," Lexi said. "The fire, the foreclosure, Raymond's disappearance. That's too much for any one person to bear." The sorrow Lexi felt was genuine and her facial expression must have reflected it because JB's furrowed brow relaxed. "Thanks for clearing that up for me."

It was time to lighten the conversation. Lexi leaned her head back and inhaled a sweet aroma. "Whatever you're baking back there, I'll take two slices and a glass of ice cold milk."

"Oh, mercy," JB exclaimed. "Thanks for reminding me." She

rushed into the back room and came back a moment later with a paper plate covered with plastic wrap. "I made this peach cobbler to go along with my special today: fried chicken-n-biscuits with black-eyed peas." She handed the plate to Lexi. "It's a new recipe. You and Kimberly have a piece with dinner tonight and tell me what you think. The big piece is for you. Microwave it on high for thirty seconds, and plop a big scoop of vanilla ice cream on top."

Lexi thanked JB and started for home.

JB could have been a top-notch screenwriter, Lexi thought. Despite her Oscar-caliber ploys of misdirection, Lexi was convinced she was the brains behind the later happenings on Cheat Mountain.

Lexi drove up the incline of her driveway, inserted her access card into the control panel, and punched in the code. As the gates retracted, her eyes were drawn to the guardian statues. Benaja and Junta...Shepherd's lions. She marveled again at how perfectly crafted they were. Every detail was magnificently chiseled from blocks of coal.

"I'd give my right arm to hear you guys talk," Lexi said out loud. She paused for a moment longer as if expecting them to answer.

She parked the Expedition next to the garage and climbed out. The mountain was desperately quiet. She checked her watch; five minutes past ten. Either Norman was burning valuable daylight—which she doubted—or Tat-Tat and Scoop were laying down on the job again.

Lexi started walking toward the ice pit. As she approached the trench area, she saw the lower half of a man's body hanging out the track hammer's rear access door.

"More gremlins?" she asked.

The man jerked and, judging from the hushed stream of expletives, he must have banged his head on something.

Norman lowered himself down onto the hammer's track.

223

"This one's my own damn fault, if you'll pardon my French. One of the studs that hold the air compressor to the frame broke a couple weeks back. The increased vibration cracked a leg weld on the receiver tank. Now I can't keep enough pressure in the tank to run the hammer."

Lexi didn't have the slightest clue what he was talking about. What was obvious, though, was that there were still roughly two-and-a-half feet of solid rock between the drainage trench and the pit.

"Can you fix it?" she asked.

"Nope. Sent Eugene back to the shop to get the spare compressor. If we can get it replaced by dark, I'll be back tomorrow morning and work clean through the weekend if I need to. Anything to get this confounded, snake-bit job behind me."

Norman excused himself, crossed over the trench and climbed up on the excavator. "Thank God, I pocketed half the profits from the airstrip," Lexi heard him say before he started the excavator, gunned the engine and began digging the loose rubble from the ditch.

Lexi's eyes became fixed on the trench. She no longer heard the roar of the excavator's engine.

Shepherd Blaylock and his men had dug trenches along Shenandoah Mountain, fortified them with wood and stone, and dared the enemy to attack; placing themselves between death and the world they loved.

Before her lay another trench—her trench—she was the breastworks; she had dared the enemy to attack, placing herself between death and everything she hoped for. And now her freedom, emotionally if not physically, was hanging in the balance.

Chapter 27

Lexi returned to the house and checked the answering machine. There was one new message. She tapped the play button.

"Mrs. Willow, this is Zelda from the *News Leader*." Zelda's voice sounded significantly more chipper today. "I found a couple more pieces of information you may be interested in. I didn't know if you're coming in today or not. If not, they can wait until next week. Hope I didn't bother you. Have a good weekend."

Lexi's head was beginning to pound—the diesel fumes from Norman's excavator were the culprit this time. She could even smell it on her clothes.

She would return Zelda's call later.

She checked her computer for e-mails from Chet before returning to the bedroom to lay down. As her homepage loaded, she watched a picture of Macaulay Calkin materialize. Below it was printed in bold capital letters, "MACKEY'S BACK IN TOWN."

She studied Calkin's picture. Though he had aged, his face still possessed that look of prepared innocence. Home alone, just like her...well, almost.

CHEAT MOUNATAIN

There were two e-mails from Chet. The subject line of the first read, 'Any News??'

Chapter 28

Kimberly returned to the house at six-thirty. When she entered the study, Lexi noted the perplexed look on her face.

"Anything I can do to help?" Lexi asked.

"The cat," Kimberly blurted. "Mrs. Madison's Persian, it disappeared. I caged her in the feline room when I got to the clinic this morning. But when I went back to examine her, she was gone."

Wonderful, Lexi thought. Now we have kitty ghosts, too. Her allergic reaction this morning was definitely not caused by a ghost.

"Could someone have taken her?"

"I asked everyone," Kimberly replied. "Terry, the techs...none of them even recalled seeing her. I searched the whole clinic. It's like she was never there."

Lexi shook her head. "That's not surprising. One thing I've learned about Monterey is, things just have a way of happening. The day Chet and I got here our truck rolled down the side yard and struck a tree, even with the transmission in park and the emergency brake set. Chances are we'll see it again before it's all over with."

"Before what's all over with?" Kimberly asked.

"Before the cavalry arrives and we all live happily ever after. At least, that's how my novel ends. Or how I think it's going to end.

"Look, I've got grilled salmon with dill sauce and steamed veggies in the warmer. And two pieces of JB's peach cobbler for dessert. Let's eat and forget about everything else."

Kimberly finished setting the table while Lexi pulled the food together.

JB's cobbler was divine; sweeter than most Lexi had ever tasted, which suited her newly acquired sugar craving to a tee. Kimberly put down her fork after eating only half the smaller piece.

"I can't eat another bite," she said. "Everything was fabulous. I'll think of you tomorrow evening while I'm staring at a plate of Terry's leftover meatloaf."

It only took a couple minutes to clear the table and load the dirty dishes into the dishwasher.

"Lexi, would you mind if I rest for a while?" Kimberly asked. "An emergency hip reconstruction on a Rottweiler this afternoon wiped me out."

Lexi felt sleepy, too. She glanced at the clock on the oven; it was only quarter past seven. "No, Please. Go right ahead. I may stretch out on the sofa for a couple minutes myself."

Lexi finished straightening the kitchen and headed for the study. Beecher was barking and spinning circles by the front door. She patted him on the head and let him out. "Get those squirrels, buddy."

By the time Lexi plopped herself on the sofa, she was struggling to keep her eyes open.

Chapter 29

Lexi was awakened by an acidic sensation cutting through her sinus cavity and assaulting the nerve endings in her brain. *Smelling salts.* She bolted to a sitting position; a thickly calloused hand slapped across her mouth and a second hand grabbed her around the throat. She felt a weight land on the sofa beside her; the firmness of a man's chest pressed against her back.

"Do exactly as I say," a raspy voice whispered at her.

Lexi tried to free herself and the hand around her throat tightened, her right breast got pinched in the crux of his arm.

"You're in danger here," said the voice again, reeking of stale beer. The stench of burnt cigarettes radiated from the hand covering her mouth. "Get out of this house. Get off this mountain. Tonight."

Lexi pooled her senses enough to realize she was still in the study. It was dark and all the lights were out.

The pressure around Lexi's neck released and something fell onto her lap. Lexi touched it...her purse. The intruder grabbed her hand and pressed a set of keys into it.

"Get in your car and get out of here," growled the voice.

The man shoved Lexi face down onto the sofa. Footsteps retreated toward the front door. She reached for the reading lamp but it was gone.

The front door clicked as the intruder departed. Lexi jumped to her feet and switched on the light at her computer table. As its glow fanned across the room, she saw that the reading lamp had been moved away from the sofa. She examined the keys in her hand. Her guest was obviously very familiar with the house; apparently her habits as well. She retrieved her purse from the sofa and felt for her wallet. It was still there.

How long had Mr. Nicotine Fingers been slithering around in here, Lexi wondered? Her thoughts suddenly shifted to Kimberly.

She raced up the stairs and down the north hall. She pushed open Kimberly's door and reached for the switch; light spilled into the hallway. The room was empty, the bedspread was not the slightest bit wrinkled.

Lexi eyed the clock on the nightstand. 9:52 PM. Her head felt dizzy. Somebody must have drugged her. She hurried down the hall turning on every light switch, searching each room. She reached her bedroom, slid open the drawer on her nightstand and retrieved the Colt. She thumbed the magazine release button; it slid smoothly out into her hand. She turned it from side to side, examining holes along its length: the spring inside was fully compressed. She pushed down on the top bullet the same way she had seen Sheriff Godsey do the night before. It moved only a fraction. Someone had reloaded her gun.

Nicotine Man? Godsey? Why? What did they know that she didn't? She would probably know the answers to those questions before the night was out.

Lexi slammed the magazine home, jacked the slide, rammed a bullet into the chamber and clicked on the safety. She rushed into her closet to the stack of clothes she had assembled earlier. She changed into black Spandex pants and a matching tank top, combed her hair back into a ponytail, donned the black lightweight jacket and stuffed the pistol in the right pocket.

Before she left, she examined the case where Chet kept his other gun. Lexi opened the top; the spot usually occupied by the Glock was empty. She suddenly wished she hadn't insisted Chet keep his appointments in New York.

She slipped on a pair of black, canvas deck shoes and set out to search the rest of the house. Kimberly was nowhere to be found.

"Maybe she got called out on an emergency and didn't want to wake me," Lexi said out loud. It suddenly dawned on her that Beecher was missing, too.

She ran through the downstairs turning on all the outside lights. No Beecher. Lexi felt concentric waves of panic rippling through her body. She willed them away. "Stay calm, Lexi. Remain focused; just remain focused."

She picked up the phone and started to dial Sheriff Godsey's office...the line was dead.

Lexi slammed the receiver back into its cradle and calmed herself once again. As if right on cue, every light in the house went dark. She stifled a scream and dropped to her hands and knees on the kitchen floor, praying that the emergency generator would kick in. It didn't.

She put her back against the dishwasher; the ripples of panic were now like coils tightening around her, choking off the air. Her whole body trembled. She became aware of the bulk in her right front pocket: the pistol. She placed her hand on it, felt the rawness of cold uncaring steel. It gave her a strange sense of comfort. Unlike her parents when they were murdered, she could defend herself. She had opportunity and she had advantage.

The Nicotine Man's warning drummed back to her. "Get out of this house. Get off this mountain." Lexi figured her chances were better outside than in, but she had left her purse and keys in the bedroom.

The house screamed of silence. There was no time for the keys; she had to get out now.

Lexi rose to her feet, crouched over and rushed to the laundry room door. She felt around on the shelf until she came across the Mag-Lite she'd loaded with fresh batteries the day before. She tucked it into the waistband of her pants and cracked the door just wide enough to ease out. There was no moonlight; the air was cool and thick. It seemed any moment the darkness could be washed away by another heavy shower.

Lexi crouched by the steps next to the access door to the crawlspace. It took several moments for her eyes to adjust to the darkness—all the lights at the stables and outbuildings were extinguished as well. There was a sound like a heavy car door slamming down near the ice pit. Someone shouted and she distinctly understood the last two words—the infamous F-word and 'varmints'.

She plotted a mental course and set out into the darkness holding the Mag-Lite in her right hand...not as a light, but as a weapon.

She cut across the front yard to the stone wall and followed it back toward the ice pit drainage ditch. When she got to the boss house, she saw a light moving around the sides of the track hammer.

Lexi switched the Mag-Lite to her left hand, and retrieved the pistol with her right. She raised the Mag-Lite and clicked the power button. A tunnel of light bored through the darkness.

"Mister, you'd better have a damn good reason for being here!" she shouted, immediately realizing what an incredibly stupid thing she had done; simultaneously giving away her position and

232

ruining her night vision all in one flawed swoop. If this guy had a partner, she was toast.

The man whirled around and the first thing Lexi saw was a shotgun.

"Is that you, Mrs. Willow? It's me. Norman, Norman Evans."

Lexi stuffed the pistol back into her coat pocket. "Norman. What are you doing here?"

"Protecting what's mine, dog blame it." Norman slid off the track hammer onto the ground. "When that pole light went out, one of those jinxters damn near crawled right into my lap. He's lucky I didn't blow both our heads off. Bet ya ten to one the S.O.B. was trying to sabotage my equipment again."

Norman patted his breast pocket and extracted a cigarette.

"Did you see who it was?" Lexi asked.

"No, but I got a chunk of his ass." Norman held out a square piece of black fabric. "I ripped the back pocket clean off his britches."

"I had a visitor at the house, too," Lexi said. "He smelled like he'd just chain-smoked a carton."

Norman threw his cigarette to the ground and stomped on it. "Well, it won't me, if that's what you're thinking. Look, Mrs. Willow. All I want to do is finish this job and get the hell off this mountain. You folks need never lay eyes on me again. I told Drexel Yeatts I could pump that damn hole dry in less than half a day. But he said you folks insisted on doing it this way."

"What?" Lexi exclaimed. She stepped toward Norman. "He told us it would take weeks just to locate a pump big enough. Said this was the quickest way."

"Quickest way?" Norman spat on the ground. "It's like plucking the feathers off an old Tom turkey with a pair of chopsticks." He leaned his shotgun against the track hammer. "That two-fisted, double-dipping bastard. I'm giving him fifteen percent of

233

my fee for the referral. That's nearly $1500. He probably threw a healthy mark-up on top of that. A slurry pump job would have cost less than a thousand."

Drexel? Lexi's brain shouted. He wouldn't do something like that; he had been her and Chet's savior through all this. The money was of little consequence. But he *had* mentioned digging up Titus's treasure and has known about Chet's trip to New York for over a month. He easily had access...it gave Lexi a wallop of disgust just thinking about it.

"Could that be Drexel's pocket you're holding?" she asked.

"Naw," Norman replied. "If I had a grip on Drexel's scrawny ass, he wouldn't have slipped away. This boy was built more like a middle linebacker."

That gave Lexi a surge of relief. The ditch issue must have been some kind of miscommunication. None of that mattered now though. She shone her flashlight on the trench. "How much longer to chisel that out?"

"We got the new air receiver installed just before dark, like I said we would. While my helper was gone, I pecked at what's left of the dam with the excavator bucket. A lick or two with the hammer in the right place ought to do it. Shouldn't take more than an hour or so to drain down."

Lexi ran her eyes over the track hammer. "Can you run these things at night?"

"Give me a minute to reposition the spots on the bucket over there and I'll dig you a ditch deep enough to strike fortune cookies."

Lexi smiled at his enthusiasm. But what if his jinxters and Nicotine Man were working together? How would Norman's presence here now change things?

Norman started the track hammer, powered back to idle and jumped down. He crossed the dam and ran around to the excavator.

Once the excavator was running, he backed away from the ice pit until the spotlights lit up the whole west end of the trench, and then shut it down again.

A thick layer of greasy diesel fumes were being held close to the ground by the humidity and dense cloud cover. Lexi's adrenalin rush was fading and she recognized a familiar pressure mounting in her skull and tried to massage it away. All of her headache medicine was back in the house. She hoped she could fight it off long enough to at least get the pit drained.

Norman climbed back aboard the track hammer. A bolt of lightning flashed through the valley to the south; the lights on Chet's runway blinked just like they had the night before.

Norman tossed Lexi a set of earphones. "Put these on and let's punch this out before that storm gets here," he shouted.

Lexi cupped the phones over her ears and found a safe vantage point to the right of the pit where the diesel fumes were less intense.

Norman extended the hammer's arm all the way down into the trench and dropped the power-chisel level with the bottom and began to pound away. His upper body was silhouetted inside the cab by the red and green lights from the instrument panel. He worked the chisel vertically five feet up the dam, and then back down to the bottom, surgically chipping away rock. Barely five minutes had passed when Lexi saw a trickle of water.

Norman saw it too and paused long enough for the dust to settle; water was seeping out of a crack halfway up the new furrow. He raised the chisel even with the crack and popped it several more times. A chunk of rock dislodged and a stream of muck the diameter of a basketball shot from the basin of the ice pit. Norman leveled the rubble in the bottom of the trench and the muck rolled like a gray tidal wave toward the opening at the edge of the terrace. He raised the hammer's arm out of the trench, lowered it to the sleeping swan position, and killed the engine.

Lexi gently removed the earphones. The quiet was welcomed, but she feared it was already too late for any headache relief. The diesel fumes had ignited the fuse. If she didn't eat one of the magic pills soon, her head was going to explode.

Lexi turned for the house; the runway lights brightened the valley again. This time, they didn't immediately blink off.

She stopped to look and, suddenly, heard a loud scream. It sounded as though it came from down around the barn. She remained motionless, praying it would turn out to be something else. The scream came again...more resigned, almost desperate.

Norman helped Lexi across the dam—there was no time to worry if the hammering had weakened it too much to walk on.

The runway lights extinguished the instant Lexi started down the hard-surfaced road. She switched on the Mag-Lite and ran back to get the Gator. Jumping into the driver's seat, she reached for the keys; they were not in the ignition. She frantically searched the cubbyhole under the dash, the tool box, and then remembered she had tossed them into the cup holder after giving Chet a lift to the Mooney Thursday morning. The pressure in her temples was still growing, but a fresh adrenalin rush might keep it from going volcanic.

With Norman beside her, Lexi backed the Gator around and gunned the throttle—its powerful halogens provided a shield of light before them, turning back the misty darkness.

She stopped in front of the barn and Norman checked the doors: they were closed tightly and properly latched. Hopefully, Paragon was safe and sound inside his stall. This was the first time she had been here since the accident without having the vision of Raymond and the others. She searched her mind; it was not there.

The darkness was completely silent again. The screams may

have come from behind the barn; sounds bounce all around the valley making it difficult to pinpoint a source. But tonight the air was holding everything close and that worked in her favor.

The blacktop turned to soft sand in front of the barn but the Gator's fat tires chewed right through it. Forty yards beyond where the terrace descended back toward the basin of the valley, the road turned to dirt. Lexi saw a faint light emanating from the old sawmill and heard the sound of a saw blade ripping into a firm log. Norman's body stiffened in the seat beside her.

Smoke lazed in stagnant layers before the halogens like a wispy, vagrant fog, turning into swirls as the Gator sped through it. Lexi patted her coat pocket to ensure the Colt was still along for the ride. Bumping along as fast as she could, she swerved to miss the well house and skidded to a stop inches from the steps leading up to the mill's cutting deck.

The high-pitched whine of the saw blade continued to scream like a jet engine. Lexi raced up the steps behind Norman. When she got to the deck, she saw the saw blade exit the trailing end of a log.

The log carriage stopped, and started retracting back toward her and Norman. As it did she saw a pair of tennis shoes followed by legs, then a torso. The head became visible: platinum-blond hair; dazed and distant eyes. ZELDA!

The carriage kicked over a few inches and began to make another pass at the blade. The right side of Zelda's body was directly in line with the cut.

Norman vaulted over the railing and raced to a bank of gages and levers. The saw blade tore into the end of the log; a spray of fine wood chips showered Lexi. She reached for the girl but the carriage was moving away; even if Lexi could get to her, there would not be enough time to free her. Zelda's eyes, unblinking, sought out Lexi's face.

The blade sped closer to Zelda's shoulder; Lexi closed her eyes and prepared herself for when she had to open them again.

Suddenly, there were two loud clunks and an immediate change in the pitch of the saw blade. Lexi looked; the carriage had stopped, the blade just inches from Zelda's right ear.

There was a burst of steam from the boiler at the opposite end of the saw house, another loud clunk, and the carriage retracted.

Lexi stepped up onto on a piece of planking and started digging with her fingernails at the tape binding Zelda's feet. Behind her, something burst through the wood railing and landed in a heap on the deck.

Porter Bandy! Bleeding from the nose and mouth, a blood-stained bandage was hanging from his left cheek. Above the bandage was an oozing gash haphazardly approximated with a bolt of thick, black stitches.

Lexi returned to the tape. A pair of hands joined her...she recognized the pocketknife and wedding band. Chet! His knuckles were bleeding.

Chet cut Zelda loose, scooped her into his arms and jumped to the floor. Lexi hugged them both. Chet stood Zelda on her feet but her knees buckled and he gently guided her to the deck. Lexi bent down to comfort her.

Chet seized Porter by the back of the shirt and jerked him to his feet. "Porter and I have a date with Sheriff Godsey."

Lexi gripped her husband's hand. "Where did you come from?"

"I came running when I heard the screams," Chet said. "I thought it was you. When I got here, I saw a woman strapped to the log and this sorry bastard at the controls. He took off the moment he saw me. I tried to stop the saw but he grabbed me from behind and pulled me off the platform."

238

"You were advancing the carriage speed," Porter groaned. He wiped the blood from the corner of his mouth with the back of his hand. "You'd a killed her."

"You were saving that pleasure for yourself, you murdering rapist," Lexi hissed.

"It wasn't Porter," uttered Zelda in a soft voice, slowly getting to her feet. "It was never Porter. That's what I came here to tell you. You had to know the truth, but he yanked me into his truck when I stopped at JB's to call you again."

Zelda was not making sense. "It was never Porter?" Lexi asked. "Then who pulled you into his truck?"

"Porter didn't rape my mother," Zelda droned. "It was Drexel. Drexel Yeatts raped my mother. Drexel Yeatts tied me to that log. Mr. Willow scared him off. Porter Bandy never laid a hand on my Momma or me."

This was not turning out anywhere close to what Lexi had expected. "So when Chet tried to stop the saw, Porter actually jumped in to keep him from killing you?"

"While Porter and I were trying to bash each other's brains in, Norman jumped in and saved the day." Chet turned to Porter. "Porter, man, I am terribly sorry. I thought..."

"So where's Drexel?" Lexi interrupted.

"At the pit." Porter growled walking away. "But he and the bitch ain't gonna find what they're lookin' for." He stopped in front of the Gator's headlights; his shadow was that of a giant. "That was me in the house this evening and at your window last night, Mrs. Willow. I won't gonna hurt ya none. It won't safe for you up here. I meant to scare ya out, that's all." Porter spat on the ground and slipped from the headlights back into the darkness.

"Why would Porter take the rap for a crime he didn't commit?" Lexi asked. "Something's still missing." She looked at

Chet. "And where did you come from?"

"I've got my own airport," Chet said. "How did Porter get in the house?"

"I left the door unlocked. And I didn't hear your Mooney. How did you land without runway lights?

"Came in dead-stick," Chet replied, "just like I practiced when I left yesterday. I flashed the lights twice to locate the pavement, then a third time to make sure I was aligned properly."

"You could have killed yourself."

"I didn't want to tip-off Drexel that I was here. There's a line of thunderstorms from Boston through the Carolinas or I would have been here three hours ago."

"Wait...you knew about Drexel?"

"Not until about noon today. Sheriff Godsey called to tell me the batteries in the flashlight we found under the house the night of the robbery had Drexel's fingerprints on them. It was the same Mag-Lite Drexel loaned me the day Norman uncovered Titus Blaylock's Pierce Arrow. I remembered it because the rubber disk was missing off the power button. When Godsey said the prints matched, all the pieces fell into place. Drexel knows this place better than anyone, except maybe Porter. My guess is he used Jimmy and Cedric as decoys to give him clean access to the silver. He was probably hidden somewhere around the house the whole time."

A flash of lightning and an instantaneous clap of thunder startled Lexi into Chet's arms. "We'd better find him," she said.

There was another burst of thunder and the sky began to dump buckets. Lexi followed Chet under the sawmill roof.

"Perfect timing," Norman said. "The rain will help flush the mud out of the pit."

"The ice pit," Lexi gasped. She hooked Chet's arm and headed for the Gator. "Come on! Let's go!"

Chet reeled her back. "Not until this rain slows. Drexel's after something in that ice pit. But he can't get at it in this."

A bolt of lightning struck and thunder exploded directly overhead. Lexi desperately needed her headache medicine and tried to bury her head in Chet's chest to muffle the sound of the rain pounding on the tin roof. But, in a few minutes, the downpour slowed to a steady patter.

Lexi started for the Gator again. Norman and Zelda got in the back; Chet drove.

He stopped to let Norman open the gate at the barn. Lexi slipped the Colt from her coat pocket and slid it across the seat to Chet. He grabbed it and shuttled it into the inside pocket of his jacket.

Up ahead the spotlights from the excavator were still burning and Lexi saw the outline of a truck on the road parked next to the trench. As Chet drove closer, she recognized it as JB's.

"I wonder why she's here," Chet said. He parked the Gator behind the excavator.

JB was standing at the edge of the ice pit holding an umbrella. "If she doesn't get away from the edge of that hole, she's liable to join whatever else is down there," he said and got out, rushing over to JB. Lexi followed him, so did Norman. Zelda remained in the Gator.

"Heard the banging," JB said. "Figured you must be getting close. The gate was open down at the road. Hope you don't mind me showing myself up."

The pit was over three-quarters empty. The rain runoff from the mountain was overflowing the drainage culvert above and streaming down the granite rock face into the pit, washing the mud off the sides and out through the hole Norman had created.

JB pointed to a lump on the surface. "Mr. Willow, do you have a hose that can reach out here?" she asked.

"I've got one in the back of the excavator that we use to refill the cooling system," said Norman. "There's a hydrant at the rear of the boss house."

Norman quickly rigged the hose, returned, and handed the nozzle to JB. "Here you go Janice."

Lexi felt her insides cringe. JANDY, JANDY, JANDY...there was no turning back now.

"Janice," Chet echoed. "So that's your real name. What does the 'B' stand for?"

JB gritted her teeth and directed the stream of water at the lumps in the ice pit. "Bandy."

Chet's eyes widened. "Janice Bandy. So I finally get to meet Jancy."

"And she's Porter's mother," Lexi added. "But I don't think she's certain who his father is."

Chet's expression quickly changed. "You mean to say..."

JB reached out and touched Chet's shoulder. "No, son. That's one mistake I wasn't able to make. Gentry Willow was the most honorable man I've ever known. Men like that don't take to floozies. Not a day has gone by that I don't regret not leaving this valley when he asked me to go with him. But things had gotten too entangled by then."

Headache or not, JB had Lexi's full attention. "My guess is Porter's father is either Deacon or Raymond."

JB stiffened and her eyes narrowed to slits. "How'd you arrive at that conclusion?"

"It dawned on me yesterday while I was eating a piece of Millie Baldwin's pie. She told me about a little meeting you and Harold had behind the school house a couple months before they got married."

"I was doing poor Harold a favor in advance," JB snapped.

242

"The last time anything but the bathroom mirror saw that old plate of sauerkraut naked, gas was twelve cents a gallon. If Christina Baldwin is truly the fruit of that marriage then, by golly, there's been a second immaculate conception."

"Since my incident with Paragon, every time I go near the barn I see these images," Lexi said. "It's a young woman and an older man having sex. But there was a third person there that day, wasn't there, Janice? One you hadn't counted on...Raymond Blaylock. He caught you having a romp with his father. Unless I'm mistaken, that was the night of the sawmill fire too. Wasn't it, JB? The night you pitted father against son. You had to hedge your bets because you didn't know which one had the inside track on Titus's gold. Deacon killed Raymond with a pitchfork, and then the two of you wrapped him in chains and dumped him in the ice pit. Later that night, Deacon put a match to the mill and the two of you made up the story about the hot ash. But the part of the mill which housed the boilers had been shut down for several days. Without the boilers operating, there would not have been any hot ash to start a fire. I'm surprised nobody ever made that connection. Perhaps they were enticed not to."

JB kept working the stream of water back and forth.

"After the insurance company denied Deacon's claim, he was left with no money, no business, a pending bank foreclosure and no sweet, young shoulder to cry on. You'd already managed to blackmail him into deeding over the store to you. Probably made him sign that over in blood first before helping him dispose of Raymond's body."

Lexi put her hand on JB's shoulder and turned her around to face. "Everything that happened up here that summer, except the foreclosure, was directly your fault, wasn't it?"

Tears flooded down JB's cheeks. "I came from nothing. Folks like you don't know what that's like. My daddy sweated blood in that mill for fifteen years, sometimes eighteen hours a day. The money he dragged home was hardly enough to feed a family of church mice. I watched him die when I was thirteen; a mill accident. Mother died the winter before. A little after I turned fourteen, some of the men folk around the mill tried placing their hands on me in ways generally reserved for husbands. I let them do it, too. Even encouraged it. But I made damn certain I got what I wanted in return, especially from the married ones. I didn't stop to consider the consequences until it was too late. I had one abortion that damn near killed me. After that, I learned my cycles and was a little more careful. Deacon wouldn't hear of a second abortion; I gave birth to Porter five months after he killed himself. Deacon is the Porter's father...there was never any question about that."

JB wiped the tears from her glasses on her shirt. "For Raymond, the physical stuff had nothing to do with it. He truly loved me. Deacon sent him to visit a mill near Bartow, West Virginia. For some God forsaken reason he came back a couple days early. Millie Baldwin spotted me sneaking off toward Deacon's house; she intercepted Raymond down at the store and told him where I was. He found me all right." JB slid the glasses back up her nose. "It was Deacon and me in the barn, just like you said. An enraged heart seeks revenge first. When Raymond started in on Deacon, there was no doubt he was going to kill him. With Deacon dead, and Raymond facing murder, I would never get to Titus's gold.

"But that's not how it really happened, was it Janice," Chet piped up. "Raymond was set up and you know it."

Lexi pivoted around toward him in astonishment.

"Gentry Willow was the person Millie Baldwin sent to the barn that night, not Raymond Blaylock. Gentry watched the whole thing from a window on the east side of the barn. He had just received his commissioning orders from VMI and was shipping out to Fort Benning the next morning. He wanted one last shot at convincing you to go with him."

Chet walked toward JB. "He arrived just before Raymond did and caught an eyeful of you and Deacon. You can imagine his surprise. He ducked out of sight when Raymond showed up. Deacon knew how much Raymond loved you. He also knew Raymond had discovered several large sums of money that were missing from the company's balance sheet. Money Deacon had embezzled. Raymond was going to expose the whole thing. Somehow Deacon figured Raymond would come back early. Probably even arranged something to get him to the barn at just the precise moment. It was a meeting he knew Raymond would never leave." Chet looked directly at JB. "Deacon knew you would make yourself available. But you had no idea what was really happening."

JB didn't reply. Judging from the look on her face, she didn't need to.

"When Raymond walked in on the two of you, an argument ensued. My father heard the whole exchange. Deacon had you pinned down. He stood there between your legs the whole time, taunting Raymond. When Raymond had had enough, he grabbed the pitchfork and rushed Deacon. Deacon was ready for him. He pulled a pistol from a holster concealed under his shirt and killed Raymond on the spot. The pitchfork in the chest was an afterthought. In a nutshell, Janice, Deacon Blaylock used you to get rid of his own son."

JB's shoulders heaved with heavy sobs. "How do you know all this?" she cried.

"My father and I had several talks before he died. You're right about one thing, JB. Gentry Willow was a truly honorable man. But that night at the barn, he was a crushed and frightened twenty-two-year-old kid. He tore out of there before he saw what you did with Raymond's body, but had nightmares about it for the rest of his life. That one moment of cowardice tainted a lifetime filled with

245

heroism."

Lexi put her arms around Chet. "You've known about JB the whole time. When were you going to tell me?"

"I learned Janice was still alive from Audrey Pepper, before we first came to look around. I had known for better than a year that the Blaylock estate was for sale but moving here had to be your idea, sweetheart. I dropped a few subtle hints. You took them and ran, and here we are. I knew if I owned the place that I could eventually set the record straight. I had to do that for Gentry."

"Hey," shouted Norman, pointing into the pit. "Looks like we've found something."

JB pulled a flashlight from the pocket of her rain parka and shone it in the pit. The spray from the hose had uncovered a partially decayed head and upper torso. Smaller this time, like that of a child.

Norman removed his hard hat. "Holy Sweet Mother of Jesus."

"That's likely little Bobby Denton, eldest son of Jim Denton, the assistant mill boss," JB said in a voice slightly more than a whisper. "He disappeared in the spring of forty-one, just after the thaw. Everyone figured it was the ice pit but Deacon wouldn't hear of draining it. He built the fence and swore he'd shoot anyone that crossed over it."

"Why ?" Lexi asked. "That was years before you put Raymond there."

JB's eyes found Lexi's face again. This time there was no anger, no sparks. Her skin had paled and was sagging. It was as if the past fifty years had caught up with her in a matter of moments. "I suspect we'll know shortly," JB answered. She turned to Norman. "Think you can lift him out easy-like with your digger?"

Chet turned to Norman "Lower me in the bucket and I'll bring him out."

One side of the pit was angled, the other more cupped. Judging from the slope of each, Lexi guessed that they didn't intersect in a common bottom but rather in an offset. The thought of Chet going down there made her extremely uncomfortable.

"I'll get a blanket from my truck to wrap him," JB said. She turned to Lexi again. "All those things happened a long time ago, Mrs. Willow. I won't right in what I did, but I did what I thought I had to survive. Please don't judge me too harshly."

Lexi couldn't give JB the comfort she was looking for and her eyes fell from Lexi's face; she pursed her lips and slowly turned away.

Norman started the excavator, backed it to the pit and repositioned the spotlights; Chet climbed into the bucket. Norman swung it out over the pit and lowered him to the surface, five feet short of Bobby Denton's body.

Chet lowered himself backward out of the bucket and sank thigh deep in the mud. He reached out and seized Bobby's pant leg but the fabric tore like tissue paper. Pushing himself forward, he sank to his chest before stopping.

"I think I just crushed something with my foot," Chet exclaimed.

"What did it feel like?" Lexi asked.

"Hollow."

Chet spread the blanket over Bobby's body, scooped him up in his arms and started to work his way back to the bucket. Norman nosed the excavator's tracks over the lip of the pit, extending the arm out another foot. Chet balanced Bobby in his left arm and reached out to the bucket with his right hand and hauled himself in.

Norman delivered Chet and the remains of Bobby Denton back to solid ground. The little boy had been down there almost ten years longer than Raymond had. Lexi turned away, not needing any reminders of what a partially decomposed body looked like.

Chet passed Bobby's body to JB and Zelda. Lexi rinsed Chet off with the hose and then followed him over to the trench. The outflow of muck through the hole in the bottom had slowed considerably.

Chet waved to Norman who throttled back his engine. "I felt a layer of cold water close to the bottom. It must be the spring. If you can enlarge the hole downward, we can probably speed this along."

As Norman inched the excavator back, chunks of rock fell from the rim of the pit. The weight of the machinery and all the hammering was taking its toll on the stability of the rock formation.

In a matter of minutes, Tat-Tat was pecking away again. A large piece of rock dropped out and the muck started rolling again. Norman hammered it into smaller pieces, then attacked the wall once more. Soon, another lump appeared in the bottom of pit next to where Chet had been standing earlier. Lexi took the hose and hit it with a blast of water. Flecks of yellow paint showed through the mud.

Chet joined her. "It looks like a piece of farm machinery."

The engine on the track hammer stopped.

"Thanks for finding my pump, folks," said a new voice. "Didn't think I'd ever see that again."

Lexi turned and faced the hammer. Someone was standing in front of the excavator lights holding a shotgun.

"Takes a licking and keeps on ticking. I bet if I threw a splash of gas in her she'd suck the rest of that pit dry in twenty minutes." The barrel of the shotgun dipped. "I was forced to plant that there one night about five years ago to keep Sheriff Godsey from catching me." Drexel Yeatts jumped to the ground and crossed the dam. He pointed the shotgun at Chet, pulled a pistol and aimed it toward the cab of the track hammer. "Come on out of there, Norman. I've had about all that racket I can stand."

248

Norman climbed out of the track hammer and Drexel pointed to a spot next to the dam. "Stand in the light there where I can see you."

Lexi dropped the hose and huddled close to Chet. She realized her husband was no longer wearing his coat; she spotted it on the ground on the other side of the trench, the 9mm was probably still in the pocket.

"You stay put, Mrs. Willow, and back away from Mr. Willow." Drexel shot a glance at JB and Zelda. "Y'all get away from that truck, too. No fast moves and we'll all live to tell our grandchildren about this."

Drexel cocked his head to the side and called, "Kimberly, why don't you make certain Annie Oakley here isn't packing that window buster of hers." He smiled a crooked smile. "I thought you may have killed poor Porter last night. He blazed by me dropping blood like a gut-shot deer. Too bad you didn't."

Kimberly crept from the shadows behind the boss house holding Chet's Glock. She patted down Lexi and then Chet. "Both of them are clean," she said.

"Making a late house call?" asked Lexi.

"Wait until you get the bill," she answered. "I'd say it'll run you about twenty million in gold. Sure beats snipping dog testicles."

"Uncle Drex's been telling me stories about Titus Blaylock's fortune ever since I was six. When you discovered the silver, I knew the gold had to be around here somewhere, too."

"So you just throw away an education, your marriage, and a medical practice? Just like that?"

"I never was the domestic type."

"What about dear old Mom? The woman in the picture?"

"That was one of Drex's girlfriends. I wouldn't know my own mother if she was sitting in my lap. Drexel raised my brother and me."

"So Uncle Drexel is the silver thief, and you're the apprentice."

"The restoration business has provided access to some stunning collections. I about wet myself when you invited me in to examine your find."

"So much for your judge of character," Chet whispered to Lexi.

Chet took a step toward Drexel. "What do we do now? Arm wrestle until a winner is declared?"

"Something like that," Drexel replied.

Lexi looked at Drexel; she was disgusted and intrigued all at the same time. "So it was you who sabotaged Chet's airplane and rolled our truck into the tree."

"The airplane thing was meant for Chet, not you. If it had killed both of you, I would have never gotten this ice pit drained. I helped your horse out of his stall, too, in case you were wondering. Hell, if I'd known we were going to dig up old Raymond, I'd have built a ticket booth."

Lexi turned to Kimberly. "Why Mrs. Madison's cat?"

"I figured Drexel overheard me telling you that story. It was a surprise to me, too."

Drexel stepped over to the edge of the pit. "Ask Porter. If there's a pussy ghost up here, he's probably had his hands all over it." Drexel cut his eye to JB's truck. "Right, Zelda?"

The acid in Lexi's stomach rose to her throat. Drexel had forged into territory beyond cruelty; he was Zelda's father, for Christ's sake.

"You leave Zelda alone," Lexi warned and searched the darkness to the right of the pit. She had one more surprise up her sleeve. "Don't worry, Zelda. He won't get off this mountain."

250

Drexel peered into the pit. "Well, well! What do we have here?" He pointed his pistol at Lexi's hose. "Stop your jabbering and grab that hose. Spray it on that clump of mud just behind the pump."

Lexi retrieved the hose and sprayed. Recognition took just seconds. It was another hand...this one clenched in a fist.

Drexel grinned. "It appears Raymond and little Bobby weren't alone in there."

JB rushed to the edge of the pit.

"Let me guess." Drexel's face was beaming. "It's the star quarterback and the homecoming queen."

Two bodies were lying crosswise along the offset in the bottom of the pit. It appeared to be a man and a woman. If standing upright, they might have been dancing. There was a gaping hole in the man's chest cavity—the hollow place Chet's foot had found earlier.

JB stood transfixed. Finally, she removed her glasses and wiped away another batch of tears. "I came to the house about ten or so, the night the insurance company denied Deacon's claim for the mill fire," she said, talking to no one in particular. "I knew he'd been drinking. I wanted to make sure he passed out and slept it off like usual. But he hadn't. He was stomping around downstairs knocking holes in the walls with a fireplace poker and cussing like the possessed; it chilled me clean to the bone. I don't think he saw me, though. His eyes were too filled with demons.

"Eventually, he lay on the sofa in what is now Mrs. Lexi's den, crying like a baby. He kept shouting, 'NO, NO, NO! DON'T DO IT! DON'T DO IT!, throwing his arms before his face as though to ward off blows. 'DON'T KILL MOTHER! PLEASE DADDY, DON'T KILL MY BEAUTIFUL MOTHER!' That was the night Deacon took his life.

"My best guess is that Mrs. Andrea threatened to leave

Monterey again. This time, Titus held her to task. But if he couldn't have her, nobody would. From the sound of things, Deacon must have tried to stop it. But he was weak. Never man enough to stand up to Titus."

JB ran her eyes from Lexi to Chet. "I don't know if Deacon actually killed Titus and threw him and Andrea in the pit, or if Titus simply grabbed Andrea and jumped in. Always knew the story about the *Titanic* was a lie. Folks back then must have believed it or didn't have the guts to speak otherwise. Like I told ya, the mills were the only work available. People had to eat. With Titus gone, everyone's future rested with Deacon. Deacon won't much, but he was better than nothing."

"Finding Titus's Pierce Arrow removed all doubt. Now you understand why Deacon wouldn't drain the pit after Bobby Denton disappeared. He'd likely have dredged up a pair of murder charges. Money wouldn't buy him out of that one."

JB turned to Lexi. "Deacon wasn't in love with me any more than I was in love with him. But I didn't kill him. I reckon I should have stayed with him that night. Truth was, he was dead on the inside long before. His demons pushed him into that saw blade. The same ones he was fighting on the sofa. Demons not even the fire of the whiskey could burn away."

Titus was planning to kill Andrea all along, Lexi thought. That's why he dug the ice pit just before electricity made it here. It gave him a place to stash her body and the means to control who came near it. Doing it in the winter meant there would be fewer mill workers around to witness anything.

"We need to get them out of there," Lexi said.

"Rat's ass," spat Drexel. "I've had enough of the nostalgia crap. You just keep working that hose across the bottom."

Lexi cut her eyes at Chet. She was surprised he hadn't

attempted some sort of heroics by now. Instead, he just winked at her.

The pump was resting upside down in the offset at the bottom of the pit, acting like a dam holding back the last foot or two of mud.

Drexel was standing by the pit holding his shotgun on her and Chet; Kimberly had a gun on Zelda. JB was two paces to Lexi's right. If she had been a few years younger, she could have made a break for it, perhaps reached the darkness behind the boss house.

Who was going to make the next move?

"Drexel Yeatts," JB said in a tepid voice. "I may be an old broad, but there's still enough of me here to blister your tail parts. You let us get Mr. Titus and Mrs. Andrea out of that hole this instant. And don't think for a second that I'm asking."

Drexel stared at her for a moment, and then rolled his eyes like a scolded child. "Norman, you heard Mother Bandy. Fire up your shovel. Mr. Willow's going for another dip. Get a piece of chain or something to lift that pump out, too."

Lexi peered into the darkness just beyond the reach of the excavator's floodlights. She hoped the cavalry arrived soon.

Chet and Norman paused at what was left of the dam. "Don't leave your weight on one foot too long or the whole thing's liable to cave in," Norman said.

"Let's get this over with tonight, gentlemen," Drexel shouted. "I've got a plane to catch."

Chet crossed the dam first. As Norman picked his way, Chet casually walked toward his jacket. Lexi knew he was going for the pistol so she needed to distract Drexel.

"When you broke in and stole the silver, it was pretty slick of you to take the computer and all of my notes. Was I getting too close for comfort?"

"Actually, I broke in to steal the computer and notes but couldn't resist the rest—I got $2500 for each of the candelabrum alone. I wasn't sure how far your research had gone until I moved your computer desk to uncover the trap door. Once you made the connection between Janice and Deacon, I knew it wouldn't be long before you figured out the rest."

"You wasted your time. I have it all memorized."

"Another bump on the head will take care of that."

Lexi should have figured as much. Out of the corner of her eye, she saw Chet stuff the gun in the back of his pants. "What are you going to do with us after you have the gold? Twenty million dollars seems hardly worth killing four people over."

"You aren't going to make me kill you, now are you?" He chuckled. "Actually, I think I'll stick you in that cozy little hole we found under the floor in your study. When I get to Rio, I'll phone somebody to come let you out."

"What about food and water?"

"I hear people can last days drinking one another's piss." His face busted out in a toothy grin. "The men shouldn't object too much. I'll even provide a funnel and a cup."

Lexi felt her lips roll back. "You're below slime, Drexel Yeatts. I'll have your name plastered across every newspaper from Bangor to San Diego. You'll never set foot on U.S. soil again."

Drexel grinned again. "I'll send you an address to forward my royalty checks."

Norman started the excavator and lowered Chet into the pit; JB tossed him another blanket. Chet covered Titus and Andrea's bodies, and then carried the two of them to the bucket. Norman lifted them out and JB took charge from there.

When the bucket came down again, Chet took a piece of cable Norman had provided and attached one end to the pump's frame, looped it around teeth on the bucket and snap-hooked the other end back on itself.

Norman eased the arm upward, lifting the pump from the bottom; the mud started flowing. Drexel motioned for Norman to deposit the pump on the ground next to him. He removed the cable and signaled for Norman to cut the engine.

"Shoot your hose at the back wall of the pit," Drexel barked at Lexi.

Lexi continued working. As the level dropped, three more lumps materialized, each about the size of a file box. One was resting on its side.

Drexel pointed and shouted, "There! Spray the hose there."

Lexi concentrated on the lumps. As the mud rinsed away, it became apparent that the lumps were duffel bags—thick leather, just like the straps she recovered the morning Paragon was pulled out.

"Norman, start your machine again and lower the bucket!" shouted Drexel; he was so excited, the words came out like a song. "Mr. Willow, check the bags and see if they've rotted. If they're still intact, slide your hands underneath them and carefully place each one in the bucket. Don't lift them by the straps."

Chet squatted down next to the bags. He ran his hands across one and gently pushed on the sides. "They seem strong enough."

He lifted the first bag, placed it in the bucket, and then did the same with the other two. Norman raised the arm and set the bucket on the ground beside the pump. Chet jumped off and joined Lexi.

Drexel propped his shotgun and reached inside. Suddenly, there was a thunderous gunshot. Lexi saw a plume of fire explode skyward in the darkness beyond the opposite side of the ice pit.

"Back away from there or the next one's gonna take your friggin' head off."

Porter Bandy stepped into the light and pointed his shotgun at Kimberly. "Drop that gun, Dr. Buchanan." Kimberly did as ordered.

"Well, well, well," Drexel exclaimed. "If it isn't the one-eyed

255

bastard son of Monterey. What a delightful evening for a family reunion."

"Keep your trap shut," Porter warned.

"You mean half-brother Drexel, don't you?" Lexi asked.

"Very good detective work, Mrs. Willow," said Drexel. "Different fathers, same fun-loving mother." He cut his eyes at JB. "I figured Jandy failed to mention her little affair with the contractor the bank hired to spruce-up the place after Deacon's death. Someone new who might be able lead her to Titus's goodies."

"He could have saved me a lot of trouble," JB said.

"He raised me, didn't he? Saved you that trouble. That's how I became such a gifted carpenter."

JB took a step toward the gun Kimberly had dropped. Porter fired his shotgun in the air again, ejected the shell and pumped a new one into the chamber—the blast felt like a sledgehammer against Lexi's head

"I told you to stay put, old woman."

JB backed away. She didn't challenge Porter the way she had Drexel; genuine fear flickered at the corners of her mouth.

"Okay, big brother," Drexel said. "What now?"

Porter picked his steps across the dam. "Get those bags out of the bucket and set them on the ground. Make one move for that shotgun there and I'll fill your ass with buckshot."

Drexel struggled LIFTING the bags but managed to get them out. Lexi noted that one of them was missing both of its handles.

"Get over next to him," Porter said to JB.

"That's far enough, folks," shouted another new voice, this one from the road in front of the boss house. Sheriff Godsey trudged around the right side of JB's pickup; Randy came around the other. Godsey had the barrel of a sawed-off shotgun trained at Porter. "Lay that blunderbuss at your feet, nice and slow."

256

Not a moment too soon, thought Lexi, relieved that Randy had finally made his entrance. But she wasn't expecting Godsey.

"You all right down there, Mr. Willow?" Godsey shouted.

"I'll be a lot better when Norman gets me out of here."

"Norman, bring him up," Godsey ordered. "Randy, gather all those weapons."

Randy holstered his pistol and passed in front of Lexi ...she gasped. The back of Randy's pants was torn and one of his pockets was missing. Lexi's internal alarm sounded. He had double-crossed her; he and the sheriff were after the gold for themselves.

Norman raised Chet out of the ice pit, letting him off on the opposite side of the trench.

"Quite a little party we're havin' here tonight," Godsey cackled. "I haven't seen this many shotguns since my kid sister's wedding."

Randy grabbed Porter's gun, tossed it to Drexel, and pulled his pistol again.

"Don't try it, Sheriff," Drexel shouted. "You might get one of us, but not both."

Now Lexi was really confused.

"What in the name of thunder are you doing, boy?" Godsey shouted.

"Folks, allow me to introduce you to my nephew, Randy—Kimberly's baby brother—and another one of my star pupils. I want to thank Mrs. Willow here for so graciously inviting him and Kimberly here tonight. It made planning this whole festivity a lot easier."

"You dirty sonofabitch," snarled Godsey.

"Sorry, Boss," Randy said, and then grinned. "Like they say, blood is thicker than..."

"Get on with it, Drexel," crowed JB. "I want to see that gold

257

once before I die."

"Since none of this would have been possible without you, dear mother, you may have the honor."

JB bent down next to the first bag and tugged on the zipper. It didn't budge. She jerked at it again. Nothing. She reached into her overalls and pulled out a large pocketknife, slashed open the bag, and thrust her hand inside. She grimaced and her hand immediately recoiled; a stream of blood trickled down her fingers.

"It's full of nails!" she shouted.

Drexel pulled the slit open. A landslide of rusty nails poured onto the ground. "What the hell!?" Drexel took the knife from JB and cut open the two other bags. All three bags were full of nothing but nails.

The laughter began as a low snicker and quickly grew into a roar. "I've waited twenty-two years for this moment!" Porter shouted. He belted out another thunderous laugh. "For seven years, I rotted in that stinking prison camp. Seven years, damn your greedy souls, all because Mother here didn't want her pretty-boy Drexel to go to jail for rape."

Porter walked over to JB. "I don't know how much you paid Treena Aupperly to lie for you. But she did it, didn't she?" He swung his arm in an arc. "LOOK AT THIS MAN, her lawyer shouted in court that day. A lawyer my very own mother had bought and paid for." Porter yanked off his ball cap and turned his head so everyone could see his disfigurements. "LADIES AND GENTLEMEN OF THE JURY, IS THIS NOT THE FACE OF A RAPIST?"

Porter replaced his cap and stepped away from JB. "I guess it won't hard to believe. They certainly had no interest in believing me. If I hadn't raped Zelda's mother, it was only a matter of time until I raped somebody. That's what one of them said. TO JAIL WITH HIM! Put the bastard Porter Bandy away where nobody has to look at him."

Porter leaned against the pump. "A man can do a lot of thinking' in seven years. Reading, too. If I had my face in a *Popular Science* magazine, the guards didn't have to look at it. We all got along better that way.

"When I got out, I built a submersible-coil metal detector, one that could cut through all the silt and mud at the bottom of this pit. I attached it to a pipe and started working the ice pit at night. It took me most of that first summer, but I recovered all three bags of gold. Still got every piece of it hidden at my camp. Left these nails for you. I knew you'd find 'em one day. Even stole 'em from Mother Bandy's wonderful store."

Porter started laughing again. "You should see the look on your pitiful faces."

"Goddamn you!!" screamed Drexel. He grabbed Porter by the shirt, swung him around and punched him in the face.

The last thing Lexi saw was Chet reaching for his gun. Porter crashed into her, their heads collided, and Lexi's brain exploded with stars again. She experienced a falling sensation and another sharp pain in the back of her skull.

She heard three distant gunshots, followed by several shouts and a scream. Lexi was aware of what was going on around her, yet felt strangely removed from it. She detected, or rather sensed, movement from the direction of the barn. Out of the darkness charged three opaque gray images; the first one much larger than the others. The ground under her feet rumbled to the rhythm of pounding hooves and a horse bellowed.

Side by side, the three images leapt over the ditch. The two smaller ones split off; the large one came directly at her.

It halted beside her and she could feel moist breath against her skin. It nuzzled her shoulder; the pain in Lexi's head disappeared.

The first thing her eyes focused on was Paragon.

"Hi, baby," she said and placed a hand on either side of his muzzle and kissed his nose.

Someone slid off Paragon's back. All Lexi could see at first was a pair of men's boots—tall, no laces, spit-polished. As her eyes moved upward, she saw a gray Confederate Army uniform, a flowing, chest-length beard and a pair of soft blue eyes.

Lexi was not afraid. "Shepherd Blaylock," she said. "We've met before."

It suddenly dawned on her. "Either you really are a ghost, or I'm dead." She touched the side of Paragon's muzzle again for reassurance, feeling again the warmth under his fine, shiny black hair.

Major Blaylock smiled; it was a kind, knowing smile. "No, Alexis Willow, you are not dead. You are more alive now than ever."

He offered his hand; a very large hand. A hand as large as...the muddy handprint on the back of her blouse from the day Paragon kicked her.

"You've rescued me before," Lexi said. "In the barn, when I was injured by Paragon."

He gazed at her horse. "A magnificent animal, strong and spirited. Just like his master."

Shepherd Blaylock then helped Lexi to her feet and tipped his hat. "Major Shepherd Blaylock, ma'am. Twelfth Georgia Regiment of the Confederate State Army. This mountain has held many secrets, Alexis Willow. Secrets that can no longer remain hidden. Limitations exist for the dead as well as the living. A bridge was needed, one that could serve both sides. For this, you were chosen long ago. The pain you have endured these past years shall not return. Though tragedy knows little of geography. Fires burn, people kill, mountains crumble. It is the order of things. The very nature of life itself is a cycle of risk, reward or recovery."

Immediately, Lexi's head became filled with images of a mountain sunrise, blue sky, and orange sunlight reflecting off soft billowy clouds, children playing in a meadow.

Shepherd smiled. "As you can now see, there remains much life within you indeed."

Lexi felt an arm slip around her shoulders and give her a loving squeeze; it was Chet.

Kimberly and Randy were huddled next to the trench; Randy's shoulder was bleeding. A large black lion was perched like a statue behind them, cutting off any means of escape. Sheriff Godsey was next to JB's truck, holding a pistol on Kimberly and Randy; his face was pale, the pistol shaking. Zelda was just to his left. JB had not moved; her right hand was draped across her chin, her eyes wide open. Behind her, the other black lion was circling, making low-pitched moaning sounds.

Chet extended his hand. "Major Chet Willow, United States Marine Corps Reserves.

The two shook and Shepherd gave a quick nod. "That was excellent marksmanship. There was a day when I could have used a soldier like you." He stepped over to Porter. "Few Blaylock souls have suffered so greatly as you," said Shepherd. "Of you, my son, I am most proud."

He placed his giant right hand over the disfigured side of Porter's face. A bright white light appeared beneath it, growing brighter until it completely engulfed Porter's head and shoulders. Porter's body began to straighten; the next moment he was standing totally erect. The light faded and Shepherd removed his hand. The purple birthmark that had covered the right side of Porter's face was gone; the sunken cheek had been made normal. His eyes—both eyes—were now the same soft powder blue as Shepherd Blaylock's.

He put his other hand on Porter's shoulder. "It is my belief that one who finds himself with such resource must seek ways to enrich the lives of those less fortunate."

Porter smiled and nodded his head.

Shepherd turned to Zelda. He didn't say anything; he simply gazed at her for a few moments and smiled. Zelda's legs became firm and her face brightened. The smile that rose to her cheeks must have originated from some secret portion of her soul. It was beautiful and filled Lexi with great joy.

He stepped over Drexel's body, not even acknowledging it. Judging from the amount of blood on the front of Drexel's shirt and ground, the mortal part of him had already departed.

When Shepherd's eyes fell upon JB, there was no longer a smile on his lips; his eyes turned the cold gray of steel. "The consequences of unbridled greed are most severe," he said sternly; he raised his right hand to his mouth and whistled loudly.

The lion behind JB butted her with its head, shoving her forward. As the lion passed Lexi, she saw the letter 'B' on its right cheek.

JB broke into a feeble dash for the bridge. The second of Shepherd's lions, Junta, crouched and leaped across the trench, cutting off her exit. Benaja stopped short, leaving JB stranded in the middle. Both reared back and slammed their feet on the ends of the dam. The ground beneath Lexi's feet rumbled. Rocks dislodged from the side of the dam and tumbled into the trench.

The lions reared back a second time; their intentions were clear. "The bridge is going to crumble," Lexi cried. Chet's arm swung from her shoulders and she felt him lurch forward.

Shepherd put his hand out again. "It is as it must be."

Chet halted.

The lions pounded the ground a third time. A wide crack raced up the side of the bridge below JB's feet. The bridge crumbled and JB toppled backward. A cloud of dust rose from the ice pit. Lexi pressed her face into Chet's chest.

Out of the corner of her eye, she saw another series of bright lights. This time, coming from the ice pit itself. Points of light all around the edge shined down into the bottom, illuminating something. The beams began to pivot, lifting the object to the top.

An odd-shaped silhouette appeared amidst the lights and moved forward. When it reached solid ground, the lights vanished. It took moments for Lexi's eyes to adjust. It was a man holding a woman in his arms.

Lexi recognized the faces; they were two of the people from her vision in the barn...Raymond Blaylock and a beautiful, young Janice Bandy.

"We shall never be apart again," Raymond said. He kissed Janice on the cheek. JB looked at Lexi, and smiled. The two began to rise into the sky, and Lexi watched until their reflection blended into the vast body of stars above.

Beecher came darting out of the darkness from behind the boss house. He dropped a tennis ball at Porter's feet and started barking. Porter tossed it up the road and Beecher went tearing after it.

"So that's why he barks every time he sees you."

Porter grinned shyly. "Animals need only love."

Junta leapt back across the trench. With his lions by his side once more, Shepherd walked toward Lexi. As they approached, Benaja and Junta changed back to their mortal forms. Junta bent down and picked up a white Persian cat wearing a teal green collar.

"At long last, rest awaits us," Shepherd said. "For that, we are most grateful. But there still remains one task." He brushed his topcoat aside and reached into a small black pouch belted to his waist.

"Within your breast resides the love of a mother, and within in your womb beats the heart of a son." He looked at Chet. "A fine, strong son he shall be."

Shepherd pressed a golden heart into the palm of Lexi's right hand. "His youth shall sow new life upon my mountain and the riches it bears will be many. But a man is not made whole by what he keeps in his hand but by what he holds in his heart. Teach him well, Lexi Willow, teach him well."

Shepherd Blaylock then closed Lexi's hand, kissed it and stepped backward. Benaja and Junta paced forward. Shepherd gazed at Lexi and smiled a slight smile again. A picture of the corral at her parents' house on Long Island appeared in her mind; her mother and father were standing at the gate. She was not riding Cherokee or Paragon this time. Rather, she was standing: an adult, dressed in black Spandex just as she was now.

Lexi wanted to run to them. She wanted to hold them, tell them how much she loved them. But when she tried to approach, the gate kept moving away from her. She halted.

Her father put his arm around her mother, both of them smiled and waved. Lexi felt their love warm a spot deep inside her. Suddenly, it all made wonderful sense. Her parents were together on the other side of the gate; in heaven, happy and fulfilled. She placed her hand on her stomach...the gate they held wasn't open to her because her life was not yet complete. This was the goodbye she was never permitted to have. A goodbye, at least, for now.

The image of her parents faded and Shepherd Blaylock's words filtered back to her again: "There remains much life within you indeed, Lexi Willow."

Shepherd tipped his hat, then he and his lions turned and walked toward the cut-stone fence overlooking the terrace, and disappeared into the darkness covering Monterey.

Epilogue

Three Months Later:

Headline: *Staunton News Leader*—Friday, August 27, 2012
by Zelda

Mr. and Mrs. Chet Willow of Monterey, Virginia hosted the First Annual Monterey Days Festival at their mountain estate on the eastern slope of the now famous Cheat Mountain of Virginia. The celebration was organized to honor the descendants of the families who helped work the numerous lumber mills of The Blaylock Mining and Lumber Company founded in 1874 by Thomas Horatio Blaylock.

Festivities included aerial tours of the Monterey Valley, face painting, pony rides, balloon clowns, and a parade of antique automobiles including Chet Willow's recently restored 1911 Pierce Arrow touring sedan. The exquisitely appointed Willow mansion, tenant houses and stable areas were open for all to review. *Staunton News Leader's* featured columnist, Alexis Willow, awarded door prizes of antique silver from the Andrea Blaylock private collection to lucky festival goers throughout the day. Catering was provided by the

Maple Restaurant and featured Millicent Baldwin's delicious new Monterey Maple Pie.

Each county resident in attendance at the event was given an authentic twenty-dollar solid gold US coin from a treasury discovered by Porter Bandy, proprietor of Porter Bandy General Merchandise. Each coin is valued at $1,325.00 and is believed to be part of the earnings Titus Blaylock skimmed from employee wages during his many years as Chief Executive Officer of the Blaylock corporate empire. Music was provided by The Keith Bryant Band of Staunton, Virginia.

Plans are currently underway for next year's event, although the schedule date has yet to be released.

-END-

The Author

Kevin P. Hayden grew up in central Virginia on the outskirts of the village named Rice; shortened from its original 1800's name of Rice's Depot. Shortly after the fall of Petersburg in April of 1865 Rice's Depot became a key staging area for General Robert E. Lee's Northern Virginia Army during an attempt to retreat into North Carolina, and served as a command center during the battles of High Bridge and Saylor's Creek. The area, only a short distance from the Appomattox Surrender Grounds, is rich in Civil War history and tales of a nation in struggle. Many of those stories were passed down by a sect of older gentlemen seated around a small table next to a wood stove in Percy Trear's General Store. Kevin, accompanied by his best friends Talmadge and Larry, was planted front and center to those conversations whenever possible.

Years later Kevin returned to his grandparents' farm. Standing in the back yard looking down toward the home he grew up in he saw Bill, a neighbor, walking up the hill toward him: a red cap on his head, slight bend forward at the waste, left arm swinging loosely at his side. For several moments that was not Bill. Instead, it was Kevin's grandfather, Wirt Chambers, who he had seen make that same trek a thousand times: red cap upon his head, bent slightly forward at the waste, left arm swinging loosely at his side. His grandfather who had passed three-years earlier.

Elements of youth, the stories from Trear's Store, people he had known in life... all pieces of narrative which started falling into place. When Kevin later made a visit to Monterey, the story CHEAT MOUNTAIN found a home.

Please visit us at **www.kphayden.com** to learn about DARKSAIL and other novels by KP Hayden. You will also find reviews, photographs and information about upcoming releases.

About CHEAT MOUNTAIN:

Alexis Willow had gotten her fill of life in the big city. So she and her husband Chet bought the estate of turn of the century industrialist Titus Blaylock—a mansion of stone built atop a terrace carved from the shoulders of Cheat Mountain overlooking the village of Monterey, Virginia in the lush Shenandoah Valley. For Lexi it was a dream come true: a fresh start in life, a horse farm to raise champion Thoroughbreds and a spacious home in which to start a family. But from the moment she and Chet arrived the remains of the Blaylock past began to envelop their lives—greed, infidelity, jealousy and murder. At the heart of it was Titus Blaylock's fortune in gold and silver, believed by many to still be buried somewhere upon that mountain, a fortune several had spent their lifetimes trying to find.

Set against a backdrop of the historic Civil War Battle of McDowell, the Confederate Breastworks and the rich mountain empire culture, Lexi has to wrestle demons from her past and choose whether to fight for the life she has always imagined or surrender to unrelenting outside influences once again. CHEAT MOUNTAIN by K.P. Hayden, author of the supernatural nautical adventure, DARKSAIL.

www.ingramcontent.com/pod-product-compliance
Lightning Source LLC
Chambersburg PA
CBHW061601170626
46811CB00001B/272